I0653719

Christmas Cherry Auction

Stepbrother Edition

4 Reverse Harem Romances

Christmas Cherry Auction

Stepbrother Edition

4 Reverse Harem Romances

Sylvie Haas

Table of Contents

Baking and Blindfolds

A Stepbrother Reverse Harem Romance

Sylvie Haas

Blurb

Cooking with my stepbrothers really heats things up.

I'm a disappointment.

A failure.

A burden.

That's how my billionaire father and his wife see me.

After getting dumped and flunking out of college, there's only one place left to go: back home. The last thing I want is to see that look of utter disgust in my father's eyes and that smug smirk on my stepmother's face, yet again. But the one thing I do want is to get over my ex and finally take control of my own life.

And I know exactly the man--or men--for the job. Getting my stepbrothers to bid on me in the Christmas Cherry Auction should get the ball rolling. It's time to make their resistance waiver. Torn between their desire to please me in every way possible and their loyalty to my father's wallet for their up and coming business proposal, it's going to take a Christmas miracle to get the gift that I really want this season.

And I know it's the gift that will keep on giving!

If you love dirty-talking men who know how to please their stepsister, don't miss this year's Christmas Cherry Auction!

One

Bianca

Chimes ring from my phone, alerting me that the first twenty minutes of sunbathing are over. I tap the Restart button and sit up to flip onto my stomach, but stop midway and carefully set my oversized, cat-eye sunglasses with cute rhinestones at the tips on my stepmom's teak side table.

I'm more worried about scratching her precious table than ruining my glasses. I don't have the funds to replace either.

Cranking the space heater up, I sip my celebratory sparkling cider and take in the penthouse balcony view of the mountains. The snow-capped peaks mimic the puffy clouds set against the crystal blue sky. Sunbathing in December may not be my brightest idea, but I'm determined to stand on stage at tonight's auction with bright sun-kissed cheeks.

Both sets.

Hopefully, my stepbrothers find out about the second set tonight.

Bottoms up for the next twenty minutes, then a long, warm, bubbly soaker bath before my deep dive beauty prep for tonight's auction at the sex club.

The freshman fifteen makes me slightly conscious of my belly as I settle in to sun my buns. I tug the bottom of my suit into my crack for better exposure and unhook my top. The warmth of the sun on my body is pure joy.

Can I be as lucky as the women who participated in last year's auction? They all ended up in reverse harem relationships with billionaires. One of the women weighs heavily on my mind since her stepbrothers bought her.

Will my stepbrothers accept the anonymous invitation I sent? Technically the auction isn't for a relationship or even sex, but fantasies are king...and I'm their queen.

In reality, my world is falling apart. Or maybe it fell apart and is drumming its fingers on the table, like everyone else, waiting for me to quit being a disappointment and figure out how to put my life back together.

Loud voices and the crash of one wooden chair into another startle me from the next balcony.

"You'd be a fucking moron to think I'd do that, Sean," my stepbrother Mark yells at one of my other two stepbrothers. All three of them live in the other penthouse. I imagine Mark shoving his long bangs to the side so the full extent of his ire can beam from his eyes.

My arm extends reflexively, my fingers tangling in my robe. There's no actual worry about being seen, there's a solid divider between the two balconies.

I'd welcome one of my fantasies playing out. My brothers would peek around the edge of the balcony and catch me—

Now isn't the time. The garbled words I think I hear from inside their apartment have my full attention... 'the invitation' and 'tonight'.

Did they figure out I'm in the auction? Is going to the auction the thing Mark would have to be a moron to do? Are they disgusted at the thought of bidding on me?

Me. Their emotional little stepsister who let a bad breakup derail her college classes. The immature girl who had to move in with the stepmom she despises. The pathetic sister who took a job as Santa's helper because they were willing to hire me on the spot.

This is the exact opposite of how I imagined tonight going.

Unable to make out the words of the brother who's still inside their penthouse, I let go of my robe, stand up, refasten my top, and tug the bottom of my bathing suit to a less invasive position.

With my ear pressed to the divider between the balconies, I strain to hear.

"You're just an asshole," Mark, the brother on the balcony says. Surely he's not this upset at Sean. Aside from Sean's friends-with-everyone nature, his baby face adds to his friendly demeanor.

Ugh! What did I miss? Is it time to abandon my stealth efforts and let them know I'm the one who sent the invitation? I bite my lower lip.

I don't want them to bid on me out of pity. It's not like I'd even benefit from the money since it goes to charity. I might actually have to donate four hours of my time to help the winner prepare for the holidays.

It's a far cry from feeling desirable. I want to be loved. I want my stepbrothers. They'd be a safe way to lose my virginity.

More realistically, I want the fantasy. Saying something now could bring it crashing down. Silence is my best bet.

Their argument continues. "How bad would it piss off Frank?" That must be my confirmation that they know I'm in the auction. Carl's the pensive brother, always crafting strategies, but what does he have against my dad?

"How long do you think it would take for rumors to surface?" Sean is in on the ulterior motives?

Is it too late to back out? Aurora and Cindy would kill me, but as I'm surrounded by luxury, I shouldn't bite the hand that feeds me. I grab my phone and send a group text to my girlfriends: *Might not make it tonight*

"I'm not sure what would be more priceless, if we all bought her or..." Sean's voice fades.

It's a game to them. An evil plot. I'm crushed.

I stare at my phone. Why haven't my girls texted back?

"I'm heading to the bar," Marks says. Their door slams.

My stomach sinks. It's lose-lose. My grand plan that my brothers bid on me can't happen if they spend their normal Friday night with friends. But if they show up, there will be collateral damage.

Fantasy might not have been king when it comes to them.

Or perhaps queen was the overstatement. Court jester? Family fuck up? The first college dropout?

I try to focus on the positive...nope. My splurge on the adorable Santa's helper costume and black knee-high boots that have white fur around the top is a waste.

I've practiced strutting in my boots so the soles are bound to show wear. I can't return them.

"Are you snooping on your stepbrothers?" The nasal accusation of my stepmom's voice smacks me from behind as her too-much floral scent invades my nose.

Gripping one hand on the rail and using the other to comb through my hair, I stand taller and turn. Her bright magenta suit is as potent as her perfume.

"No. Why would I do that?" The elevated pitch of my voice and the way the words spew from my mouth betray me.

"I could ask that of most things about you. Like why you threw college away just because your boyfriend found someone new. It's quite—"

"I didn't throw college away."

"Two F's, a D—"

"Stop." Pinching the bridge of my nose, I take a deep breath.

"How do you plan on taking care of yourself without a college degree?"

"I'm filling out applications. I'll find somewhere to go." Vulnerability eats at me as her eyes rake up and down my body. I cross my arms and look at the mountains.

"Now, to earn your keep, I need you to pick up the invitations for my gala." She hands me a business card I hadn't noticed she was holding. "They're open for one more hour, and the guest list is on your desk. They need to be delivered to the post office tomorrow at the latest."

I laugh.

That was the wrong thing to do. She's serious.

"It's hardly funny that the printer forgot to emboss the filigree on the envelopes. Their delay puts me perilously close to only getting the invitations out two months in advance."

I laugh again, although it's actually a scoff of disbelief if I was forced to categorize the sound.

Her scowl indicates it's still the wrong thing to do.

"The post office closes at two on Saturday," I say, as if she cares about mortal constraints.

"I suppose you can't sleep until two then."

Tension in my jaw has to be nearing teeth-shattering levels.

No matter how much I despise my stepmom, I appreciate that she's the one who convinced my dad to let me stay here.

I don't know if he agreed, but he's out of the country so there wasn't much he could do.

My real mom, who I always lived with, just moved in with a guy. She says it's too early in the relationship for me to complicate things by moving in, which basically means I've become her baggage.

So, my stepmom's offer of penthouse living, where she might consider me her personal assistant, won out over being homeless.

"I have plans tonight. Would it be okay if I get the invitations in the mail on Monday?"

Her eyes pause on my belly. "Now isn't the time to be slack about commitments and let yourself go."

I relent, to avoid a lecture. "Let me get dressed. I can pick them up and still go out with my friends. I'll tackle the addresses in the morning."

"There are exactly one thousand invitations. Make sure your handwriting stays pretty."

Crap.

Turning off the space heater, I grab my belongings and stifle my desire to stomp to my room. It would only give her one more reason to chastise me.

Signing up for the Christmas Cherry Auction was a dumb idea. My father's right. I'm too lost in daydreams like my mom. I might as well have plucked petals from a flower to ask the universe if my stepbrothers could love me.

Aurora and Cindy's messages finally come in and offer another perspective. I have to attend...or they'll kill me.

But Aurora's last message hits another sore spot. My ex. *Don't let Damon get the best of you. Put on your big girl thong and be outside your building on time.*

I wish he was the problem.

I don't want to be the pawn in some rude game my brothers are playing.

Me: *My stepbrothers want to irritate my dad by bidding on me.*

Aurora: *WTF?*

Cindy: *They're idiots. Let's beat them at their own game.*

Me: *How*

Cindy: *We'll run their bid up and all they'll get is four hours of holiday prep help, exactly as you signed up to do. Your dad can be proud that so much money will go to charity.*

She has a point. I can stay in charge. They'll have nothing on me, which means... The least I can do is fulfill my responsibility.

The musky scents of my stepbrothers' colognes linger in the elevator when I enter.

Swoony fantasies about elevator sex—

No. My stepbrothers are a great starting place for this new leaf I'm turning over. No more fantasies. Watch out world, Bianca's embracing a new reality.

I don't have a thing for my stepbrothers.

I don't, not anymore

11

I stop squeezing my thighs together.

Time to move on...as soon as the elevator stops spinning.

Two

Mark

"Try flipping the script," Sean says.

"Try driving with your mouth shut." I'm thankful I can see the bar. I need a drink before I blow a gasket. Bianca occupies all of my thoughts. She makes me tingly…and I'm not a tingly kind of guy. She makes me think of houses with white-picket fences and other things that don't fit into my jet-set lifestyle.

How can I want her so badly when she's exactly what I don't want? Mom had a streak of disastrous relationships before meeting Bianca's dad. I don't ever want to hurt a woman the way men hurt her.

"Instead of you pulling Bianca out of the auction, what if we let it go on as planned and I win her?"

"You won't because I told you not to." I can't deal with the thought of what he wants to do with her. His intent can't be far from my own, which I can barely tamp down. And if either of us screws our stepsister, we stand to complicate our family and business in one harsh blow.

"Let's say I got the high bid. I could fund the entire goal for the women's shelter."

"No."

"Why not? You want to be the shining star? You want to control what Bianca does with the four hours of her volunteer time?"

"Bianca's not taking part in the auction."

"What if you don't get to decide what she does with her life?"

"I'm not letting our eighteen-year-old, as in she's legally an adult, stepsister sell herself."

"Don't patronize me."

"Don't interfere with my plan."

Sean's exasperated sigh as he turns into the parking lot amps up my need for alcohol.

"The only part of your plan I agree with is that we get some drinks in you so you can calm down, hopefully not make a fool of yourself."

"What about Bianca making a fool of *her*self, or of our family? Have you thought about that?" I slam my door and beeline for the bar.

The rush of Sean hurrying over the gravel lot and his continued pleadings don't help any. "Trust me. I've thought about her walking across that stage and what she thinks will happen."

My cock thickens as he forces the thought into my mind. "We have to think of what's best for the family."

"You're assuming she wants the same thing we do. She's not like us."

The bartender nods as we enter. I hold up two fingers, and he gets to work on my usual.

"She loves luxury as much as the rest of us. She'll need a career." The ease with which lies flow from my tongue should bother me. What I really want is to lock Bianca in the highest room of the tallest tower and keep her for myself. She wouldn't need a career. She'd need me and only me. But I've seen how relationships change men, ruin their drive for success. Then they start a family and become domesticated.

I'm not ready to be tied down. And her father's been a generous mentor when he's not busy being a prick.

"Everyone loves luxury, but all she talks about in her future is a family. You ever notice she doesn't mention a career or lavish trips?"

"That doesn't mean she doesn't want them."

"But it means that when she looks at her future, there are things more important than professional success."

The bartender brings me two Rusty Nails. They'll either calm me down or they'll seal my coffin when I make a scene at the auction.

I can't stand the thought of anyone, even my brothers, buying Bianca. Even if it is for four innocent hours, I'd lose my fucking mind. Which means there's only one solution. If I can't get her out of the auction, I have to win the bid.

That's a dangerous path. If I buy her, I'm responsible for her. A lot can happen in four hours. But I'm not the settling-down kind of guy she wants. I've crafted my entire career around never being limited to one location. A fucking catch-22.

Three

Carl

Sean and I decided that he should go with Mark to the bar. It's a chance for Sean to figure out what has Mark so riled.

I suspect he's as obsessed with Bianca as I am, but we've never spoken about beyond-sisterly feelings, or how we'd deal with one of us dating her.

My ulterior motive was to go straight to the auction and make a game plan to try to keep Mark from turning this evening into a fiasco and embarrassing Bianca.

The last few days since she's been back in town have unlocked my creative genius. I've had more breakthroughs for work projects and an idea for a special feature to add to our app.

I've never been the type to credit a muse for my inspiration but when I think of her, the world comes alive.

I can't let Mark fuck this up. I need Bianca in ways I've denied. And from what I've heard, her boyfriend broke up with her. That shouldn't be a green flag for me, but fuck if I don't want to help ease her through the heartbreak.

The doors to the sex club are locked. The bodyguard outside shakes his head when I try the handle, even though he told me that I couldn't go in yet.

He glances at his watch. "Five more minutes."

I note his name embroidered on his barely-big-enough black polo. "It's an emergency, Winger."

"What kind of emergency?"

"I have to talk to my stepsister. It's a private matter."

"Is her life in danger?"

"No."

"Is there a death in the family?"

"No." Although I seriously wonder if somebody's life might be in danger if they bid on her. That's not likely to carry any weight with Winger.

Five minutes pass and I expect the door to open from the inside, but to my surprise, Winger pulls keys from his pocket and unlocks the doors. I decide not to voice my thoughts that he's a dick for making me wait.

As I make my way through the club, I ask the wait staff where the women for auction are and get mixed answers anywhere from no one's allowed in with them to waitresses pointing in the general direction of the stage.

I head for the door beside the stage where a bodyguard with a similarly strained polo to the guy outside, although this one named Mammoth, steps in front of me.

"I have to talk to Bianca." I point as if I know where she is.

"The only talking they want to hear tonight is the auctioneer rattling numbers each time you raise your paddle."

"She's my stepsister."

Mammoth smirks.

"It's not like that." Except it is. That crazy inspiration I get from Bianca is unlike anything I've ever experienced. Probably the taboo nature. Stepsisters shouldn't have such long legs, tiny waist, and plump tits. She's a hummingbird in a family of vultures. She's a relief.

I have to shake the thought of settling down with her from my mind. Monotony stifles creativity.

"Sign-up is over there." Mammoth extends his tree-trunk sized arm.

I follow the direction he indicates and get that out of the way in case it's necessary. Then I stake out the front table since others are filing in.

I pat the bidding number against my thigh, lift it, and imagine I'm the winning bid. Exhilaration shoots through me. My cock swells before I get control.

I can't imagine what her dad would think. The charitable donation defense would go over better than the truth of making sure no one got their hands on her because she's mine. It's very clear in my mind how this needs to work.

Mammoth walks past. I pop up once he safely has his back to me and I head for the side door.

"Do not touch that handle," he booms.

"Look dude, it's my sister. I need to talk to her."

"What's your name?"

"Carl."

"Your message?" His crossed arms indicate he doesn't give a fuck what my message is.

"It's personal. Just tell her I need to talk to her."

He vanishes, then comes back and shakes his head. "The lady said no."

Four

Sean

Mark opens the car door and hurls himself toward the entry of the Aubergine Affair sex club when I've barely stopped the vehicle. Two Rusty Nails were not enough to take the edge off.

I jump out of the car, circle around, and barely catch up with him by the time he's made his way inside to the tables directly in front of the stage where Carl is sitting.

Mark growls, "What the fuck is that?"

Carl gives a half smile and flashes the bidding paddle as he stands. "In case we have to bid."

"Do not bid on Bianca."

"It's one way to get her out of here." The undertones of Carl's excitement confirm that she's gotten to all of us.

"If anyone's going to bid on her, it's me." Mark seems to think he gets to call the shots. He's the oldest, but that hasn't mattered for a long time.

"That's up for discussion," Carl says.

Mark reaches for the paddle, but Carl jerks it back throwing his other hand against our brother's chest. "Get your own damn number."

"Or we can go in together as one big happy family," I reason.

"Then we're doing it under my number." The corded muscles in Mark's neck flex.

Why the hell does he choose to be agreeable now? I regret my suggestion. Keeping the peace is usually my priority but I won't pass up a chance to officially win Bianca, to lay claim to her. There's something about her that all the other women I've dated don't have.

I change my approach. "Or we can bid against each other and drive the price up. It's all about charity, right?" I give them a wink and walk off to register.

Mark follows me, grumbling the whole time, then we meet back at the table.

"So...what would you do with Bianca for four hours?" Is anyone ready to admit what's haunting each of us. The silence shuts that conversation down.

"We've got to get her out before this shit storm starts." Mark is barely calmer than before.

"It's only going to be a shit storm if you make it one," Carl says.

Mark charges off and is met by a bodyguard who refuses to let him in the back. As Mark seems to be returning to our seats, he puts a hand on the edge of the stage and I think he's going to jump up, but the bodyguard jumps up faster and towers over him. "Do you need to be escorted out of here?"

I cringe internally, wondering if the first wave of the storm has hit. Nobody gets away with talking to Mark like that.

I'm shocked when Mark lifts his hands. "Have it your way."

He returns to the table. "I'll do the bidding and handle her afterward."

If I'd drawn a line in the sand, Mark just crossed it. "She's not a piece of property to be handled."

"She put herself in an auction. Are you oblivious to what these men would do with her?"

"It's not just about protecting her from other bidders. I want more than four hours of her time." Did I just pull the pin on a hand grenade? My heart's about to explode. My brothers and I have come to blows on a few occasions. If I wasn't cool-natured, it would happen more often, but this time I'm the antagonist.

Mark says, "She's our step-sister."

Carl stumbles on a few words before he finally says, "You want a relationship with her? Have you thought about how it would affect Mark and me?"

The jealousy in his words betrays the simple questions.

My phone buzzes. After a glance I dismiss it.

Carl asks, "One of your girlfriends?"

"Fuck you."

"That's what she wants." Mark makes a lame joke but he's not wrong.

"It's just a friend."

"A female one?"

"I'm capable of having female friends."

"Enough that you don't need to add Bianca to the list." Carl won't be swayed easily.

"She wouldn't just be added to a list. I want to explore things with her."

Mark might be experiencing an aneurysm, but until he drops to the ground, I'll assume he's okay.

Carl says, "A few hours ago you didn't even know she was in the auction. You're going from zero to fucking her awfully fast."

Mark growls, "Not a chance."

I've confessed my feelings. I'm in now. I have to win this. "Give me one good reason I can't date her, aside from she's our stepsister."

Mark slams his fist on the table. "She has dreams we can't fulfill. Besides her father would pull his investment if we gang banged his princess."

Did he just admit his feelings? "We?"

Five

Bianca

"Not a chance." The deep, gravelly voice carries onto the wings of the stage where my friends and I are waiting. Unmistakably a pissed off Mark.

So, all three of my brothers probably came since the bodyguard let me know Carl was here. I declined to talk since I didn't want anything to mess up my chance to participate in the auction. If they think it's disgusting, that's their problem, not mine.

Could I be happy with a different set of billionaires? It's like being in the mood for a triple-chocolate brownie and being offered a cherry lollipop.

I pull the velvet curtain to the side a couple of inches to find my brothers and see why Mark is yelling. It's not unlike him.

He's now in a seat at one of the front tables, a bodyguard standing interestingly close to him.

Mark leans forward, head bowed, his forearms on his knees, a bidder's paddle clutched in his hand. Carl and Sean have paddles too.

Hmmm… in my fantasy, they're a package deal. How would it work with just one of them? Such a problem would be a blessing.

I wiggle as veins of excitement shoot through me. The bodyguard steps away. If Mark's anger was dialed up anymore, he might just burst into white-hot flames. Not good.

The other brothers wear strained expressions but not as intensely as Mark.

My attention is drawn to motion as he rises. Our eyes lock as he unfolds himself from the chair and strides toward the stage.

My pulse pounds in my ears.

The bodyguard catches his arm and steps in front of him. The two men square off. This could go wrong. Should I swallow my pride and intervene?

I close the curtain and turn to Aurora and Cindy, hoping they'll offer good advice.

"I shouldn't be here. That argument I heard with my brothers earlier, I'm messing everything up."

"No, you can't leave. You've been so excited about this." Aurora and her cheery demeanor can barely break through my nerves. The announcer's voice booms over the PA system, rattling me to the core.

"You have to go," Cindy says. "You're first."

The key issue here is that if I don't go first, Cindy will be. She was clear that she didn't want to be first or last. She wanted to be sandwiched safely in the middle.

"I don't think I can go through with it. Mark's going to cause a scene. If I just leave, we can pretend like none of this ever happened."

"Think of the women's shelter," Aurora says.

"I'm sure you two will raise enough."

"And you don't want to be a part of that?"

She knows how to get at me. My stepmom is really big on fundraising, and I'm trying to be more of an adult and emulate her selfless actions. Even though, for the most part, I could never be like her. But that's one thing she gets right.

The door slams and adrenaline spikes through me that it's Mark. It's not.

"What are you doing here, Wendy? Aren't you getting married today?"

We're not close friends and I heard it was going to be a small ceremony. Who knows, I might have gotten the date wrong. She's in sweats so that's no help. But her frantic expression hints that she might have bigger problems than I do.

As she wrings her hands and takes a few deep breaths, I note what Jefferson, the emcee for the evening, is saying. "Thank you for showing up. Let's make this bigger than last year. In case anyone isn't aware of how this works, the women have agreed to volunteer four hours of their time to help with holiday preparations, nothing more...unless mutually agreed upon."

Wendy's shaky voice pulls me back. "I couldn't do it. I couldn't be a piece of property getting traded as part of a business deal. My dad, my boyfriend...if they don't respect me now, how do I think they ever will? I had to stand up for myself?"

"I had no idea that's why you were getting married." I feel dumbfounded that people still do that.

Aurora hugs her. "You want to be a part of the auction? I couldn't decide between two dresses so I have an extra."

Wendy's voice wavers. "I hate to admit this, but I came here on purpose. I saw the contract. My virginity was part of the deal my father offered to his pervy friend. I want to officially break the contract."

"We can't guarantee who will win you, but remember, you don't have to have sex."

"I know. Thanks, ladies."

Aurora nearly whispers, "Everyone from last year's auction ended up marrying the guys that bought them."

Wendy grimaces. "I doubt I'll be that lucky, but as I ran through the room, I saw quite a few guys I'd be happy to make a deal with."

"Well, last year was an anomaly," Cindy says. "I don't know that we can count on that, but the auction is for a good cause. And well, quite frankly, what better way to lose our V-cards than with experienced guys. I mean, if it all pans out. If not, we just clean a house or wrap presents for four hours."

Aurora pulls us in for a huddle. "It's showtime. They just called Bianca..."

Did they?

Aurora continues, "Cindy is second, and I was going to go last, but you can go before or after me, I don't care."

Jefferson emphasizes my name over the PA. "Let's give a round of applause for Bianca Sinclair."

The roar of the crowd grows. My confidence ticks up one notch. I tug my skirt down.

Aurora slaps my hand. "Enough of that. I know you think you're not pretty enough, not skinny enough, but you're skinnier than all of us. And it wouldn't matter if you weren't. Don't let your stepmom get in your head. Walk out there, chin high, tits out, and let that money roll in."

She slaps my ass then guides me to the edge of the curtain.

As she pulls it back, my eyes land on the front table where my three brothers are still sitting. Mark has gone from irritated to feral. Our eyes lock again and he lifts from his chair, but a slight shift from the bodyguard causes Mark to sit. What the hell did that dude say to him to get him under his finger?

I'm conscious of teetering my way to the center of the stage, breathing a sigh of relief when the auctioneer starts rattling numbers, but then it starts to blur.

My brothers raise their paddles. Other people do too, but it's my brothers. They keep bidding on me. Up and up. I can't understand a word the auctioneer says except for the occasional repeated number.

Then suddenly... "Sold!"

The room spins and I fear that I'll faint. Won't that be disappointing. Thankfully, Jefferson wraps his arm around me. Could he tell? I lean into him.

How did I miss all of the bids? How did I miss the "Going, going, gone"? Was that even said? How much did I go for? Who won me?

"Get off the stage." The low, growly reverb of Mark's voice answers my question. He's getting up from his chair, and the bodyguard doesn't stop Mark from hopping on stage this time.

Chaos erupts from the back of the room. Whoops and hollers, but it can't be about my bid. I pull my eyes from Mark as he stampedes toward me.

It's Aurora's brothers, the rock stars. They have a concert tonight. Why the hell are they here?

I look to the side and catch Aurora staring wide-eyed, then suddenly I'm swooped off my feet.

My hands flail to stop my fall, but strong, thick arms wrap around me, curling me into the contours of Mark's chest. My flail lands my arms around his neck. Our faces are inches apart.

Through the anger, the intensity, I see something more intriguing...desire.

He barks at Carl. "Go wrap up the payment."

As Mark moves furiously toward the exit, his chest rises and falls with heavy breaths. He's even harder than I imagined. Electricity zings through my body. Will it be just him, or all three?

"What the hell were you thinking?"

The sexy stepbrother fantasy bubble bursts.

I'm too embarrassed to answer. I've successfully pissed him off.

I shouldn't be lost in the woody musk of his cologne tinged with alcohol. I should be gathering my senses. All of them, the logical ones included.

Gathering a moment of clarity, I toss out my prefab answer. "It's for charity."

The chill from his demeanor is colder than the winter evening. And the storm in his eyes rages deeper than the front that's supposed to blow in.

He continues to Sean's car but doesn't set me down. "You're half naked. Everyone knows what you're hoping for."

Apparently not, but I don't say anything. I'm saved by Carl and Sean rushing to our sides. Cindy's running out behind them with my bag.

"Why aren't you on stage?"

Sean takes my bag.

"Aurora's brothers demanded they be allowed to buy her right away."

Oh no, Cindy was worried about the order. Low rumbles from the street catch everyone's attention. Motorcycles file into the parking lot.

"Get the fucking car unlocked," Mark demands.

Sean holds the keys up. "Chill, we already paid. No need to scare her."

Sean cups his hand over mine, pulling it from around Mark's neck. "You want him to set you down?"

"Get the fucking car unlocked. I'm not setting her down until I can get her away from the horny-as-fuck rock stars and now this motorcycle gang."

This isn't the way I fantasized he'd want to protect me.

His voice grows louder as he turns, our faces just inches apart.

"Did it not occur to you that the auction was moved to a sex club for a reason?"

Any threads of my fantasy that were hanging on unravel. Is he going to chastise me for the four hours he won? This isn't the kind of tongue-lashing I hoped for.

Six

Sean

The members of the motorcycle club barely glance at Bianca. They're looking for someone and she isn't that person. Their dismissal of her puts Mark at ease enough that I get the car unlocked, the passenger door open, and convince him to put her inside.

He buckles her seatbelt. I rub the back of my neck, waiting to see if he'll go for a kiss. I'm the only one who admitted to wanting her. I'm clearly not alone in my feelings though, and that complicates every fucking thing.

Crisis averted for now as his bulky torso backs away from the car, no kiss.

I say, "Carl, you drive Mark home, that'll give everybody a chance to cool off."

"I don't need time to cool off," Mark says.

"Then why are your fists clenched?"

He furrows his brow and lifts his hands, surprise barely hidden on his face as he flexes his fingers. Mark's voice fails to ease. "It was all falling apart."

"Stop. You're scaring her. Can you see that this is not the look of a woman who's pleased? Do you know what that looks like?"

My phone dings. I glance at the screen.

Mark takes a jab at me. "Is that one of the many women you've pleased?"

In the dim lighting of the parking lot, can he tell that my glare conveys, 'Not in front of Bianca'?

I turn the spotlight back on his asshole behavior. "Nothing's falling apart. You made a giant donation. You're fabulous. You should be happy you won Bianca, and we're taking her back to our place."

Carl huffs. "Come on Mark. You need to chill."

Mark steps toward Carl's car while pointing at me. "Don't try anything. We'll be on your tail."

I slip into the driver's seat and set my hand on Bianca's in a semi-friendly gesture. "He'll calm down. He was just trying to protect you."

"I'm an adult."

"That's the problem." I work my fingers around her palm.

"Can we just drive quietly?" She squeezes my hand.

Why do we fit so well? The backs of my fingers touch her thigh.

My cock shifts into Erection mode, and I have to take my hand off hers so I can shift the car into Reverse then Drive.

True to Carl's word, he stays on my tail.

I resist the urge to reach up and brush her cheek, cup her chin, pull her closer, and plant a kiss on her lips. They'd see that through the back windshield for sure.

We arrive home at the same time and file into the elevator. The silence makes the elevator ride last about an hour longer than normal even with the keycard that takes us directly to the top without stopping at any other floors.

The doors open and Bianca steps to the left towards mom's penthouse.

Carl gently says, "We're over here."

"I'm staying with your mom. I thought you knew."

That's an interesting piece of information Mom forgot to mention.

"Not anymore," Mark says, missing the point that we're trying to be respectful.

Carl is more skilled with his words. "What Conan is trying to say is that we need to talk. Will you come over, please?"

"I get it. I shouldn't have shamed the family." She pulls her hair in front of her cleavage. That should be a sin. The only thing that belongs between her tits is my tongue or my cock.

"You didn't shame anyone." I step closer, but she parries with a step back, a step away from me.

I offer all that I can. "Bianca, we need to talk about what happened and what we all expect or what we all hope will happen now that we won you in the auction."

"I won her," Mark says.

Seven

Bianca

Being locked in Mark's bedroom is the less important half of my fantasy. The key part that he missed was that I wanted him on the same side of the door as me.

If I'd known my brothers had something to sort, I could have gone home.

Their discussion sounds like another argument, but other than raised voices, I can't make anything out.

How could Mark be so mad at me?

I slump onto his bed. His bed—a place I've longed to be, a place I imagined getting tossed onto as he climbed over me. I take off my boots and bring my feet onto the bed, slipping them under the covers, as I sink into the plush mattress, pull the top sheet over me, and nuzzle my head into his downy pillow.

I breathe in the musky scent. It's missing the alcohol from earlier. Is that why he's so upset? The alcohol? I rake my hand over the silky sheets and onto a different fabric. I lift my head, assess that it's a t-shirt, and bring it to my face.

I'm shameless at this point. If they're going to take a minute, so am I. There's one part of my fantasy I can control—having an orgasm in my brother's bed. Fantasy will always be king.

I stare at the door, focusing on their grumblings, making sure they're not approaching, and slide my hand between my legs.

My phone dings. Damn it.

A text from Damon, my ex: *What's up*

His level of stupidity.

Damon again: *Want to hang out?*

Not unless you want to give me an orgasm. I set my phone aside.

Ding.

You've got to be kidding me. Can my evening get any worse?

It's not him this time. Aurora added Wendy to the group chat with Cindy.

Another ding. Aurora: *I'm hidden backstage at my stepbrothers' concert. How is everyone else?*

Me: *LOL. I'm locked in Mark's room, but not in a good way.*

Aurora: *How is that not good?*

Me: *I have time to text you, which means I'm not busy with them. They're arguing about something.*

Aurora: *(hug emoji)*

Me: *I can't believe your stepbrothers showed up. Were our expectations too high?*

Aurora: *I never thought I'd have a chance with my brothers in a million years but I'm downing some liquid courage since they bought me*

Me: *I'll cross my fingers for you to get to uncross your legs! (wink emoji) (eggplant emoji)*

Aurora: *same*

At least one of us has a chance. I type back: *They'll have to let me out by morning so I can address their mom's invites. Or if they take too long, I can text her and tell her they're keeping me from doing it. Stepmom to the rescue.*

Aurora: *Want me to help with the invites?*

Me: *Sure*

Aurora: *We can swap stories*

Me: *Not the story I was hoping for*

Aurora: *count on our damn brothers to screw things up*

I time myself 'pretend' addressing an envelope then use my phone calculator to determine how long it will take to do that times a thousand. Aurora and I agree on a time to meet.

I drop the phone and remember I'm in Mark's bed...alone. It's amazing how many things I can fail at.

Sliding my hand between my legs, I press gently. I've been so wound up all evening, it takes nothing for the swirl of an orgasm to start building. I grab a pillow and put it on my chest. It's not heavy enough to be one of my brothers, but it's better than nothing.

The bedroom door flies open.

39

"You should have knocked!" The first part of my statement comes out as more of a pant but I'm screaming by the end as I scramble to sit.

I stare at the three of them huddled in the doorway. Do they realize they barged in on a private moment?

Would it change their reaction if they did? I'm pretty sure I can't stoop any lower. Being at a low point is oddly liberating.

For a moment, I savor the way they're staring at me—like they want me.

Eight

Carl

Bianca's moan and what seemed to be her hand between her legs stymy me. Did we walk in on her... No. Surely she wouldn't... My muse is a naughty one, perhaps Erato or Thalia. Why the hell am I pondering Greek Muses when mine is right here?

"Unless you boys have plans for me, I have to get home. Your mom needs me." The taunt in her tone hints at a sassier side I'm not used to.

Her fingers toy with the edge of the sheet as if waiting for us to call her bluff.

I'm quick to say, "We're not done. We need you—"

Mark cuts me off. "To explain why you were in that auction."

Damn him. Is he completely unable to pivot? Walking in on her hand between her legs should have moved us past the question we agreed he could ask first.

Sean's phone buzzes. He ignores it.

"I already explained—to raise money for the women's shelter."

"Why were you dressed like that?" Mark doesn't relent.

She tosses the covers back, and for a fleeting second, I'm expecting to see her perfect tits, to find out how rosy or dusky her nipples are. But it's all red and white fabric. The only things she's taken off are her boots.

Sean's phone buzzes again.

Bianca pauses but Sean waves a dismissive hand. She answers Mark's question with a light tone. "Some of us are in a festive, *giving* mood."

"Giving?" I step into the room. Mark follows and Sean stops on the other side of him.

She rolls onto her side and throws her legs over the edge of the bed as she sits.

Sean's phone buzzes yet again.

"See what your damn girlfriends need," Mark says.

"I don't have a girlfriend." Sean pulls his phone from his pocket and swipes messages from the screen. "It's nobody important."

Bianca's phone buzzes.

Relief washes over Sean's expression. "See. I'm not the only one who gets texts."

Mark raises an eyebrow at Bianca. She grabs her phone and flusters before poking at the screen several times and setting it aside. If she always pokes it that hard, I might understand why the screen is so cracked.

"Who was that?" Mark asks.

"My ex. It's no big deal. We've all been in other relationships."

Sean rubs a hand over his face, and Mark asks, "What does he want?"

"The question should be what I want."

"Okay. What do you want?"

"He dumped me, and I want to get over him. That's why I was at the auction tonight, other than charity, of course." Bianca's response shuts Mark down.

Sean says, "Looks like I'm not the only one ready to move on. Get over your ex how?"

She grabs her shoes and pushes off the bed, walking toward us. The come hither look I swear she's giving us is replaced by an eye roll.

Sean, usually the gentlest of the three of us, grabs her arm. "How can we help?"

She pulls away and slumps with a heavy exhale. "I can't believe I have to spell this out to my older brothers."

Words fall from my mouth before I can stop them. "Were you hoping to get laid?"

Mark, being ever so not helpful in this conversation, says, "No."

Bianca laughs as Sean and I simultaneously say, "Shut up, Mark."

"Don't fucking tell me what to do." He pushes the two of us aside, steps toward Bianca, cups her chin, turns her face upward, and lands his lips on hers.

When he finally pulls away, he says, "Did that help?"

Nine

Bianca

Mark's words meet my ears, which means he can't be kissing me anymore. The pressure of his lips lingers on mine. I lift a hand in disbelief, covering my lips before I force my eyes open.

Shoot. I must look like an idiot. I clear my throat and move my hand to my hair, pretending to straighten it.

That kiss did a lot more than make me forget about my ex. I forgot how to speak.

Everyone's staring at me. Am I going through with this?

Mark grumbles something then barges past his brothers. The door to their penthouse slams a few seconds later.

I wait. There's no other sound.

He's gone.

How on earth did I screw that up? I stare at my feet, curious how my previous low point has been surpassed. If Carl and Sean hadn't closed the space in front of me, I'd rush out too.

Forcing my chin up, I let my eyes move from Mark's picture of the Colosseum to the Eiffel Tower and Stonehenge and several other noteworthy landmarks. It's Mark in a nutshell—always on the go.

Sean breaks the silence. "Did that help, Bianca?"

Did he kiss me too? No, he didn't. He's reiterating the unanswered question. Maybe this whole thing was too confusing for all of us. Maybe I should have told them that I wanted them instead of anonymously sending them an invitation. That was a spectacularly vague effort on my part.

But two of them are still standing here waiting for my answer, which means it must matter. Surely this time, I can't go any lower. I muster the 'can only go up from here' bravado and meet his gaze.

"Yeah, that's a step in the right direction."

Carl smirks. "A step in the right direction...so Mark wasn't enough."

Oh, shit. Mark's ego would take a hit if they told him he didn't succeed.

"That's not what I meant."

"Help us understand." Sean takes one of my hands, caressing gently. Why does that spark the reminder that I have a thousand invitations to address? That our parents would be horrified to know I lust after my stepbrothers? That I seem to have no purpose in life other than to fail at things.

"It was...just..." I pull my hand back and scramble for a lie so I don't have to admit how much it met every expectation. "Mark's kiss was great...it's just weird since we're related."

46

Carl reaches for his collar, unfastens his tie, and slides it from his neck. "What if you couldn't see us?"

He moves behind me, positioning it as a blindfold.

Sean's body presses against me from the front. I'm sandwiched between two of my stepbrothers. My entire body throbs with need. How wrong is it to want this?

"I can make you forget a lot more than your ex," Sean leans down to whisper in my ear.

"Can you make me forget we're related?"

His kiss proves he can. I lose track of who's who. A hand brushes up my side. I'm moaning against Sean's mouth. His tongue takes control of our kiss the way I want him to control me. I want to be able to surrender all of my worries.

A hand comes from behind and massages my breasts before trailing down and working its way under my skirt, leaving my panties in place as fingertips slide over my sex. My hips buck shamelessly in response.

The bliss I'm basking in intensifies as he moves his hand faster and faster.

Someone nips my ear. The hand exploring my neck, my back, and my arms has me wondering how many erogenous zones I have.

The sweet nothings destroy my ability to hold back.

"We can make you forget everything. All you have to do is let go. We'll take care of you."

I splinter into a million pieces…to his words, to the mouth on mine, to the fingers working magic between my legs.

When I drift back, my body is no longer braced between them. I'm being carried, set on a chair, and kissed gently.

"Can you come for us again?" Is that Sean?

My head is turned to the side and a mouth is on my neck. The other brother's lips are on mine. The neck kisses trail downward until there's warmth on my sex. I'm lost in blindness.

Why didn't he take my panties off? I fumble to get my skirt out of the way and my panties down.

Carl says, "I guess that's a yes."

Firm hands grip my wrists on either side then swing my hands wide and pin them behind my head.

Warm breath heats my sex—panties still in place. Then the breath is gone. Lips and kisses make their way from one thigh to the other. My hips make their best guess when they can buck into the kisses.

He, whichever brother it is, finally takes pity on me. Pressure on my sex makes me aware of how wet my panties are already. His moans indicate that's a good thing.

"So sweet. I could do this all day." The movement of his lips as he speaks drives me closer to release.

I'm not going to admit that I don't think I could handle 'all day'. It doesn't matter. I'm lost in 'right now' as I fall apart once again.

They take turns making me come. It finally seems like I'm getting something right.

When I wake up, I'm not wearing the blindfold. It's dark. Bodies are on either side of me and I have to wiggle just right to slip out of bed. I manage it without waking anyone.

The faint sound of my alarm filters into my awareness. That's what woke me up. I'm grateful it starts quietly and gets louder. My brothers haven't heard it yet. The faint phone glow from the other room is just enough to help me navigate from the bedroom we ended up in.

I shut the alarm off, and with the little bit of screen light, find my dress and thank my lucky stars that my walk of shame is only to the next penthouse.

As I open the door to leave my brothers' apartment, the elevator dings. I hope that the sound isn't enough to wake the guys, but the door is ripped from my hand.

Mark's standing there. His eyes are bloodshot. He's only in his boxers and his damn happy trail has me salivating. When did he come back? Did he join—

A click from my right draws my attention to my stepmom as she looks up from her phone, shocked.

I follow her horrified gaze to the elevator where Aurora and Cindy are exiting. I didn't realize Cindy was coming too, and I don't have time to celebrate that the invites will go even faster.

"Mark?" My stepmom's comment dictates where all of us look. "What is going on here?"

"I was just...um..." He is rarely speechless, and holds up his shirt, which if my brain can be trusted, he was not holding a few seconds ago. Carl is close behind, grinning. Mom can't see him.

Mark resumes his normal composure. "I dropped this in the hall."

Carl winks at me. "Mark had one of those wild nights. Our lovely stepsister was just returning it."

Their mom motions to me. "Your friends have to go. My invitations won't address themselves. And don't walk into the post office looking like a little Christmas whore."

She turns her ire to Mark. "Why are you still standing there? Cover yourself when there are ladies present even if your sister doesn't know how to dress like one."

Mark and his happy trail step into the lobby. Nerve endings spark to life where his arm brushes mine.

"Don't speak to Bianca that way. The clothes don't make the woman. You—" Mark defends me.

Then he gets yanked backward. I don't know what happened, but their door slams, and I'm left to deal with their mother by myself.

Ten

Carl

I yank Mark by the underwear to get him away from mom. We crash into the wall under his unbalanced weight.

Shoving off of me, he adjusts his boxers. "Bianca was here all night?"

"You would have known if you hadn't run off."

"My head is fucked." He rakes a hand through his hair.

"That's the only explanation for going off on Mom like that. But thanks, man. I was about to defend Bianca. You'll get Mom's wrath instead." I playfully punch his shoulder.

"I'm already going to have to deal with Mom. I want Bianca. I want to get her out of here."

"You have an interesting way of showing it. You should have stuck around and joined us," Sean says from the kitchen.

"You had sex with her?" Last night's level of anger returns.

I answer, "No, but if she needed to forget her ex, I'd say, 'mission accomplished'. She was game for both of us, messing around. What do you guys think about sharing her?"

"How would that work?" I ask, variations of sex acts already vivid in my mind. It's the public life stuff that poses issues I'm not sure any of us are ready to deal with.

Mark finds relative calm. "We should invite her over to discuss what this is."

"She has to address invitations for mom this morning. Carl and I offered to help but she declined. She's going to let us know when she's finished."

I furrow my brow and start to say something but Sean cuts me off.

"Yep, we're at her mercy. Just sit and wait."

I'm not sure what he's up to but after Mark's hissy fit last night, I'm fine with getting petty as fuck and leaving him out of our actual plan. Sean and I arranged to drive Bianca to the post office.

The hours tick by slowly until the moment I've waited for. Invitations are mailed. Her friends are gone. Now the elevator ride back to the penthouse. I watch her in the mirrored wall.

Her smile. Her innocence. Her fun nature. I'm captivated. She's everything this family isn't. And she's exactly what I need. Figuring out how to play this has wreaked havoc on my brain. I can't lose her. I just don't know how to keep her.

For now, we can have fun.

Through her sundress, I cup her ass, giving me a perfect handhold. Why she's wearing a sundress in December is beyond me. She steps to the side and I follow suit until she's pinned against Sean. Her mischievous grin eggs me on the whole time.

I tug at my collar, "Sorry, I didn't put a tie on today."

With the mirrored walls, I can see Bianca from several angles. It's the way it should always be, I should be all-knowing about her. A ding pulls us back to reality. I step away.

The doors open and the fuck if Mom and Mark aren't standing there. Mark is livid. Mom gasps in horror, "What are the three of you...?"

"Just goofing off," I say playfully. Sean pushes Bianca past Mom.

"Your father is coming home around ten this evening. I told him fresh gingerbread would be waiting. I'll be at the spa getting a tune-up before he gets back."

"Yes, ma'am. I'll get some gingerbread made," Bianca says. It takes me a second to process that Bianca understood my mom was telling her to make it. I thought my mom would have it delivered from the bakery. Fuck, she has Bianca under her thumb.

I come to Bianca's defense, "What if she has plans?"

"She can speak for herself. Her father works very hard to afford this lifestyle. And when she goes back to school, he'll pay her tuition. I'm sure she'll be happy to do this small favor for him."

Bianca says, "I love baking. It's no problem."

"Yes, and Bianca already offered to do the baking for the family holiday party since she'll be home."

Mark says, "When is that?"

"The twenty-second." Mom reminds him with a stern look.

He grimaces. "Shit. I think that's when I'm heading to Poland with my friends. They have a stellar holiday light display from what I've heard."

"It would be nice to have you home."

Does Mark hear the sadness in Mom's tone?

She continues, "Please check on that. But more pressing is today's schedule."

I don't want to argue with Mom. I'll let Mark be the bad guy. "We'll make it work."

"Make what work?" Mom asks.

"We asked Bianca to give input on our app since women are our primary demographic."

"I am a woman." Mom juts her chin out.

"Yes, and we'll ask for input from you when we have the app perfected a little more."

Mom beams with pride then quickly turns serious as she points toward the elevator. "That should be fine as long as she has time to bake. And don't let your father see you acting childish like that again."

We all voice agreement.

"And don't forget the homemade—"

Bianca cuts her off, "Whipped cream. I know how he likes it."

I like whipped cream. My dick is hard thinking about Bianca's tongue licking it off of me. I angle myself so mom can't see my reaction. "We better let Bianca get to work, she's got a tight schedule."

"So much to do." Bianca heads toward Mom's penthouse.

Mark asks, "How long will you be gone, Mom?"

Her hand hovers over the elevator buttons. "Why does that matter?"

I can't afford to let Mark's irritation derail us. I answer. "We want to make sure the kitchen's cleaned up."

"I'm going to tea with friends after the spa, I'll be gone until at least eight."

"Great." We all head to the door with Bianca.

Mom's voice pierces the air, "Why are you going with her?"

"Maybe she can teach us a thing or two."

Eleven

Bianca

I breeze through the kitchen, setting the ingredients on the counter. Carl studies me from the doorway.

"What are you doing?"

"Making sure we have everything for gingerbread."

"You don't have your phone or a recipe card."

"I have the recipe in my head."

"Seriously?" Sean asks. "How many times a year do you make gingerbread?"

"Usually just once."

"And you memorized it?"

"Yeah. I love baking. I love taking care of the people around me. Gingerbread's always been one of Dad's favorites. I memorized it long ago. And it looks like we're missing butter."

"That's pretty damn impressive. We've got butter at our place," Carl says. "But what was that mention of homemade whipped cream?"

"Yeah, let's play house." Mark finally pipes up. I wondered how long he would simmer over not being a part of last night. "You better make extra."

"You aren't going to dine and dash like last night, are you?" I tease.

"I had to take care of something."

Sean steps closer and pushes my hair behind my shoulder, planting gentle kisses on my neck.

"I'll be happy to taste test for you." His kisses tickle, and my shoulder hikes up. He winks as he steps back. "And I'm sorry Mom assumes you'll bow to her needs. We'll talk to her. But for now, how much time do you need for the gingerbread?"

"Since I don't need to shop, and I want it to be warm when Dad shows up, I don't need to start for a few hours. Why don't we go work on your app?" I make finger quotes. After all the orgasms they gave me yesterday, it has to be my turn to please them.

Carl pulls out his phone as he laughs. He taps the screen and angles it toward me. "We really do need your help. This is our app."

"Oh." My excitement sinks. "What could I possibly help with?"

"We'll show you."

My heart rate escalates and my panties are drenched as I step into their penthouse.

Carl turns his computer on and a logo similar to the one on his phone populates the screen. He launches into an explanation. It's cute seeing how excited he is.

"When we get this up and running, it will be the top-of-the-line clothing app. We're going to partner with everything from stores that have brick-and-mortar locations to online stores, and even local boutiques like Peaches and Jeans."

"What does it do?"

"You scan your body in, preferably wearing a bathing suit or underwear at most, so the computer can truly assess your shape. When you select clothes you're interested in buying, you can try them on virtually and get the best visualization on the market of how the clothes will fit you specifically. Everywhere from the rise of the jeans to the fit of sleeves. Every detail's been incorporated."

"Ready to get started?" Carl looks at me expectantly.

"Is that your way of asking if I'm ready to get naked?" I can't stop the giggle. For all we did last night, I was blindfolded.

Sean says, "Only if you're comfortable."

This is a good opportunity for the next step. No blindfolds.

Sean notices my hesitation. "If you'd feel better, we could all strip to our skivvies." He's already undressing.

"And we're not even going to make this sexual," Carl says. "I do need to test the app."

It's one of the most ridiculous things I've ever seen—me and my three stepbrothers nearly naked and each of them sporting varying degrees of erections. I grab the edge of the desk to steady myself. It's a lot to go from blindfolds to a lit room.

"Sorry," Carl says, rubbing his hand over the strained front of his underwear. "You're just so fucking beautiful."

How much of a next step will this afternoon be?

"Let's get started." Carl guides me to a greenscreen.

"Unclasp your hands," Carl tugs my fingers.

I have to willingly relent and end up keeping my hands in front of my thighs.

"What's wrong?" Sean asks.

"Just standing here...you can see..." I can't meet any of their eyes, especially Mark's. He's sitting on a barstool nearby. I'm not sure how he'll fit into what Carl, Sean, and I had even though they asked if I'd be fine with including him.

"Are you embarrassed? Sugar, you may have had a blindfold on last night, but we didn't."

Carl cups my shoulders. "Don't slump. Your body is beautiful."

My hands slide up and down my arms. "I'll look better once I lose the weight I put on in college."

"What the hell?" Mark surges toward me.

"As soon as things calm down. I'll go on a diet."

"No. No. No. You don't need a diet," Sean assures me.

"Your mom would disagree."

"She doesn't matter. She overreacts." Mark brushes his thumb over my cheek.

My eyes fall shut. I want to believe him, but it's a fact that I gained weight.

Carl says, "If we haven't proven that we're fine with you just the way you are, let us help you with a few more orgasms."

Mark slides his hand down but I stop it before he gets to my belly.

"You don't have to prove anything. I hear you." But the importance of image has been seared into me far more than a few orgasms can wash away. "Let's do the app."

I swallow my pride and let them document my body from all sides. I'll have them retake the pictures when I lose weight.

Carl moves behind me, circling his arms low on my hips. "It won't affect the way the app puts clothes on your body, but I want the scan to document the way you blush after an orgasm. How about it?"

I close my eyes and lick my lips saying what I'm pretty sure is the right thing to say. "Shouldn't I reciprocate first?"

Sean steps in. "We're not keeping score. You wanted help getting over your ex, we're doing that. You don't owe us anything, although helping with this app would be great."

"I'm pretty sure guys keep score."

"If guys kept score with you, that's their problem."

Heat overtakes my cheeks.

"What's that for?" Mark asks.

"What?" I've probably delayed this as long as I can.

"Why are you blushing?"

"There hasn't been anything to keep score of."

"What?" Carl circles in front of me.

"I haven't had sex, or even an orgasm with a guy... And I don't want to talk about it. Don't make it a thing."

"It is a thing." Mark's possessive expression is back.

"Fine. It's a thing we're not going to talk about. Now let's do the app."

Everyone stares at me, indeed making it a thing. I cringe. Waving my hands, I say, "Shoo. Get your camera. Either we do this or I leave."

They scamper into position around the camera.

We scan my body, they let me select different clothes to virtually try on. It's exciting to see how it works. Then Carl pulls me onto his lap.

"I had a special feature designed. Want to see it?" Nervousness taints his words.

"It sounds ominous."

"Nothing bad, just something you inspired."

"Me?"

Based on Sean and Mark's reactions, I'm not the only one who's confused.

With a few clicks of the mouse, the computer simulates a pregnancy month-by-month. I'm in love with my belly but when my hand goes to my core, it's sadly disappointed. I'm only pregnant on-screen.

"That's amazing." The tears of happiness welling inside of me make it risky to say much more.

Sean says, "I didn't realize you could be even more beautiful."

Mark adds, "Well done, Carl."

"I'm glad you like it, Bianca." Carl dismisses his brothers. "I wasn't sure I'd get to show you."

To be a mom, to have a baby inside of me, that's my dream. But wait. "How did I inspire this?"

"I want to get you pregnant, Bianca."

Surely that's figurative. I'll check Urban Dictionary later for an alternate meaning. His dick is like a rolling pin underneath me. So thick, so hard. I can't focus on the screen anymore. I catch myself rocking my butt over his shaft.

"He's not alone," Sean says. "And I know you want kids."

I croak out, "Yeah."

Mark is a wrecking ball through the beautiful moment. "We can fit them into your career plan."

Thanks for the reality check, bro. "Yeah, lots of women do. Speaking of which, I should go check on my college applications. Alone."

Batting the guys away as I slip my sundress on, I hold back tears. Of course, he thinks I should have a career plan. Of course, they all do. They're all so successful.

Telling them I don't want a career will disappoint them. I need a second to regroup.

Exiting their penthouse, I turn towards my stepmom's. I choke on the memories of her judgment. I don't want to be in this space, in this world where image is everything, where perfection is everything, where success is everything.

Detouring myself to the only space that doesn't reek of them, I cry my way up the stairs to the rooftop.

Twelve

Sean

The click of the stairwell door is a gift letting me know Bianca didn't go check on her college applications. What the hell went wrong?

Sobs come from above. I look up, ready to catch her tears but the door to the roof slams shut. I'm taking the stairs three at a time.

I told Mark and Carl to give me a second with her but they're not likely to listen. I have to hurry. Before I get to the roof, they're following.

Bianca's only a few paces past the door. The brisk winter wind whips past us, reminding me there's a storm blowing in. I wrap my arms around her, first and foremost, making sure she's secure. Her chest heaves against me.

My need to protect her soars to new heights. How can I convince her that she means more to me than any other woman I've dated? I can't even explain it to myself. But if I can't have her, I'll be single and miserable forever.

"I..." If I tell her I love her now, it might seem forced. Damn it. "I hate to see you upset. What's wrong?"

"All of it. We're related...and my school...your business...our parents...just give me space."

I back away. My brothers have stepped on either side of us, and also leave space. Moonlight shines on her wind-kissed cheeks.

Carl says, "We can work this out."

"There's nothing for you to work out. You're already successful. We're in totally different parts of our lives. I'm the one floundering around. I can't even follow my dad's rules correctly: finish high school, get a degree, establish my career. I'm not like all of you."

"Frank's rules...are they what you want?" Carl asks.

"I don't want to throw my life away. There are tons of people who would love to have their college paid for. But it's not what I want...going to college, I mean."

This is huge. Our parents have no idea. I've heard them talk about Bianca's failures, and it irritates me to no end. The only way she's failing is by not pursuing her own path. She's trying to please everyone else. The struggle resonates deeply. I love keeping the peace, but there are limits.

"Being a mother isn't throwing your life away."

"I know that, but they want me to be successful. Like Mark said, I should be fitting kids into my career, which means I need the career first."

"I'm sorry, Bianca. I thought you wanted that." Mark sounds truly sorry.

I shove Mark out of the way. "Success is about knowing what you want so you can strive for it and celebrate when you get there. I'll get you pregnant right now if that's what you want. Fuck what everyone else thinks."

Carl and Mark say something but I'm only listening to Bianca.

The wind catches her dress, blowing it into her face. My cock is rock hard at the sight of her bare legs that wrapped around my head so sinfully last night, and her panties...damn...her virginity. My balls ache with the need to fill her with babies.

She fusses to get her skirt down, but I take it as the universe saying, "Get her clothes out of the way. Time to get her pregnant."

Carl adds logic to the equation. "Hold on. Before we start talking about pregnancy, we should clarify what this is. Mark, are you just in this for fun, or for everything?"

"I'm older than you two. I saw Mom's relationships. They were perfect until they weren't. Commitment changes people. Why can't we play this out slower?"

"He's right," Bianca says.

"There's not a single doubt in my body that I'll do whatever it takes to make you happy, Bianca." I don't need time.

"What do you most want out of life?" she asks me.

"You're not going to let me say, 'pleasing you', are you?"

"No." She's more firm than normal.

I don't understand why she won't relent. Is my brother's indecision the hold up? "What I want doesn't matter. Let's just trust our hearts. What does your heart say, Mark?"

He paces. "Life is bigger than gut reactions. Our parents would disown us. They'd yank the funding from the app. We'd probably get kicked out of the penthouse."

Carl cuts in. "That's all true. So you have to ask yourself, what's more valuable to you, our parents' approval or Bianca's happiness?"

"That's a loaded question. Of course, I want Bianca to be happy. But the three of us can't agree on most shit. How are we supposed to make a relationship with a single woman work?"

Carl offers, "We'll figure it out as we go. I like a plan, probably more than anyone else, but if we wait, we might lose her."

"I don't want to hurt her," Mark calls over his shoulder as he leaves. "I have to make a call.

Bianca points at him. "This is what happens when I'm involved. Everything gets messed up. You guys are arguing because of me and my silly fantasy that we could have something. That you would bid on me at the auction, and we'd end up with a happily ever after."

"Your fantasy?"

"That's why I sent you the invitation."

"You sent that?" Carl says.

She slumps. "I didn't want you to know it was from me. I was afraid you wouldn't come."

"It's always because of you that we'll come. Mark needs time to sort this out. He's afraid of commitment. But if Carl and I can make this work with you, he might warm up."

She gnaws at her lower lip. "I don't want to be the cause of family strife."

"Bianca," I use both of my hands to cup either side of her face and hold her windblown hair out of the way. I have to be sure she's paying attention. "Let me make love to you. Don't worry about Mark or the future or anything. Let me show you how much I love you. And if you want Carl and Mark to be a part of it, I would do that for you. I just want to make you happy."

"At what cost?" Her exasperation crushes my heart.

"There's no cost too high, but I don't want your first time to be up here."

She turns to Carl and her expression shifts, or maybe it's the moonlight glinting in her eye, but I swear something changes. Her shoulders pull back. Her jaw sets. Her eyes meet mine with an intensity she's never hit me with.

"Don't make decisions for me. Everyone keeps talking about me like I'm not here."

"I'm sorry. What do you want?"

"I want to have sex right here, right now."

"Hell yeah." I grab her by the waist and sit her on the ledge, pressing a thigh between her knees, encouraging her to spread for me. Then I lock my lips with hers.

"Thank you for this," I say between kisses.

Thirteen

Bianca

The agony of wanting something that I fear plays out as Sean tenderly kisses me, caresses his hands over my body, and makes room for Carl to join in. The three of us are so perfect, and yet we're still missing a piece.

"You don't have to close your eyes, Bianca."

"I need to." I can't look at them—the men whose hearts I'm going to break. I'm going to fail them like I failed everyone else. I hate that they're so kind and generous. When I dared to look into Sean's eyes earlier, I saw nothing but sincerity. And Carl, there's something between us, like a constant spark. Not just sex but inspiration.

That's how I got this idea.

"How do you want Sean to take you? You're in control."

I don't care as long as we stay up here. I'm free when we're on the roof. I'm enough, or at least Carl and Sean make me feel like I am. But I can't look them in the eyes.

"Let me hop down and bend over."

They stop me before I spin around, each taking their turn caressing my body, tweaking my nipples, kissing my lips, my neck, my arms. They back me against the ledge and Carl drops to his knees. "Can I do this first?"

My eyes shift from his gaze to the gentle brush of his fingers over my shoulder, down my arm to the intertwining of our fingers.

Staring down at him, I understand how much power I have. I'm not used to being in control. Is this what it's like to be surrounded by people who love me for myself?

He unties the sash from my sundress and hands it to Sean. "Let us take away all of your worries. Just exist."

And once again, I'm blindfolded.

Carl grips my waist, trails his hands down my sides, my hips, and wraps his fingers around the backs of my legs. Gusts of wind remind me of my freedom, of my position on top of the world.

"You ready?"

I barely register his question but manage a nod and my cheek brushes against Sean's lips.

Carl's fingers tuck between my legs, pulling my panties to the side, and the wet warmth of his tongue sends jolts of excitement through me. It's different when there are no clothes in the way.

Sean pulls away, and when I reach for him, he takes my hand. A second later he presses it on his bare chest, his heart.

He steps closer, straddling my leg as he presses his body to my side. The thickness of his cock on my side has me more eager than ever to reciprocate.

Carl grips both of my thighs and dives in, eating my pussy like it's the tastiest dish he's ever had. I'm too weak to resist. I give in to gluttony. I'll take as many orgasms as these men will give.

My cream coats his face as I come undone.

"You are the sweetest, Sugar."

A nickname? Why does that feel so intimate?

The heat of his body moves up mine as he stands, his face hovering in front of my blindfold, his warm breath letting me know his lips are poised to let me take in my own scent. I'm consumed by myself, and him, and the rock of Sean's hips.

It doesn't really work to have three people kiss, but Sean tries. He's in on the mix and groans as he licks my release from where Carl's transferred it to my lips. He slides a hand between my legs, slipping easily between my pussy lips, into my center, and another orgasm gathers.

Where are my panties?

"You're so fucking wet. Are you ready for my cock?"

"Yes. Yes, please." Panties not needed.

He spins me to face the ledge, helping me place my hands. Lifting my skirt, he wraps his arms around my hips, continuing to work my clit, driving me to the sweetest surrender I might ever have as his tip nudges at my entrance.

"I'll take it slow. Tell me if I need to stop."

He's respecting the conversation I don't want to have. "I'm ready."

The wind whips past, reminding me the city is laid out at my feet. I don't need my ex. I need my stepbrothers.

There's a sound I can't identify, then Mark's voice. "Have you thought this through?"

Sean's tip pushes a tiny bit farther, spreading my pussy lips. Now is not the time for thinking.

"I know exactly what I want." Sean inches in, stretching me. "She feels better than you can imagine." Sean slides his shaft back and forth in tiny motions.

"I'm here for this. I'm sorry I took so long to get my head clear, Bianca." Footsteps bring Mark closer and he kisses the side of my face.

I cry out as Sean thrusts inside of me. His hands clamp around my hip bones as he freezes. "I'm sorry. I lost control."

"Don't stop. I want that. I want you to mean it."

I didn't know my body could be taken to these heights. So many hands and mouths. I splinter apart over and over again. White heat and stars and rainbows, everything beautiful.

My body contracts around his thick shaft. The surges of tightness, not just from him sliding in and out, but from me reflexively begging him for everything, begging for that baby he said he would give me.

He growls as his cock swells. "If you don't want to be pregnant, tell me now."

I thrust my hips into him. The warmth of his release coats my sex, spills out, and trickles down my thighs. It's a shame any of his seed is wasted. I know what I want—his baby.

I lose track of the other two until Carl speaks up. "You look so fucking hot taking his cock."

"She should take cock more often." Mark agrees.

"She's taking mine next," Carl demands.

Fourteen

Carl

"You're going to have to hold on a second, Mark." I hate to think of it as getting in line, but he can't keep running off and think he deserves time when he returns. Sean and I are invested.

I bend down, kiss Bianca, then move my lips to her ear. "Are you ready for round two? It's a lot for a first time."

"I want it."

I stand her up, facing me, and rub my finger along the edge of the blindfold. "Do you want to take this off?"

"No. It helps me focus."

"Do you want to take this off?" I run a finger down the buttons of her dress.

"I think it better stay on too. You don't need to do anything special."

"Everything I do for you needs to be special."

She smiles nervously and I kiss the tip of her nose, then her forehead.

"I just want to do this with you now while we have the chance."

I'm not sure what to make of her "have the chance" comment. Does she not understand Sean and I are in this? Mark, I still don't know. I can't make heads or tails of where he is with his commitment phobia.

That's not my problem. I turn Bianca's back to me and set her hands on the ledge.

"You ready to let me have a piece of that pussy?"

"Yes."

"We want you to be ours forever."

"You don't have to say that. I want this. Remember, I'm in control of my life. I want to have sex with all three of you."

Why the fuck is she resisting?

"Sugar, we've got you."

"Then prove it."

"Don't fuck this up, Carl," Mark says. Is he worried that she's as commitment-phobic as him?

I glare, grateful Bianca can't see. Then I lift her skirt and admire the glistening streaks of cum running down her legs. I notch my cock at her sopping-wet entrance. Just the tip. I slide in and out.

"You like that?"

"Uh-huh."

"You want more?"

"Yes."

"Then ask me for it."

"What?"

"Ask me for it. Tell me what you want. You're in control of your life."

She hesitates but when I pull away she relents. "I want more."

"More what?"

"I want more of your cock."

I make love to her the way she wants. Later, I'll do it properly.

I don't last much longer than Sean, her release triggers mine. She's that tight, but also, there are three of us and this is her first time. Why is she asking for it to be like this? Blindfolded, turned away, 'have a chance'...is she keeping her distance? Not letting it get personal? Fuck! Are we toys to her?

"Thank you," Bianca says.

I stroke my finger over her cheek. "This isn't the kind of thing you say thank you for."

"Maybe when it's that good, I should."

My cock twitches at her pseudo-compliment, but I have to make one thing clear. "You don't ever have to thank us. It's our job to take care of you."

Fifteen

Mark

Watching Sean and Carl fuck Bianca should give me time to come to my senses. I can't.

I'm wrecked. Her father will pull his company's support for our app, and the dominoes will fall. He's too fucking influential.

But while my brothers were seducing Bianca on the roof, I ran downstairs to make a call to the realtor I've been talking to. I closed the deal on the perfect home in the perfect neighborhood. As soon as I give Bianca the keys, it won't be possible to hide this insane relationship.

I stare at the cum running down her leg and the darkening spot below her where it's pooled. She's so fucking full of cum, and she's about to get a massive load. I'm sure as hell not missing out on my chance to get her pregnant.

"Mind if I taste how divine you are?"

"You'll taste a lot more than just me."

I throw my clothes to the ground as I step behind Bianca. Lowering myself to my knees, I slide my hands up and down her legs.

I can't wait for the feast in front of me. I dive in, settling my lips and tongue on her sex.

Damn, if she isn't worth every bit of risk our relationship poses. I want to be the man for her, to protect her. That's why I bought the house. It's the rashest thing I've ever done. And now that my lips are on her sweet sex, I can't be sure of my motivation.

Am I so hung up on her that I'm still not thinking straight?

Her body spasms, her cries escalate, and she releases with a little squirt on my face. Sweet surrender. She's mine.

When I step back, I drag my hand over my shaft.

Watching her come over and over again for my brothers, I know she regroups pretty damn fast. I slide my cock in.

"I can't believe I can take more."

"I don't want to wear you out. I'll be fast as long as you promise I can take my time later."

"I promise."

My chest swells that she's making promises to me. I hope she'll feel as at home in the house I bought as I feel inside of her.

I piston slowly at first then pick up my pace.

Her cries let me know she's headed from simmer to a full boil, and when she comes undone, she strips me of all my power, all of my ability to protect her because in that moment, I'm reduced to primal need. I have to get my seed inside of her. I thrust hard and fast. I will make her mine even if it ruins me.

Her body stiffens before her release. I take that as my cue to come with her. We're one. We're perfect. She's worth everything.

I wrap one of my arms under her to support her spent body and brace the other against the ledge. "Are you going to let us keep you forever?"

"You're ours, Bianca," Sean adds.

She wiggles out from under me and takes off her blindfold. Sean hands her a shirt to wipe the excess baby batter away.

"Guys, we don't have to pretend this can work. Our parents will never understand."

Carl's head whips from where she's cleaning to her face. "Who cares?"

My blood is boiling. She's right. They'll never understand. Our relationship will cause a rift in the family.

"Get your head out of the clouds, Carl." Bianca's dismissal is a gut punch we all need.

Sean offers, "We don't have to tell anyone right away. Let's take our time. If you are serious about not wanting to go to school, you don't have to. If you want to help with the app, we can teach you things that need to be done, specific skills. Or just let us do it all."

Bianca gnaws on her lower lip. "My dad thinks I don't listen, but I've heard him say it a million times, never mix business with pleasure, and this was definitely pleasure."

She deals such a massive blow, I'm winded.

Sean says, "Then let's keep it as pleasure, but let us keep you."

I find my voice. "We'll lose our biggest investor, but we can deal with that. It's not like we don't have our own—"

Bianca interrupts me. "You did what I asked. You helped me get over my ex. Now, I need to clean up and get the gingerbread going."

Carl steps in front of the stairwell door. "Wait. Did you just use us?"

"You knew what it was from the start. I needed help and you helped me."

"That's not what this was. I love you."

I've never heard Carl speak those three words or sound so hurt. It sucks. It matches how I feel. Glad I'm not the one to put my heart on my sleeve. Except that's a lie. I want to tell her, and I was going to do it with the house. But now?

Bianca's voice is oddly flat. "It's what I want it to be."

How can she be so cold?

She slips past the three of us.

Sixteen

Bianca

I lock the penthouse door. My brothers are still on the roof, no doubt, trying to sort out what just happened.

Pangs of guilt tear at me for pretending I don't care.

I can't stop my reaction to them, but I can stop this madness before it ruins their relationship with my father. It's my first step to being an adult and thinking about someone other than myself.

My next step...move out. I can't always rely on someone to care for me. Their mother has made that clear, and she has the track record to prove it.

While I set all of the ingredients for gingerbread on the counter, I call Aurora.

"I know we have a lot to catch up on, and I promise I'll tell you everything, but I have a huge request."

"What's going on?"

"I need a place to call my own. I was wondering if I could move in with you. I know that's not exactly my own, but I'll pick up another part-time job. I can make enough money to cover half the bills, and rent and whatever else. I need to prove that I can take care of myself for five fucking minutes."

"You know I'm there for you, except I'm not actually there. I'm going to be on the road with my stepbrothers."

"Crap. What have I missed since this morning?"

"We can talk later. You're welcome to crash at my place, and if you can help with the rent, that would be great. When do you want to move in?"

"It won't take long to pack my suitcases. How about tomorrow morning? My dad gets back in town tonight. I'll let the whole family know that I'm moving out."

I add foil cupcake holders to the counter so I can save a few treats for Aurora.

"You don't sound very happy about it."

"It feels like my life's been tossed into a blender. That thing with my stepbrothers exploded, but how can it work?"

"That's a good question."

"It's crazy, right—thinking my fantasy could play out? How can any of us be sure it's real?"

"That's the difficulty of falling in love—ugh, let's table that love word. I've heard it enough times today."

"How many?"

Clunking around from next door tells me the guys came down from the roof.

Aurora sounds as flustered as I am. "Enough to know that it's being tossed around too easily."

"Why is this so hard, Aurora? I just need to prove to myself that I can take care of myself."

"I'll always have your back."

Hanging up with her, I have a sense of pride. I'm going to live the way I want. No more letting my dad use his money to dictate what I do. I have to make this work.

Mentally rechecking the ingredients, I curse at myself.

Butter.

Fuck my life. Swallowing my pride, I head next door to borrow butter.

Their voices hit me in the lobby before I realize their door is open a few inches.

Carl says, "We can make it work."

Mark adds, "Yeah, we lock the deal in. This investment from Frank's company, it's a huge pat on the back. It'll draw in a lot of other investors. We need to capitalize on that."

Sean adds, "We can't lose sight of our priority."

Right, their priorities. It must be nice to have siblings you're close to. They can refocus so quickly.

As I suspected, they were just telling me things they thought a virgin needed to hear. We don't have anything real. They didn't rise to success by letting every pair of spread legs lure them in.

Having heard enough, I knock on their door.

"Hello?" I say sheepishly, pushing the door open. "Can I grab that butter?"

"Hey, yeah." Carl hops off the kitchen counter and heads to the fridge, "How much do you need?"

"Half a stick."

He hands me a full stick. "We told Mom we'd let you teach us. Mind if we come over?"

"You don't have to do that. She won't expect you to learn to cook."

"We could just hang out."

Sean adds, "We can sift the flour or tie your hair back and make sure it's out of the way."

I'm not sure if it's good or bad that they're pretending nothing happened.

Mark says, "And we can forget that awkward post-sex moment. We're all still willing to make sure you're sufficiently over your ex."

A laugh bursts out of me. "We're good?"

"Nothing serious, that's how you want it?" Carl asks.

I nod.

"Then we're good." Carl's response almost seems canned.

Surely it can't be this easy. "Well, I'm going to be making gingerbread." I wave the butter over my shoulder as I walk out. "You're welcome to help, but I have priorities too." Will they catch on that I heard them?

It doesn't much matter because, in seconds, Mark scoops me up, carries me into our parents' penthouse, and sets me on the kitchen counter, "Looks like you've got everything ready."

I like being in his arms way too much.

"I have things to do. I don't just sit around waiting for orgasms all day."

Carl laughs but there might be a note of seriousness. "You could. That option is on the table...or the counter." He drags a hand up my thigh, then grabs a dish towel with both hands, rolls it up, and takes a chip clip out of the drawer.

"What are you doing?"

He places the rolled dish rag in front of my face, holding it at my eyes, and uses the clip to fasten it behind my head. "We need to have a little fun with our chef. Let's play Name That Spice."

His statement is followed by a distinct scent being wafted under my nose.

"Cloves."

"Very good."

Sean seems to be bumping him out of the way, jostling my knee in the process, "And this?"

"Nutmeg."

"You're making it too easy. She had those on the counter." Mark's voice seems to come from the pantry. Seconds later a new scent is offered.

"Rosemary."

"She does know her spices." Mark sounds impressed.

"She also knows that's an herb, not a spice." I join them in talking about me like I'm not there. That gets a hearty laugh from all of them.

Somebody pushes the hem of my skirt up and then traces a finger over my thigh, but it's not just a finger. "Are you rubbing something on me?"

"Can you tell from the texture?" It's still Mark.

"Oil?"

"I thought maybe we could lube you up."

We all know the last thing I need is lube. But they might not know about laundry. "Don't get any on my dress."

"I guess we better take it off."

There's plenty of time. Another romp would be nice now that we're all non-committal. How bizarre has my life become?

Fingers tug at my buttons and soon, they have me standing, they're peeling my dress off.

"This too?" One of them runs a finger under my bra strap.

"Yes."

A finger slides into the waistband of my panties and pauses.

"Yes."

It's easy to say yes when I don't have to look at their faces. Their potential judgment. Deep down, I know I'm thinner than most girls. I know I'm pretty by most standards. I'm just not enough of either of those for my stepmom.

The blindfold keeps me from mistaking a sideways glance as disapproval.

I hear squishy sliding. "How much oil did you put on your hands?"

"How do you know that's what I put on my hands?" Mark asks.

"There are only so many things that make that sound. Hold it under my nose." I wait. "That's canola."

"Damn, you're good, but then again, you already knew that."

I grab his hand while he's letting me sniff the oil and determine that his entire hand is coated. I push it away. "Wash that off."

"It's massage oil."

"I'd need a shower if you coated me with that."

"Oh, dejected." Carl lifts me back onto the counter.

I hear the refrigerator open or is it the freezer? I can't tell.

"How about this?" Sean's fingers touch my collarbone, then ease something cold onto it.

I shiver. "Is that ice?"

"It is."

He trails downward, circling my breast until he makes his way out to my nipple. If I wasn't perky already, I am now. My nipples have to be rock-hard. His mouth latches onto my breast, warming the sensitive skin he just cooled.

"Wow." I tangle my fingers in his hair.

"How about this?" His fingertips touch my knee, then ease the coolness onto my skin, making a slow zigzag toward my sex.

I have goosebumps, and heat is racing through my body all at once.

Closer and closer. Kisses trail up my other thigh until the kisses and ice meet in the middle.

The ice disappears. His warm lips nuzzle my curls. Then he eases the ice cube between his lips, dragging it up and down my slit, "Oh my God, that's so cold."

He pulls away. "Too much? I can warm you up."

"Keep going. I—"

"Holy fuck!" Mark's shock doesn't fit the ice-play thing.

"What the hell?" Who is that? Rustling obscures the voice. I don't know what's happening, but the coldness is gone, and so is the warmth. Everything's gone, even the blindfold gets ripped away.

My eyes squeeze shut against the bright light. The guys are standing in front of me.

"If you were younger, I'd tan your hide."

Oh shit, that's my father's voice. I grab the muffin cups, slap them over my nipples, and clutch my arms over my chest. My dress and other clothes got tossed across the kitchen.

"For Christ's sake, you do realize the glass pan is see-through?" My father is pissed.

Mark shoves the pan to the counter and grabs his pants and my dress.

I want to laugh at the thought of our parents seeing Mark's cock through the pan, but there's nothing funny about this.

"Why didn't you call?" Mark pulls his jeans on and the other two wait for me to get my dress on before they unhand the bag of flour and jar of molasses to get their clothes.

"We didn't know we had to ask for our children to be finished with whatever the hell this is."

Mom says, "Frank got an early flight and I canceled the tea. We texted you but no one responded."

"You boys get out of here. We'll talk later."

The guys each look at me which is sweet, but infuriates Dad. "Now."

"I'll be fine."

With only myself and our parents, Dad says, "Young lady, I thought I was doing you a favor, letting you regroup after flunking out of college, but apparently, this is just pandering to your immaturity. Pack your bags and find somewhere else to stay."

I rush to my room and shove everything in my bags. A text to Aurora confirms it's okay if I head to her place now.

Our parents are in the living room but I don't meet their eyes. I just leave.

Seventeen

Carl

"We get your point," Mark says after Bianca's dad lays into us for a solid twelve minutes without breathing. "We accept full responsibility. We're older. We know better. She didn't force us into anything and we didn't force her into anything. It was a slip in judgment not to use more discretion with what happened."

"Oh, Son, discretion wouldn't solve the problem. You can't fornicate with your stepsister." Mom is beside herself.

Mark's about to blow a gasket.

We had a plan to give Bianca space to keep our relationship fun. We didn't want to force her into something serious even though the three of us brothers are very clear on wanting her. But a key part of the plan was to keep it quiet until she warmed up.

Our parents walking in on us unraveled that plan.

I've tried to play this out several ways in my brain, but despite Frank's lengthy monologue, there's not enough time to come up with a plan that will please everyone. We need a voice of reason.

"Let's look at this logically. We're not blood relatives. No matter how uncomfortable this is, it's no different than any other woman we could've dated."

Frank opens his mouth but I hold my hand up. "I get it. She's our stepsister. That makes it different. But it doesn't change how we feel."

Sean says, "Bianca wants to have room to make her own decisions."

"Damn foolish ones," her father says.

"We're—"

He won't let me continue. "You boys are old enough to think of the practical matters."

"Having the woman we love by our side at work and home seems pretty damn practical." Mark's taking a stand.

"The practical matters I'm referring to are your relationships with your clients. The practical matter of needing clients to buy your app, to support your app, to promote your app. If word gets out that it's run by a bunch of sex-starved, inbred idiots, you'll be the laughing stock. You must always think of your customers."

Mark's and Sean's expressions indicate their patience is wearing as thin as mine. We love Bianca and we'd rather spend time with her than with her father. "We only need *the right* customers."

"And who are those?"

I'm going out on a limb with Mark. "The ones that aren't assholes."

"You may be older than Bianca, but you're still younger than me. You don't understand the way the business world works."

"You don't understand that times are changing, old man." Shit! I might have gone too far.

I rush out, needing to get to Bianca. My mother shrieks something about watching myself, and Frank yells something I tune out. I can't deal with them anymore.

But when I get next door, it's silent.

"Bianca." I'd understand if she yelled at me or was crying. What I'm not prepared for is for her to be gone. Her room is in disarray as if she packed quickly and left.

She was worried she would ruin everything, but she didn't ruin it.

She had an unexpected lesson for us. One we should have handled years ago so she wouldn't be subjected to such scrutiny. Mark, Sean, and I need to become fucking adults. We've got to man up for what we want.

We want Bianca.

Eighteen

Bianca

Hauling myself up the stairs to Aurora's apartment, I'm not sure I'm cut out for working in a diner. I'm merely a messenger passing orders in one direction and plates and cups in another. I'm not doing the fun part of food, the creation, or sharing in the excitement.

But it's a job. It's also less temporary than being Santa's helper at the mall and stocking shelves for last-minute shoppers at the department store. I've been working myself to the bone now that I have to pay my own bills.

I'm almost dead after one week.

Dropping onto the couch, I open my phone. It's safe to do that now that I've blocked my family. I sent them messages letting them know I needed time to myself but my brothers kept calling and messaging anyway. They want to make sure I don't forget about the Christmas dinner. I let them know I'm not going and that they should arrange for someone else to cook.

There's an opening for a nanny in the local jobs listings. That would be perfect. I'd get to try out all of my cooking skills and take care of kids. I rub my belly, remembering how good I looked simulated-pregnant.

My period should start in another day or two. Unless I got pregnant already. I still can't believe how caught up I was in the moment.

My fantasy stepbrother game was strong. Have unprotected sex with all three of them. Everything will be fine.

I'm exhausted. I could use a foot rub.

I try to think if there's any way to mimic one. I toss my phone aside and head to the shower. If the showerhead's cord is long enough, it would work. Anyway, I need to get cleaned up, rest for a couple of hours, and then head to the department store to stock shelves.

The warm water steams up the bathroom before I'm naked and enjoying the warmth running over my body. Grabbing the showerhead, I lean against the shower wall so I can lift my foot, but the enclosure is still cold.

Not a fun kind of cold like the ice cubes.

Using the water to warm the wall, I lean again. It's awkward. I'm tired. I'm pissed that everything reminds me of my brothers.

Letting my foot return to the floor, I drift the showerhead to my sex. An orgasm would be better than a foot massage anyway.

The pulsing water is a distant second or is it a fourth to the guys? My orgasm builds slowly, almost too slowly. I close my eyes, remembering how their hands and mouths felt on me, and their cocks inside of me.

I had to guess sometimes since we used blindfolds, but it seemed Sean's touch was usually the gentlest. Carl was more likely to try to excite me. Then there was Mark. His grip was firmer, more controlling, and that's what kicks my orgasm into gear.

I lean forward, bracing my free hand on the shower wall. I'm almost good enough at pretending to imagine that this mimics the position of the rooftop. My orgasm builds a little faster. It's still not the same. Nothing will be the same as them. I'm probably ruined.

I spread my legs and try to get comfortable. It takes a second to get into it again.

Then the tiniest fireworks show ever erupts inside of me. It's comparable to lighting a single Black Cat after going to the city fireworks display.

Whatever. I finish showering, dry off, and crawl into bed. My drifting-off mind sandwiches me between the guys. I startle awake. They're not there.

In a pathetic attempt at positivity, I remind myself that I'm in control of my life. Yay! It's what I want.

Those heights of pleasure I attained—they give me something to work for. I know how good life can be. My future adult self will get back there someday.

Nineteen

Mark

Elvis's *Blue Christmas* is playing on the PA system at the store where I'm buying decorations. Memories of Mom listening to it over and over again filter into my mind. I thought she just liked Elvis.

Now I get it.

I grab the box of blue ornaments with silver glitter. If Bianca's silence wasn't so deafening, I'd make a blue balls joke when I get home.

My fears that I wouldn't be able to commit, and take care of her, and be enough for her, have come to life. I bought a fucking house and it might as well be empty when I walk in the door and can't say, "Honey, I'm home."

How did I go from the idea of the penthouse being nothing more than a landing pad between trips to buying a house, having a white picket fence installed, and wanting to say that classic line every single day? And that's only when I absolutely can't work from home.

The irony fucks with my head.

Putting up a tree and going through the motions of decorating appease the piece of me that Bianca will realize we're soulmates.

Would things be different if I hadn't held back? If I hadn't let business get in the way? If I'd just admitted that I wanted her instead of pulling that macho big brother shit?

And if we'd revealed our relationship to our parents differently, would they have been less shocked? Yeah, that's a given. There's not a worse way to have let them in on our little secret than by defiling Daddy's little girl on the kitchen counter. The penthouse reeked of bleach for a week with Mom trying to eliminate our sin.

She's doing better now, insisting that we continue with plans for the family's holiday dinner. Mom thinks I canceled my trip to Poland for her. I let her have it.

I won't be leaving the city until I hear from Bianca.

Carl drives us to the penthouse on the day of the party. Snow is starting to gather on the road and the sidewalks have been shoveled.

"Do you think Bianca's going to show?" Sean asks. She's not returning calls or texts.

"Mom hasn't heard from her. And without a car, she'd need a good rideshare driver."

Carl says "I can't blame her for not wanting to face our parents again, that was pretty rough."

"I think she could have dealt with getting caught. But her father kicking her out? Too much." This will be the first time I've seen Frank since *that day*. I promised myself not to throttle him, but I'm popping my knuckles as we ride up the elevator.

The second we're in their apartment, I give a polite hug to Mom, confirm that Bianca isn't there, and storm over to Frank.

"You need to get shit straight with Bianca. We don't know that she's safe. We don't know that she's alive." I pull my voice down. "We love her even if you don't. Give us a fucking chance."

"Whoa, that's a big word."

"Do you need me to define it?"

"I don't know what's wrong with your generation. It's going to hell in a handbasket. All of you think you can share women...your sisters no less. Earlier this week, the social media rag, SmorgasSmut had stories about semi-local rock stars and hockey players sinning with their stepsisters."

"It's not a sin to love someone." My voice is too loud and angry.

Mom pats my arm. "Now, now, Son. Let's be civil."

"I can't be civil when this prick doesn't give a fuck about his daughter."

Frank points to the couch. Sean and Carl sit but I don't budge. A staring contest ensues and I know it doesn't matter who wins. He will in the end. He has seniority.

Sean scoots to the middle, freeing up the end for me. "Come on, man. Let's have a conversation."

So we do. Sean, Carl, and I sit shoulder to shoulder, squeezed onto the couch.

"Don't ever talk to me like that again and don't ever accuse me of not caring about my daughter. I have a tracker on her phone. I know where she goes all day every day, and she is perfectly safe, but she has some lessons to learn and so do you."

"What the fuck?" I jump up.

"Sit down," he yells.

My pent-up energy has me about to explode. I circle behind the couch and grip the back of it to keep myself from punching him. "Where is she?"

"If she wanted you to know, she'd tell you."

"She should be here. It's our Christmas dinner." My irritation borders on petulant child.

Mom defends Dad. "Bianca was included in the group chats. She's choosing not to be here."

"Where the hell is she?"

"Lower your voice, Mark."

"I'm not lowering my voice. You're the scumbag who doesn't value your daughter any more than any other asset. It must perform. It must be perfect. She must be perfect. You two have ruined her."

"Son. She has a lot of growing up to do. She's still a teenager."

"Don't patronize me."

Sean uses his ultra-calm voice, which tells me instantly that he's anything but calm, but he has a knack for this. "Let's focus on Bianca's safety. Can we be sure that she's safe? Does she have people she can talk to?"

"I can assure you she's safe." Frank's assurances don't mean anything to me.

I rush over, yank his phone out of his hands, and toss it to Carl. "Find her."

Carl springs to his feet and is out the door the second the phone hits his hands. He has some computer gadgets in the car. Hopefully enough to get into the phone.

I point at her father. "Don't move."

"You stole my phone."

"Unlike you, I will give up everything for your daughter. Her happiness is the only luxury I can't live without."

"You might want to think about those luxuries before you keep running your mouth. I own this building. I can evict you."

"If you paid more attention, you would have noticed we moved." I storm out, and Sean is only a pace behind me. I yell over my shoulder, "We'll give your phone back when Carl gets what we need."

It's true. Frank has a tracker on her. We can see everywhere she's been. She's busy all day, all night. My poor sweetheart barely has time to sleep. We make note of the address, an apartment complex, then decide to keep Frank's phone in case she leaves before we get there.

Carl offers a piece of wisdom. "We haven't talked about the possibility that Bianca's already carrying one or more of our babies. Now is not the time to point that out to her. Are we clear?"

We agree to focus on getting her back first.

Based on the dot on the phone, we narrow Bianca's location to two possibilities, upstairs or downstairs, of the apartments in front of us.

Aromas of cinnamon and sweets guide me to the upper choice. Her schedule is ragged and yet, she's baking?

As I'm about to knock on the door, a man's voice halts my hand. "I made the biggest mistake of my life letting you go, Bianca. When I set out to find myself, it was because I was young and foolish. I didn't know what I needed."

"I've been doing a lot of self-discovery too. I guess it's what we do at our age."

"I'm sorry I let you go. It turns out that when I looked for myself, I couldn't find me. There is no me without you. Bianca, please forgive me for whatever pain I've caused you." This dude must be her ex.

There's no me without you. That's pretty good, but I won't stand by without a fight. I bang on the door so hard the windows rattle. The whole fucking apartment might shake. We've got to get her out of this place. This isn't the kind of life she deserves.

"Open the door, Bianca."

"Go away. You're supposed to be at the Christmas party," she yells to us.

"Who is it?" he asks.

"My stepbrothers."

Carl angry-whispers, "She told him where she was, but not us."

That's not helping my irritation issues. "Open the door. We're here to take care of you."

The lock on the door clicks but the swing of the door is caught by the chain, after a few inches.

"Let us in, Bianca," I keep my voice low.

"Don't cause a scene."

Sean says, "You belong with us."

Idiot ex has the balls to say, "If she wanted to be with you, she would."

The hair on the back of my neck prickles, and not just because I'm getting covered in snow. If it was possible for me to go into Hulk mode, I'd knock the door down.

Carl says, "Your choice, Bianca... We can have this conversation in front of your ex who foolishly chose to dump you, or we can have it in private."

"Give me a minute."

"Now." I've lost my patience.

"Damon, you better go. We'll talk later."

"I'll stay. I'm here for you, B." Damon doesn't know how close I am to strangling him. His use of a nickname makes it more likely. And when Bianca steps out of sight, the rope holding my restraint in check, frays within a strand of snapping.

"Let him leave peacefully." Bianca eyes us through the slim opening.

A strand of relief fortifies my restraint. I hate to back away even an inch, but I do, and sure enough, she slides the chain off to fully open the door, and her ex, who looks like a decent guy, is standing beside her.

His eyes go wide when he sees the three of us. "Those are your stepbrothers?"

"Yeah."

I swear he shrinks several inches as he tries to slip between us, which is fine.

Bianca ushers us in, and we do our best to shake the snow off rather than track it inside. Keeping us at arm's length, she asks me, "Aren't you supposed to be in Poland."

"I canceled the trip because I was worried about you."

"No need to be so dramatic. I'm fine. Better than ever." Her expression softens.

"Then you didn't show up for the holiday dinner..."

"It was a choice to keep negativity out of my life. I'm sorry it messed up your plans."

"You didn't mess up my plans. I finally found what I've searched the world for...happiness...you."

"Mark—"

He cuts her objection short. "But I didn't protect you. I never thought I'd be the guy to fail his woman. It's the worst feeling ever. I'll never fail you again. Let me take you home."

"I am home." She holds her arms wide. "I can take care of myself. I'm making it on my own. I have multiple jobs. I'm doing my things my way."

"Perfect. Do your things, your way, at the house I bought for you."

She draws back in surprise.

Carl speaks up. "Please give us a chance, Bianca. We stocked the kitchen with all the gadgets the clerk at the store said you could ever need. The only thing missing is you."

"Assuming I'll spend a lot of time slaving over food could be offensive."

"We didn't mean it like that."

"I know." A hint of a smile graces her lips.

I wink. "We got extra soft dish towels."

"Moving in is a big step." She's hesitant but not refusing.

Carl warned us not to mention the possible pregnancy. I'll tread lightly. "Maybe not as big as another step we may have already taken."

Her lips purse almost imperceptibly through a long breath.

Twenty

Sean

We're kind of on probation, but Bianca moved in, so we're headed the right direction. She's ended things with her ex, and her need for personal space gave us time to talk to our parents about how they treat her.

She looks up from her book when I join her on the balcony. Her fingers barely peek out of the blanket she's snuggled in, and hold the page she's on.

Snow falls gently, collecting on the rail. The storm coated the entire mountainside and it glistens in the sun.

I can see why she'd sit out here to read. "I can't decide which is more gorgeous, you or the landscape."

She pats her messy bun. "I warned you. Messy hair, don't care."

The warning is part of her testing if we're truly comfortable with her simply being her. She's so used to being judged, it's hard for her to accept that we love *her*, not the incidentals.

I lean down, kissing the top of her head. "Just kidding. The only reason there are only eight wonders of the world is that you weren't born when they put the list together."

She bats me away. "Now you're just being cheesy."

Arguing wouldn't convince her that I'm being sincere.

She blushes. "Stop staring. Did you come out here just to bother me?"

Oops. It brought out her playful side though so we're good.

"Ready for your first Christmas present?"

"I thought we were swapping gifts tonight. I need five to fifteen minutes to get yours ready."

"That's oddly specific, but your presence is all we need right now."

She snuggles into my chest, her book secure in our bond as I scoop her up.

I set her on a barstool where Mark's laptop is open and the video from our parents is paused on the screen.

The exact moment she sees it, her smile vanishes. Scrambling to shrug the blanket off, she trips and drops her book. We're all there to catch her but she swats us away. The book doesn't fare as well.

It bounces off the counter and crashes to the floor, pages bent.

"I don't want to talk to them. Christmas was going so good."

"Hey," Mark grabs her shoulders. "You're not talking to them. They're talking to you."

"Even worse." She shrugs away, grabbing the book from my hands as I smooth the pages.

Carl catches her arm. "It's a video. They're apologizing."

The ticking of the huge clock on the living room wall counts the passing seconds that count the many ways she was hurt by them.

Did we fuck this up?

She kicks the blanket from around her feet and steps away. I wish I could undo the moment, wrap her back up in the soft pink blanket, and rediscover the sweet smile she had when snuggled against my chest.

Grabbing the blanket from the floor, I return it to her shoulders. "I should have prepared you. We talked to our parents. Did our best to explain how their expectations and judgment hurt you. And that you'll take your own path."

She angles her head up to listen.

Carl adds, "They were surprisingly receptive."

Mark gives her the zinger. "And we told them that if they lose you, they lose us because we've chosen our side."

Tears well in her eyes.

I continue. "They wanted to come over to apologize, but we asked them to respect your space until you're ready. The video was your father's solution. And I truly think you'll like it."

We pile onto the couch, Bianca positioned on Mark's lap, flanked by Carl and me, and we watch the video with her.

Mom spells out the scary and humiliating years when she didn't have enough money to feed us and had to beg friends to let us stay with them. It's why she pushed so hard for Bianca to get a degree. Some of the keeping-up-appearances tie-ins were a little harder to grasp, but she meant well and promises to tone them down.

Frank has a harder time opening up but makes a show of writing a check for the amount he planned on spending on Bianca's education. It's hers to spend however she wants.

Carl keeps the tissues handy for Bianca. I snatch one as I head to the counter. I don't want my brothers giving me shit over a few tears to mar the moment.

"There's one more thing." I grab the envelope our mom sent. Ditching the tissue and resuming my place on the couch, I position the envelope for everyone to read the outside:

To my beautiful (on the inside) children, please open when you are all together.

"She sent this. Who wants to do the honors?"

Carl says, "Bianca should since she sparked this transformation. Are you okay with that?"

When Bianca nods, I set the envelope in her hands. She slides a pink fingernail under the edge of the flap. I hadn't noticed her nail polish matched her pajamas until now.

Finding four pieces of postcard-style stationery, each with one of our names, Bianca hands them out. We quickly determine that Mom has made the same handwritten promise to each of us. She'll always be there for us, no matter the situation, no judgment, no questions asked.

I grab another tissue...so I can blow my nose. I'm not used to this level of emotion in our family. Interesting, everyone seems to do the same.

"That's an incredible gift. I need a minute." Bianca is running out of the room before the words are out of her mouth.

We get our gifts out from under the Christmas tree while she's gone. "What do you think she's doing?"

"By the sounds of her footsteps and the door, I think she went to the bathroom."

"Good thing we didn't follow." Mark cracks himself up. It's good to see him relax. He's finally found the thing he's been searching the planet for, and it was at home.

Bianca does an abrupt halt when she enters the room and we're not on the couch.

"Over here." I wave her gift in the air.

"Your present will be ready in a few minutes." She glances over her shoulder.

"No worries, this isn't your real gift anyway."

"Real gift?"

"This one's sort of utilitarian, and will need a little bit of an explanation."

She takes the package from my hands and unwraps it, holding up two new phones.

"I got you a new phone because yours was a little broken."

"A little? The screen was nearly unusable."

I kiss her nose. "I was being kind."

"And the other phone?"

I take it from her and send a text to all of them. Carl and Mark's phones buzz from nearby but Bianca's is farther away.

"That's my new number. I played it off that night my brothers razzed me about girlfriends, but they were partially right, I had too many *friends*. Now that I have a new number, only the important people can get in touch with me."

"Hearts will be broken." Mark can't resist the opportunity to harass me.

"As long as I never break the one I care about." I pull Bianca onto my lap. We're lost in a kiss when a timer sounds from the other room.

"What's that?" Carl asks, striding to find it.

"Ah! Wait!" Bianca calls. "You all have to get your present at the same time."

"Where?" I ask as she crawls off of me.

"The bathroom."

"Our present's in the bathroom?" Mark stops beside Carl and I join them.

She shrugs.

Carl surges forward first but Mark muscles past him, their shoulders banging into the hallway walls. I'm hot on their heels as we file into the bathroom.

A single pregnancy test stick is on the counter. Mark lifts it. "Fuck yeah!"

A pink plus sign. "We're having a baby!"

Carl says something but I'm running down the hall to wrap our new mama in the biggest hug ever.

Our brothers join us, and too many kisses are swapped to keep track of. Then Carl asks, "How did you know it would be positive?"

"Sore breasts, tiredness, nausea...all the fun."

"This is better than my wildest fantasy. Being a dad feels like I'm king of the world."

While my brothers argue over who the father is, I say to Bianca, "I need to make love to you. Is that okay?"

"If you're worried about having sex while pregnant, I've checked five different websites. They all say it's fine."

"If you want a blindfold, we can use the ribbons off the Christmas tree," Carl says, dragging his fingers over a velvety blue ribbon.

Tangling her fingers with his, she says, "I don't need a blindfold. I want to see it all."

She's giving us gift after gift. I only hope I can make her as happy.

The three of us guys strip then I spread a blanket and pillows over the carpet. Mark eases Bianca onto the pillows and slips the bottoms of her pajamas off. She lifts her arms out of his way as Carl maneuvers her pajama top over her head.

I'm about to take her nipple into my mouth when I remember what she said about the signs of pregnancy. I sprinkle light kisses over her nipples and breasts instead then work my way down to her pussy.

Her curls are soaking wet, glistening with the lights of the Christmas tree.

Mark works his hands over her leg, pulling it wide for me. "You hungry?"

"I'm starved." I settle between her legs and drag a finger through her sex. She tries to suppress a giggle. I ease two fingers inside of her, pump them in and out, and let my thumb brush over her clit with each stroke.

Mark and Carl caress the rest of her body and keep her lips busy. She draws Mark near, licking his shaft like she plucked one of the candy canes off the tree.

My cock hurts too much to draw this out any longer than necessary, so once she has the first orgasm, I lick my fingers, give her a minute to rest, then sink my shaft deep inside of her.

The warmth, the tightness, and her moans, are the best Christmas gifts ever.

Epilogue

Carl

Four years later

The kids are at Aurora's house for the afternoon since Bianca hasn't been feeling well.

Our first pregnancy was triplets and then two years later, we had another baby, and another year out, I'm certain Bianca's pregnant again.

She doesn't think so. She said it's a stomach bug, so I sent her to the doctor. And planned a little fun with my brothers.

We have such a close relationship with the doctor and office staff, that I convinced them to run a pregnancy test with the bloodwork, and only give the pregnancy test results to me.

When the call comes in, Bianca is stretched out on the couch across the room. It's nearly impossible to hide my excitement while she's staring at me curiously.

"Who was that?" she asks when I hang up.

"A business deal. Good things are on the horizon. Why don't you get another nap before Aurora brings the kids back."

"I'm feeling a lot better, but I can squeeze one more in before the circus resumes."

That's the go-ahead I need. I slip out of the room and call our parents. I invite them over for dinner and the plan is in motion. My brother and I want our important people present for our big reveal.

I hear her making a call, and since she has it on speakerphone, I hear that it's the doctor's office. "Your results just came in. The good news is that you're not contagious."

Panic races through me. This could be my only chance to surprise Bianca with a pregnancy reveal. I race into the room as the nurse continues, "Nothing to worry about, just rest."

"That's a relief," I say, playing off my seeming overreaction.

Pulling Bianca's fuzzy pink blanket around her shoulders, I rub her back as she drifts off to sleep.

By the time she wakes up, Aurora is in the backyard with Mark, Sean, the kids, and our parents.

Before Bianca can see any of that, I say, "We have a little surprise for you. Some friends and family are over."

"Why?" She rubs her eyes and looks toward the backyard, but I've closed the blinds.

"You'll find out soon enough."

She runs her fingers through her hair. "I'm a mess. Do I have time to clean up?"

"Trust me. You're perfect." My eyes drop to her tummy, and I'm busted.

Her hands fly to her pajama top. "Is it dirty? I should change."

That was close. "You don't need to change a thing. It's just a few people who love you dearly as you are."

She accepts my hand, letting me guide her to the back door.

"What the heck?" she exclaims when she sees everyone.

My brothers and I are too excited to delay the reveal.

I spin her around, sit her on top of the cooler, and kneel in front of her.

"What are you doing?"

"Something that we should have done a long time ago. Bianca, I kept wanting to make this right and perfect and I kept letting you talk me out of it while you said you needed to get your life in order. But look at everything you've created."

I motion around us, and we have everyone's attention at this point.

"You've made these beautiful babies. You've brought our family closer than ever, and you've provided the most welcoming home for my brothers and our children.

I don't have to worry about my mom taking offense. We've talked to her about how much we value everything she did for us.

"Bianca Sinclair, will you do me the honor of fulfilling the most important contract, the most important investment, the most important alliance of my entire life, and marry me?"

Sean steps next to me and kneels. He drags his hands up and down her bare leg. "I hope you'll do me the honor of allowing me to be a part of this crazy endeavor and marry me too because I can't imagine a life without you."

Mark kneels on the other side but bumps me a little so he can get slightly more to the center.

"Bianca, no one's ever challenged me the way you have. No one's ever made me lose control and like it. No one's ever made me so happy to settle down. You make me feel completely insane. But I can assure you, it's of sound mind that I too want to marry you. And I hope you'll take all three of us as a package deal because, well, let's face it, visitation rights are going to get complicated if you don't."

"Oh my gosh. Yes to all of you!"

Tears well in her eyes, and her hands cover her mouth while we embrace her.

Mom steps up beside us, cutting into the moment. "I don't mean to pry, but do any of you have a ring?"

"We planned this in a hurry, but we'll get rings, Mom."

"A hurry?" Bianca's brow furrows.

"It's the other surprise that's the ticking clock," Carl explains.

"Another surprise?"

"You're pregnant."

117

And we live happily ever after!

If you'd like to go for an elevator ride with these naughty stepsiblings, grab the BONUS SCENE by signing up for my newsletter.

Visit my website: https://SylvieHaas.com

Carols and Consent

A Stepbrother Reverse Harem Romance

Sylvie Haas

Blurb

My rockstar stepbrothers are every girl's fantasy. And if I were to reveal my naughty secret, I'd admit they're my fantasy too. But years of being used by people who simply want access to my brothers have caused me to distance myself.

Am I foolish to think the Christmas Cherry Auction will give me a moment to step free from their celebrity shadow?

Apparently, I am, because when they're supposed to be putting on a concert, they swagger into the auction. They drive the bids sky high. And they win.

Four hours of my time!

Will one night with these four heartthrobs get them out of my system, or tangle our lives forever?

If you love dirty-talking men who know how to teach their untouched stepsister a very important holiday lesson, don't miss this year's Christmas Cherry Auction!

Sensitive readers: Please be advised that this story includes a scene of consensual non-consent, also abbreviated as CNC. To be clear, the characters agree ahead of time that they want to do this and have a safety option if anyone changes their mind in the midst of the scene.

One

Big D

Smack. My phone goes tumbling to the floor as I stumble backward. It takes me a second to register that I missed the doorway into the backstage meeting room.

"I think you were aiming for that big opening, not the door jamb, slick," Jack says, as all three of my brothers laugh.

They wouldn't be laughing if they saw what I *think* I just saw. I grab my phone from the floor. Damnit. My phone turned off when it hit the ground.

"If you break your fingers walking into a door jamb, it's on *you* to tell the audience the show is canceled because our keyboard player is a dumbass."

I don't bother looking up to acknowledge Calvin, who's the oldest, and a little cocky about being lead vocals and guitar.

"Go to hell." I tap my thumb against the side of my phone. Why the fuck does it take this thing so long to power on?

Joining my brothers, I sit on a stool for our pre-concert check-in. If there are any last-minute changes, I'm fucked. The image that seared itself into my brain seconds before I ran into the door and dropped my phone is occupying all of my brain space.

"What the hell has you so flustered?" Jack asks. He's the bad boy of the band, but it's a façade.

"Hang on." I want to be sure before I say anything.

"Do we need to make a 'no phones' policy for when we're on stage?" Calvin mocks me.

The screen powers back on, saving me from arguing with him. I tap into the social media app and try to remember the name of the gossip group from the hole-in-the-wall town less than an hour away. One of our fans just invited me to it. *Smut* something.

I type *S-M*— There it is. *SmorgasSmut.*

And there she is, Aurora, our stepsister.

Not the little kid we always gave over-the-top support to. Not the gangly teen with a passion for theater. Not the bubbly, innocent sister—my brain short circuits.

Fuck-Me red lipstick, way too much for her light complexion. Long, blond wavy hair styled to perfection. And that smokey eye-makeup. Shit.

My cock forgets that she's been our sister since she was three. That we share a last name since our dad adopted her. My cock shouldn't be getting hard.

She shouldn't be wearing that sexy red and white strapless number. I shouldn't be wanting to lick up her red and white striped thigh-high stockings to find her sweet spot.

Our band's success has required us to be on the road a lot the past few years. It had helped me try to ignore how little Rory had grown into such a gorgeous woman. But damn. We're back home and she's...off limits. I know that.

The tension in my jaw is enough to trigger a headache. I shift my lower jaw from side to side, then rub a hand inconspicuously over the strain in front of my pants.

The stage manager enters and starts talking. *Yada, yada.*

I have to figure out why Rory's dressed like that, and why she's being gossiped about. I scroll to read the comments. "She's in a fucking auction?"

I almost drop my phone again.

"*She* and *auction* in the same sentence. Sounds like something I'd like." Jack steps beside me. I scroll back to the picture.

"Oh damn," he says. "That's Rory."

"Tell me something I don't know."

"She's in an auction?" Jack's as dumbfounded as I am.

Her body glitter sparkles almost as much as her light blue eyes. Will I go to hell for wanting to roll around with her and get that sparkle in inappropriate places?

Brian, the stage manager, tries to cut in. "The opening act's about to go on. Time to focus."

"Aurora's in an auction?" Calvin says coming over, ignoring Brian.

"It's some small-town thing." I'm trying to sort the details through the comments people have posted. I'm not the only one who's ready to bid on my sister.

"Shit! The auction is at a sex club." My chest tightens. No way in hell my little sister should be in a sex club. I do some mental math and confirm that she's eighteen. Not that I need to. I know the exact day she turned eighteen.

"What's the name of the sex club?" Calvin asks, his fingers poised on his phone.

"The Aubergine Affair. The winner gets four hours of help with holiday prep but apparently last year, the winners got—"

"Stop," Calvin says.

"Just telling you the facts."

"Save it for in the car. The Aubergine Affair is thirty minutes away."

"You can't leave." Brian blocks the doorway.

"Tell the opening act they're getting extra time." Calvin's never looked more serious.

"That's not how this works."

"It does tonight."

Calving reaches into the cabinet and grabs his keys. "Let's go."

We've blown past Brian and are halfway down the hall. He's pissed. "You can't just leave."

If my brothers are having the same thoughts as me, I pity anyone who tries to stop us.

Travis keeps his voice low. "What are we planning to do with her when we win her?"

"I'm sure as hell not asking her to wrap presents." Jack matches my sentiment.

Two

Aurora

"I need to help Wendy." I grab Bianca's shoulders to get her to focus. "You're raising money for the women's shelter."

I slap her butt and nudge her onto the stage.

In seconds, Wendy emerges from behind the privacy screen, holding up the front of her dress. She spins around. "Zip please."

"I've got body glitter too."

She glances over her shoulder as I zip her up. "I noticed."

"Want some?"

"Is there any left?" She laughs.

"It's possible I overdid it, but I plan to sparkle." My smile hides the frustration of never really being seen once someone hears my last name. My stepdad officially adopted me, since my dad walked out of my life when I was little, and I've lived in the shadow of my stepbrothers ever since.

Jefferson, the auction emcee, has been given strict orders not to utter Bengtsson; I'm simply Aurora tonight.

"Do you hear how much the bid's going up? This is crazy." Cindy makes sure we're listening. "Twenty-five thousand and climbing. Bianca raised the full twenty thousand."

"Is it her stepbrothers?" I dust Wendy with body glitter while she puts the cute red gloves on.

We stand side by side and check ourselves in the mirror. It was hard for me to decide which dress to wear, but the tutu style skirt won out. It's fun and helps me channel my love of theater.

I'm packing as much into tonight as possible, complete with a little song and dance number to Marilyn Monroe's *Diamonds Are a Girl's Best Friend*.

We join Cindy at the edge of the curtain. The poor girl's shaking.

I wrap an arm around her. "You're going to be fine. Those bidder paddles are hot, just like your bottom's going to be before the evening's over."

She pulls back and puts her hands over her face. "I don't know if I can go through with this."

Turning toward Cindy, I tease. "We convinced Bianca. We'll convince—"

Jefferson's voice elevates. "Going, going, gone. Bianca is sold to bidder number three."

A ruckus at the back of the room draws my attention. Leather, flannel, ripped jeans, swagger—Big D, Jack, Travis, and Calvin. I can barely breathe. "My stepbrothers..."

"What?" Cindy says. "I thought her brothers were winning?"

"No. My stepbrothers. They're here. No, no, no." The velvet curtain slips from my fingers.

Cindy says, "They have a concert tonight. They can't be here."

Wendy checks. "It's definitely them."

As she holds the curtain open, Mark growls orders at Bianca and is carrying her off the stage.

Cindy thinks fast. "Somebody grab Bianca's bag. I think they're leaving."

"All right, everybody." It's Big D's voice followed by a loud hand clap. "We've got to get back to our concert, so what's the 'buy now' price for Aurora?"

This can't be happening. Flashbacks of the high school talent show pin themselves in my brain. My helpful big brothers catcalled and cheered *before* my performance. It drew the audience's attention to them. I had to wait for their fans to calm down before performing Annie's *Tomorrow*.

It was one of the moments that led me to distancing myself from them. Along with so many times my peers pretended to be my friends in hopes of getting to meet my brothers.

Tonight was supposed to be safe. I don't want to wait until tomorrow for the sun to come out. I want to be seen for me. I grab Bianca's bag. "I'll take it to her."

I step out from behind the curtain, startled by how quickly Calvin made his way to the front. He's the oldest and always in charge. Probably barged through everyone with his lean build and broad shoulders. And if they met his gaze, yeah, he has a super power with those intense eyes.

"Sorry bro, I'm not up for bid yet. Besides, I've got to run this out to Bianca."

Calvin hops on the stage and takes the bag before I can resist. "Who can take this to Bianca? Our stage manager's already blowing up our phones. No time to waste."

"You can't just come in and change the order of the auction. Cindy is next." Annoying little sister isn't a good look or sound for me, but I'll own it.

Jefferson speaks into the microphone. "Anyone object to a 'buy now' price of five hundred thousand?"

The crowd goes wild. My head jerks toward Jefferson. He's serious.

I'm numb. My brothers can easily pay that. How can I deny the women's shelter getting such a huge donation?

Jack, the youngest, and the bad boy persona in the band, hops on stage and holds his hands to the side. "Anyone object?"

I object to him having his shirt unbuttoned. Those ripped abs and his sly smile make him irresistible.

I blink hard as he turns, extending an offer for a handshake toward Jefferson. Not again. Why won't they just let me do my thing? Channeling Marilyn, I try to own my fifteen seconds of the spotlight and I slap his hand away.

"I do! I object!"

If only the brief contact hadn't sent sparks of excitement racing through me.

"Why?" Jack's brow furrows as he rubs his other hand over the skin I touched.

"I'm supposed to have my time on stage. I'm supposed to get bid on." Pesky little sister is shining her brightest, but I applaud her for finally standing up to them.

"You want to get bid on?" An air of disbelief taints his words.

"Yes, but..." Why can't I force the rest of the thought from my mouth—*but not by them*. Now is a terrible time for my secret crushes to surface. Where are you now, pesky, defiant little sister?

Jefferson pivots. "Cindy, would you mind if Aurora goes next? And could you run this out to Bianca?"

He's keeping the show rolling, which is his job. Poor Cindy. She takes the items from Calvin and rushes outside. I hope she doesn't use this chance to back out. When the door opens, there's a deep rumble growing louder by the split second. Motorcycles. A lot of them.

Under Calvin's guidance, Travis hands a bidder paddle up to him.

Jefferson says, "This is indeed her time to shine. You're welcome to bid from the audience."

Small victories.

"Let's start the bidding at four hundred thousand." He initiates the bidding before I can tell him I need to start my music.

"No, that's not how this works." I toss my head back in frustration.

"Any lower and we're just wasting time. They have a show to get to." Jefferson's statement of fact doesn't help.

My brothers are messing everything up. Like always.

Hordes of leather-wearing bikers, complete with leather chaps, dome spike helmets, and beards, storm into the auction. What now?

Heat rises in my cheeks. Will I make Rebels'—my brothers' band—twenty thousand fans wait?

Jefferson must notice I'm trying to relax the tension in my shoulders. "Then again, what would it hurt to include everyone in the fun? Several of you were bidding on Bianca. Here's your chance to get back in the mix. Let's start Aurora where Bianca left off. Thirty thousand, do we—"

Several paddles fly into the air. The incoherent increases in dollar amount whiz past as my brothers drive it up. The higher the number, the longer it takes for anyone else to bid.

It's bittersweet to be partially responsible for such a huge donation at the expense of my dreams.

I'm sold.

To my stepbrothers.

I'll give them the designated four hours of help to get ready for Christmas, just as the auction advertised. And I'll hate them even more.

My little fantasy about losing my V-card to swanky billionaires will go die with all of my other crushed dreams.

Jack tosses me over his shoulder, but I beat my fists against his back.

"Calm down, Sis. Just having fun." His hands linger on my waist while I get my bearing on my heels.

Forcing myself to stop swooning at how his fingers wrap around me, I muster, "You're not the kind of fun I was hoping to have tonight."

"Ouch!" His smirk does things to me I can't control. My own body is betraying me.

"Time to go." Calvin interrupts our moment. Which is *not* a moment because he's my stepbrother.

I rush off the stage to grab my stuff and wish Cindy and Wendy well but Wendy is frantic and blurts out, "That motorcycle gang that came in..."

I nod.

"My stepbrothers are in it," Wendy says.

"You've got to be kidding me. Bianca's brothers, then mine, and now yours?"

We both turn to Cindy. "Any chance yours are showing up?"

"If I could only be so lucky." Cindy is more open about having a thing for her stepbrothers.

"Come on, Rory," Calvin calls loudly.

Damn him. "How many times have I said I'm done with that nickname?"

I hug my friends before my brothers cart me away. To do what? Watch their concert? Hang out in a corner with my V-card while they screw their groupies?

Great.

Three

Calvin

"What the hell was that?" I say from the driver's seat, my eyes meeting Aurora's in the rear-view mirror. She's sandwiched between Jack and Travis. I'm jealous.

"A fundraiser." Her sass makes me want to pull the car over and spank her.

"What exactly were you selling?" My eyes drift shamelessly downward and I thank the mirror for not letting me check out my stepsister's cleavage.

"My time." Her evasive answer makes my palms itch. A good smack on the ass would teach her... Hell, it would make my dick even harder. She's always been feisty. That's not likely to change, but it is likely to be fun.

Jack scoffs. "Christmas *Cherry* Auction. You do understand what was really being auctioned?"

She starts to answer, but Big D cuts her off. "And we won you fair and square."

With the help of the mirror, I shoot Big D a warning glance. The four of us had time on the ride over to clear up that we want her. In every way. But we're not discussing it with her until after the show.

"Don't remind me. I can already see the headline, the billionaire rockstars make a giant donation to the woman's shelter. Yay!" Irritation drips from her words. "You could have let me stay there with my friends."

"Not a chance." I can barely hold back from telling her our plan.

"Then take me home."

"We have a concert to get to. You did your good deed raising money for a charity. It's time for us to put on a show that pays the bills for a lot of hard-working people." Big D reaches between the seats and tries to take her hand, but she pulls away.

"You should have just stayed at your concert."

None of us has an answer. Should have...yes. But seeing her in that picture from backstage, before the auction, all four of us broke. I've never spoken to my brothers about my feelings for her, but I wasn't alone.

Did testosterone take over, to make us think we could convince her that we want her? Why is the one woman who doesn't swoon over us the one we're interested in?

We've always adored and protected her, but things are different now...seeing her as a grown woman. She still has our attention. She's fun and sparky. She's perfect.

Before I know it, my mind dives into the dark parts of my desire. I want her to be the mother of my children. *We* want to keep her knocked up.

And we have no idea how to get her to see us this way.

We had to get her off that stage because no one's going to fuck our little sister for money. I pull through the security gates to the private entrance.

"I still don't see why you're forcing me to watch your concert," she says as we walk quickly, guiding her inside.

"You're not watching the concert."

She stamps her foot down, halting our forward momentum, crosses her arms, and says, "You interrupted my fun evening with friends *and* you're not going to let me watch the concert? Great way to ruin a girl's evening!"

Oh, I want to ruin her, all right, but not in the way she's thinking.

"You're going to stay backstage," Jack says.

"I'm not staying backstage. I'll call an Uber."

She pulls her phone out of her purse.

"You're not going anywhere."

"Then the four hours I owe you start now. Oops, they started thirty minutes ago."

I hoist her over my shoulder and carry her to the meeting room where a member of our security team is stationed. I'm sure we had security in pursuit when we left unexpectedly, but this guy's in place.

Brian intercepts us as we put Aurora in the room. "We've been stalling, but they're running out of their best songs. You've got three minutes."

"You heard the man." Aurora makes a shooing motion. "You better get on stage."

God, I fucking love her sassiness. I want to resist just to get her worked up, but I holler over my shoulder to the bodyguard, "Nobody goes in or out except us."

"Tick tock," she says, "I'm only your hostage for three hours and twenty-nine more minutes."

Her dress shifted when I had her over my shoulder. Her tits are spilling out just a little bit more, A slight tug and I'd be able to see those tight little nipples. I physically turn my body toward the exit.

The bodyguard is staring at my chest. I look down. My black leather jacket and t-shirt are covered in glitter. I try to wipe it off, but my hands are covered, too.

She looks like a damn glitter factory exploded. She's always loved things that sparkle, and that's what I love about her. She sparkles, even without the messy addition.

I stride out of the room, Jack flanking me with Big D and Travis following. "We've got to forget about her until the show is over."

Jack laughs, "Tell your erection that."

Four

Aurora

The good news is that my brothers will be occupied for the next couple hours, running out the clock on the four hours I owe them.

I browse the room. The globe lights around the mirror and makeup on the counter indicate it's a dressing room, but the bulk of their stuff is somewhere else. It's kind of funny. My brothers have more makeup than me...except for glitter.

A set of Travis's drumsticks lay haphazardly on a couch next to hand written sheet music. I pick one page up. The words under the musical staff aren't English. He's into some weird stuff. He's the withdrawn, black hair hanging into his eyes, type—but on him, it's ridiculously sexy.

I've tried to keep my distance from my brothers, but the tabloids mentioned something about him tapping into the Viking roots of our family. I toss it aside.

Nobody knows what goes on in his head. He's probably as misunderstood as me. People wonder why I don't use their fame to catapult my career, but I don't share their dreams. I love theater, same as when they were younger, but I love working with kids. I work at the children's theater and want to run it someday.

Picking up a pair of Travis's drumsticks, I find they're heavier than I expected. Then again, they'd break if they weren't pretty sturdy. I try spinning the stick in my fingers, and it goes clattering to the floor. I try flipping it in the air and catching it, only to hit my head.

Fine, I'll give him credit for his show-off skills.

I look in the mirror. I'm the epitome of classic beauty: long blond hair, pale blue eyes, hourglass figure. Trailing a finger over my collarbone and down my chest, I wonder how my evening would have ended if my brothers hadn't intervened.

It should have been perfect. The Christmas Cherry Auction getting moved to the Aubergine Affair sex club made it a given that I would lose my V-card.

Were my brothers the only people who didn't get it? Or were they being the overprotective brothers they've always been? Will I ever shake free from being their little sister?

I lift one of my feet to a stool and start humming the classic stripper tune, slowly unzipping my boot. *I'm Sexy and I Know It* by LMFAO comes to mind.

I shift my weight to pull the boot off but lose my balance and almost twist my ankle. Thankfully, I fell against the countertop.

I zip my boot and return to the couch, trying to pronounce the weird words on Travis's music. Fail. Snapping a picture, I plan on finding a translation app.

For now, I'm done.

I head to the door, open it, and a thick arm shoots across the doorway, followed promptly by the bulk of the security guy, bodyguard, whatever he is.

"You're not going anywhere."

"I'm being held against my will." I try to lengthen my spine so that I come up somewhere higher than his armpits.

"Sorry, ma'am. I have orders to keep you here."

"Did you just ma'am me...Hudson?" I resort to the name on his lanyard when I fail to think of something clever.

"Yes, ma'am."

"You do realize I'm younger than you?"

"Yes ma'am."

Okay, that's not working. "I'm their sister."

"I'm aware of that, ma'am." He is the most polite, obnoxious person ever.

"My brothers don't have any right to keep me here."

"That's not for me to decide." He steps forward, leaving me no choice but to step back. When I'm clear of the door, he grabs it and pulls it shut, forcing me to my solitude.

Walking absent-mindedly around the room, I find bourbon under a t-shirt with Travis's stuff. I survey the rest of the room. Nothing else to drink.

Glancing at the closed door, I lift the bottle. "Thank you very much. I would love a drink."

I pour myself a shot and promptly down it. Wow! It's way smoother than the cheap stuff I've tried.

Pappy Van Winkle...what a silly name. But tasty. I bypass the glass and drink the last bit from the bottle. Were Travis's lips here? It didn't take long for the alcohol to start lowering my inhibitions. My fantasies refuse to be repressed any longer.

"Well, Pappy, maybe this doesn't have to be a terrible evening after all."

Pappy doesn't answer. I guess that's a good thing. If he does start talking back, I need to check myself.

"With a little more of your help, I might be able to convince my brothers to help me with the V-card issue." My brothers are sinfully gorgeous, experienced, and owe me for messing up my evening.

I grab my phone and add Wendy to a group chat with Bianca and Cindy then send a text: *I'm hidden backstage at my stepbrothers' concert. How is everyone else?*

It turns out Bianca's evening failed as badly as mine, and she has to address invitations for her stepmom first thing tomorrow. I offer to help. It'll give us time to swap stories.

The second shot must be taking hold because I'm considering a new, wild scenario. What if my brothers bought me because they know exactly what I was hoping for in that auction?

Five

Jack

I bolt off the stage and motion for Hudson to step away from the door. My brothers are still taking bows, but there's nothing I care about on that stage. Everything I want is behind this door.

I throw the door open and Aurora's holding an empty bourbon bottle to her mouth like a microphone, singing a slurred rendition of *All I Want for Christmas is You*. Her vocal talent is clear despite her drunkenness.

When she leans forward and points at me, my cock goes rock hard. I step closer and take the bottle from her hands.

"How much did you drink?"

"All of it."

"How much is all of it?"

"There was hardly anything left."

She walks her fingers up my chest and again sings the only line she seems to remember. It's a damn shame she's drunk, and my sister.

My brothers file in behind me, and Calvin demands, "What the fuck?"

Big D stops beside me. "Mind if I join in?"

Calvin steps to the other side. "She's drunk. What kind of men are you?"

"Her brothers." Travis overemphasizes the relation as he walks past us and flops on his chaise.

Yeah, but no. We're only related by our parents' marriage. Which should be enough to keep me from reacting the way I am.

"Jack's the..." Aurora giggles, and before I realize what she's doing, her delicate little fingers are on the crotch of my pants. No hiding how hard I am for her.

"The cocky one." She squeezes gently and I'm desperate to lose my morals, but my bad boy persona is a stage and publicity thing.

I cough at her unexpected move. She's bold and fun, but I've never seen this side of her. I've also never seen her drunk.

She says to Travis, "I read the tablets...tab...tabloids. I know exactly the kind of men you are."

"The tabloids don't know shit about the real us." Travis's head tips back.

"You're the tortured, broody one." She lolls her head toward Doug. "Big D's the playboy."

He catches her hand before she gropes him.

She pulls free and points toward Calvin. "And you, Mr. Bossy Pants..."

He cuts her off. "Yep. I'm the bossy one. I'm the oldest. I've always been responsible. Time to get you home."

"Not yet." She giggles while trying to appear defiant. "No sir, you're responsible so you owe me." She rambles about messing up her evening, overexplaining without explaining anything.

"What do we owe you?" Calvin taking her bait is a bit of a surprise.

"Everyone knows what the Christmas Cheery...Cheer...Cherry Auction is for, and you bought me. Now you have to fuck me."

Bam! She said it. The thought that's haunted me from the moment I heard she was in the auction. She was in it for sex. My chest tightens. My fists ball. If we hadn't bought her...

Travis, for the first time ever, moves fast and is at Aurora's side. "That's not how this works. We won four hours of your time, and apparently you're going to need to use four hours to sleep this off."

"But—"

"You're in no condition to do anything but sleep it off."

"You're not the boss of me. You can't do this."

"Come on." I try to help her to the door, but she slaps at me.

"You should have stayed here and blabbed along to music that's so loud no one can hear your crappy lyrics. We could have all had a good night."

"You don't mean that."

"You ruined my night. You owe me. You're always screwing things up. I hate you."

She's kind of cute-drunk, but her words, albeit impaired, sting. Is there something to them? She wouldn't say that if she was sober, would she?

"We'll take you home, let you sleep it off." Travis's eternally dark and broody expression makes him hard to read.

Calvin adds, "We're taking her back to our place. Make sure she doesn't get into trouble."

"It's now or never, Pappy. I have to help my friend address invitations in the morning."

My balls threaten to blow a load at her calling Calvin Pappy. Jealousy? I'm totally fucked, in the wrong way.

"We'll take you wherever you need to be in the morning." Calvin's stoic response dismisses the nickname, but I'm stuck.

What if the truth in her earlier statement is that she wants to fuck us? I can't let that go. "We'll drop you off in the morning, but when you're done, you have some explaining to do."

Six

Aurora

Putting the last zip code on the final envelope for Bianca's stepmom's invitations, I sit back and relax. "I can't believe we finished all thousand invites."

Cindy came, too, which was a huge help.

Bianca says, "Thank you so much. I wouldn't have been able to enjoy my brothers last night if I had to do these all on my own."

I'm truly happy for her. Even though she didn't have sex, she had a lot of fun. Cindy did, too. And rumors are swirling about Wendy's brothers clearing out the sex club for time with her, but she hasn't messaged us yet. Even though the guys took me home to change clothes, I brush stray glitter off an envelope. "Three out of four isn't bad."

An uncomfortable silence is met with sympathetic smiles. I've killed the mood. "It's fine. My brothers are going to get an earful when they pick me up. They want to talk about last night."

Cindy pats my hand. "They may just be worried about image, like my brothers. Their night with me has to stay super-secret. They're already in trouble with their coach for a rowdy weekend. Their huge bid last night is all they can afford the media to publicize. The fun side of being a celebrity is great until something goes wrong and then the public scrutiny is vicious."

"I can't imagine living like that." A great reminder that shacking up with my stepbrothers has drawbacks. Our parents already can't separate stage persona from real life. It's been a sore point for years.

Bianca puts the pens away and grabs my hand. "You're bound to find out someday, Aurora. You're so talented. Have you heard back from the *Mama Mia* audition?"

"The director lost interest in me when he found out my brothers will be out of town." Such is my fate. My brothers interfere even when they don't do anything.

Bianca organizes the invitations in a box to take to the post office. "I'm sorry, sweetie."

Cindy asks, "Are you still auditioning for *Wicked*?"

"I'm going to focus on theater management, getting my foot in the door at the children's theater. People should be less worried about whether I bring famous brothers to the table."

Cindy gives me a hug. "Your time will come."

"You'll be brilliant whether you're on stage or managing it." Bianca toys with another piece of my glitter that's stuck to an envelope. "I better get these to the post office before my evil stepmother sees that you added your personal sparkle."

"My brothers are waiting for me."

"Consider the audition, though," Bianca encourages me as we head to the elevator. "Having a big role like that under your belt can't hurt."

"You're right. Why punish myself? I want that role." Perhaps this director won't ask if my brothers will attend a performance. And so what if they do? Being cast in a big role will only help my ultimate dream of running a theater. I pull out my phone and reply to the email confirming my audition time.

The elevator ride down from the penthouse gives me time to consider the immediate topic. My brothers. Rather than give them an earful about ruining my night, I'll get a rideshare to take me to my car. I don't owe them anything.

Seven

Travis

Our tour bus pulls up to the building where Aurora was helping her friend and I motion for my brothers to stay put. "I'll get her."

I crave a few seconds alone with her. Taking the steps out of the bus, the sparkle on my boots catches my attention. If only I could explain that she permeates my soul the way her glitter left its mark on everything.

My brothers and I had the most bizarre but honest conversation of our lives. We all want Aurora, even if it means sharing her. We live together, work together, play together, and we want Aurora to be a part of that, at any cost. We're not naïve. The public will be cruel.

It's one of many things weighing on our minds.

Calvin's on the phone with our tour manager discussing our potential world tour. I'm undecided on it. My Viking roots are calling to me and a world tour would mean less time to develop the concept. It would also mean we're even farther from Aurora.

She's exiting the elevator, pointing past me as I enter the lobby.

"The tour bus? Really?"

Her friends give her a hug, whisper something, and she waves for them to leave.

"Hello, Aurora. It's good to see you too." I don't mean it as sarcastic as it comes out.

"Why are you in the tour bus?"

"We're on tour. It's the only way we'll have time alone with you."

"What is that supposed to mean? We fit in the SUV last night. Where is it?"

"One of the stagehands is driving it. We have a show an hour away."

"I'm not getting on the tour bus."

"Why not?" I try to take her hand, but she shrugs away.

"Because I have things to do."

"We need to talk about last night."

"I'll spare your vocal cords the lecture. You didn't like my behavior. Thank you for taking care of me. You're such great big brothers. I'll get a ride back to my car." She's fucking sassing me.

I love it and hate it all at the same time. I crave her closeness. I crave her enthusiasm. I crave being able to sort out my very confusing feelings for her.

Shoving all of that aside, I strategize how to get her on the bus.

"We should have asked if you could spend a few days with us instead of just showing up in the bus."

"I have an audition, and I have a job."

"Do you have work today?"

Her bravado vanishes. "No."

"I'll help you run lines. And I promise, we aren't going to lecture you about last night. We have a proposition for you based on something you said. And if you object, we'll get you back for your audition."

"Promise?"

"I'd never lie to you."

With hesitation, she makes her way to the bus. She sits in the seat closest to the door and I take one opposite her. I drum my thumbs on the arm of my chair. It's my nerves. I don't know how we're going to explain this. That we want her.

Now that she's sober, it could go over like a lead balloon.

"What's that you're humming?" she asks.

I didn't realize I had been. Was I actually loud enough to be heard over the road noise of the bus? I get too lost in my head sometimes. Most of the time.

"It's a Viking chant I'm working on."

Big D pipes in. "Yeah, doing his broody, melancholic Viking shit. It all sounds like either a death march or a war chant."

Calvin is quick to add, "It's something he's doing on the side. The band is still going strong. Making bank."

"Is that why I'm here? So you can tell me how popular you are?" She glares at me.

"No, we want to get to know you better," Big D says.

"Okay, then you need to know that I have an audition. A job. A life. I'm more than just your little sister."

"What are you auditioning for?"

She sighs. "I shouldn't tell you because you'll interfere, but you could ask around and find out anyway. *Wicked*."

"That's awesome. But why not take our help?" Big D asks.

"If you show up, everyone will think I got the role because of you. Please don't mess this up for me. I truly love theater, and I can't enjoy it if all of the focus is on you. I just want to trust that I have what it takes."

She doesn't have to explain to me that she's all grown up. I lean forward. "We didn't realize we were causing problems when we came to your shows. We can change. We can give you your own space. You're an adult. Trust me, we know that. And if any of us hadn't realized it, we did at the auction last night."

"Then why didn't you leave me alone, let me do the auction my way?"

The words catch in my throat. Now would be a great time for some bourbon. I force the words out. "If someone had bought you last night, would you have had sex with them?"

"That's none of your business." I toy with the sash around my waist, giving far too much attention to the white snowflakes set against the blue satin.

Jack says, "I beg to differ since you grabbed my crotch and said we needed to fuck you."

She shrinks back. "Did I do that?"

"Even gave a little squeeze." Jack raises his eyebrows at me.

Now that we're solidly into the topic of last night, I'm nervous about seeing what she'll admit to.

"What the fuck! You're not auditioning for *Wicked*." Has Calvin listened to anything that was just said?

I cringe at the photo as he holds his phone up. My brothers and I did a lot of theater growing up, even as we formed the band. If our music hadn't taken off, we'd still be doing theater. We all love putting on a show. But not for the slave driver who's running *Wicked*.

She throws her hands up. "I told you about the audition two minutes ago. And I expressly said I didn't want you to interfere. Did you listen to anything I said?"

She waves her hands in front of her bowed head.

I've never wanted to punch Calvin more than at this moment.

Aurora stands up. "No, this isn't happening. You don't get to parent me. We have parents and their lack of appreciation for the arts is bad enough. This is my decision. Stay out of it."

Eight

Jack

We've put Aurora on the defensive, which is exactly wrong. I move closer to her, sit on the table, and block her view of Calvin.

She waves me off. "And to think I wanted to... Don't you have groupies to impress? I shouldn't have agreed to get on the bus."

"We're just trying to help," Calvin says as his phone rings and he excuses himself to go to the back room of the bus.

"You guys have career blocked me. You've cock blocked me."

"Whoa!" I put a hand on her shoulder. "We've cock blocked you?"

"Well, in a way. It's the same thing as careers. Either people love me or hate me because I'm your sister. I love acting, the pure art of it, and want to do it with people who share my passion. I don't want to be asked if my brother could do a promo spot for a show or if one of my brothers would be interested in a double date. I'm never seen for me."

Travis is taken aback. "Sorry, Aurora, I had no idea. But I hear you about following your passion with like-minded individuals.

That's why I'm looking into the Viking stuff regardless of what The Rebels fans think."

Big D offers a sympathetic approach. "Look, there are good and bad directors in the theater world, like every profession. The wrong one can be a miserable experience. We spent our time vying for audition spots and taking whatever was thrown our way. Even when our band started taking off, some of our managers made us miserable. You've got to be careful with these people. Calvin was just trying to point out that we have experience. We know that director is bad news."

Aurora seems to listen when he mentions our struggles. She was probably more aware of our successes, not our failures.

"Yeah," I say, "It's hard to make your dreams come true. Taking on stage personas is how we hang onto our love of acting."

"So with your spectacular acting skills, you chose to be cocky?" A lightness shines through her tone.

"Us? You were the one grabbing crotches last night. Haven't you heard of consent?" I chuck her under the chin.

She purses her lips. "Sorry. I know it's not a good excuse, but the bourbon may have given me too much courage."

"You're forgiven. Now, we've made your life miserable, so as you said, we owe you."

"You can't control other people's obsession with you. Just no more jumping in to save the day, unless I ask."

We all voice agreement.

"But there is one more thing you mentioned last night that we'd like to explore."

Nervous excitement flips through her eyes. "Could we just forget about last night?"

"Sweet Aurora, your sassy little mouth said something last night that I'll never be able to forget."

Her eyes fall shut and her breaths quicken. She grins sheepishly. "Remember the bourbon."

"You mean Pappy? And how you said it to Calvin?"

"Does he hate me for that?" Her hands cover her mouth.

I slide onto the arm of her chair and pull her hands from her mouth, allowing my finger to skim over her lips. "He'll have to speak for himself, but it made the rest of us jealous."

"Jealous?" She licks where my finger touched.

"Not only did you torment us with that nickname, but you said we had to fuck you."

Did all of us stop breathing? Road noise fills the void. Everything hinges on her response.

Big D breaks the silence from across the table. "Is that what you were hoping for at the auction?"

Travis adds, "You can be honest. Look how much clarity we're getting now that we're opening up to each other."

She nods but turns her gaze to her fingers, fiddling with the ribbon around her dress.

"So you were hoping that whoever bought you would be worthy?"

"Something like that."

"A *Pappy*?"

She laughs. "Please don't ever remind me that I used that term."

"But it was—"

"No." She shakes her head. "Can't go there with my brothers."

I step in front of her and extend my arms. "Can you go here?"

Her brow furrows, but she nods.

I scoop her into my arms and carry her to the couch. Her long, golden hair fans around her as I lay her on her back.

"If..." I emphasize the word, "the winner was worthy, would you have wanted him to take you missionary style?"

Our eyes lock and I swear I can see my future. The sparkle in her eyes returns, so I swing a leg over her, pinning her beneath me.

"Would you have wanted him to crawl on top of you and make slow, sweet love?" I lower my hips.

Her answer is barely a whisper. "Yes."

"Or maybe you'd prefer this." I hoist her up and she squeals, clinging to me. Her embrace is too good to pass up, but I'm running with my plan. Flipping her over, I settle her on all fours, grip one hand around her hip to hold her up, and press my other hand on her back, forcing her shoulder down. My strained erection presses into her winter version of a sundress, and I resist

158

the temptation to get her skirt out of the way even though I'm still clothed. "Being ridden hard and deep from behind."

Travis kneels, lowering his lips to her ear. "So what is it?"

"I don't know."

My cock throbs inside my jeans. Good enough. With her holding the position, I release my grip and inch her skirt up. "Say the word and I can make you sing the praises of all things holy."

Big D positions himself against the wall next to us. "It's your call, Aurora. You pick the position. You pick the man. We're here to please you."

Pulling her body upward, I rotate her to sit across my lap. I kiss her hair then tuck it behind her ear and nibble. My other hand rests on her thigh, my fingertips inching closer to her pussy. "Anything you want, just know that I'd love to get my mouth on your pussy. Make sure you're good and ready for a cock. Whatever you prefer."

A beat passes before she says, "I don't know."

Big D, Travis, and I divert our eyes from her to each other.

I consider the possibility that's weighed on me. The true struggle I had with her taking part in the cherry auction. "Have you ever had sex?"

"I haven't."

"So the whole cherry auction thing was for real?" Big D fails to hide his excitement.

Her shoulders hunch up. "If I didn't feel a connection, I could have just done four hours of cleaning or holiday prep. That was for real."

"But if you did connect?" I wrap my arms around her waist.

The blush that takes over her cheeks is brighter than any of the sparkly makeup she wears. She looks at me from under her eyelashes. "You said to be honest, right?"

"Always."

"I was hoping to lose my V-card."

"And you were mad at us for ruining your plan?"

She nods.

"People say we're the naughty ones." Big D's grin is about to split his face in half.

I hold back my frustration that she was willing to have her first time with a stranger. Crisis averted, as I hold her in my arms. My possessive streak soars way beyond big brother protectiveness. She's mine. In every way. And I intend to prove it.

Nine

Aurora

Jack's steel rod of a cock is underneath me. Did he already know I was a virgin? It doesn't matter.

The big question is, did the bourbon kill too many of my brain cells? I've all but admitted that I've had a crush on the very brothers who've annoyed me for so many years. Am I willing to choose them for my first time?

Them?

How do I pick one? They way the three of them are surrounding me has me feeling like sex on a swivel. Maybe I channeled Marilyn all too well. I recall the movie excerpt where all of the men are clamoring for her. She's the center of attention.

Jack's arms tighten around me as he nuzzles his head against mine.

Is that what I want? All of them? Nobody said anything about one. What about all four?

Jack tucks a finger under my chin, pulling my attention from the door Calvin is behind. Our lips are mere inches apart.

"I could help you figure out the answers to those questions."

"*We* could," Big D is quick to point out, stroking his stubble. Is he imagining us together?

"We're all here for you, Aurora, even Calvin. See what it's like to be loved by all of us."

"Is that the way you do it with groupies?"

Jack's breathing deepens. I might've missed it if I wasn't sitting on his lap.

If I'm going to bare my secrets, so are they, although their sexual habits are more public than mine. "You said we should be honest."

"We've never shared a woman," Jack clarifies.

Travis is tense. "People spread rumors. You were backstage. Did you see any women?"

"I figured it was just because you had me back there."

"That's how it is every time." Travis is painfully clear.

"So why me?"

"It's just something we know."

Big D leans in. "Let me kiss you."

I nod. My tongue darts over my lips. This is real. I lean forward and close my eyes.

He cups my neck and his lips fall softly on my cheek before he rests his head against mine.

My cheek? My eyes flit open. He's holding me so tenderly I don't want it to end. I close them again and sink into his touch. We simply exist for what feels like an eternity before he pulls away.

My lips part, hopeful for more as he angles his head. Our lips meet. He accepts my offer for more than a chaste kiss. The passion. The acceptance. They're everything I dreamed of.

I could lose myself in this forever.

He pulls away, resting his forehead against mine. "We want to make you happy. Go on tour with us. You'll be the highlight of everything we do."

How can a kiss make me want to re-evaluate everything? My factual answer is half-hearted. "My audition is on Monday."

"If it's that important, we'll get you back in time. Let us worship you until then." Travis's smile is forced.

"But consider who you'd be—"

I put a finger to Jack's lips. "Shh. No talking me out of it."

Doug reaches up and angles one of the lights on me, then reaches to the side and does the same with two more. "If it's the spotlight you want, we'll put you in it."

"I don't need fame."

"But you do need answers. Ready for your first lesson so you can make an educated decision?" Jack winks.

"As long as you promise."

He places a finger on my lips. "We promise to get you back to your audition if you insist on going."

Doug takes my hand. "Are you sure you're okay with this? All of us?"

"How could I refuse? You're every girl's dream."

"Are we your dream?" Travis is sweet to clarify, but does it really matter? He's not typically the guy who needs his ego stroked.

"We're being honest with each other," Big D reminds me.

I nod.

"Lesson number one, continued from last night." Jack repositions me on his lap, spreading my legs over his thighs. Shoving my skirt out of the way, he takes my hand and presses it against the front of his pants. "You remember how hard you make me, Baby?"

As if I'd need a reminder. Playing up my innocence, I ask, "Has it been this hard the whole time?"

Jack's mouth goes slack. "In the interest of honesty, I took an extra-long shower and jacked myself off thinking about you."

I flash a teasing smile. "I was joking. But thanks for the honesty."

He shakes his head. "Guys, anyone else willing to admit how badly they need Aurora?"

"I wrote a song about her," Travis says. "Then I imagined making slow, sweet love to you under the stars."

"So yeah, he jacked off too." Jack shifts his attention to Big D.

"Winning you in the auction left me in a world of hurt...every hour on the hour."

"Impressive." I wonder if he's joking.

"Enough about us. Why don't you get her zipper, Travis."

In a combined effort, my dress is unzipped, pulled out from under my bottom, and slipped over my head. Jack rubs his finger over my bra. My sensitive nipples tingle like never before. My sex aches, and I'm pretty sure I'm so wet, Jack's pants will be soaked.

"I'm not sure what to do."

"Enjoy being in the spotlight while we get to know you better." Jack drops one hand between my legs. His finger teases over the damp silky fabric, giving him the most wicked smile I have ever seen.

My breaths fall in sync with the movement of his fingers. My body takes on a mind of its own, bucking and tightening as he reads my every reaction.

Doug tilts my face to the side and locks lips with me. His tongue explores my mouth. I love getting attention from both of them. I love the spotlight more than I thought.

Travis is watching from the side. Then I think it's his hand that slides onto my thigh, works up my waist, over my back. I think he's the one who tucks hair behind my ear, but I'm losing track.

Kisses are harder to cling to as Jack's fingers move inside my panties to massage my clit, taking me to the edge. I'm about to lose control. The whimpering is coming from deep within me.

Doug's hand is cupped behind my head, holding me close through all of my gasps and moans.

The orgasm crescendos so huge inside of me it's an explosion of energy. My body shakes as my brothers carry me through blissful oblivion, my conscious remnants drifting until I finally settle back into the moment.

They've each eased their touches. Doug rests his cheek against mine, still cradling my head in the nook between his neck and shoulder. Travis's fingers trail lazily over my back. Jack mutters, "I love—"

"What the hell?" Calvin came back.

My arms cross reflexively, hiding my chest as if we've done something wrong. Have we? And was Jack about to say that he loves me?

Ten

Calvin

Hanging up with the tour manager, I'm undecided about the proposed schedule. Rory has changed everything. I'm the brother who can find the logic and stay level-headed through anything, but now...she's clouding my judgment.

What does that mean for my gut- and heart-driven brothers?

And what would an intimate relationship do to our already broken relationship with our parents? They think my brothers and I are depraved because of our stage personas and they think she's destined to poverty because she's more concerned with the art of acting than money.

I call them, as I always do when we return to our hometown.

It goes straight to voicemail, as always.

I keep my message short. They won't respond. They never do.

"Hi, Mom and Dad. We're back in the area. Would love to see you over Christmas. Our manager's trying to convince us to do a world tour. Maybe you have insight on cities we should—"

A cry from the other room stops me cold. Shit! I hit the End Call button. Is Rory having an orgasm?

Throwing the door open, I'm paralyzed as I watch my three brothers make Aurora come. What happened after I left the room? Weren't we trying to convince her not to audition for that prick?

"Our sister's a pro at having orgasms. I've never heard anything like it." Big D tries to calm me. "Turns out sis hasn't had sex."

How far did they go? Jealousy, irritation, and desire have a battle of the bands inside of me. "I'm in there working, and you're..."

I've scared Rory. Shit. I stop myself. Breathe.

"Relax man, it's not like you didn't know we all wanted her," Jack says.

I shove Doug out of the way and caress Rory's bare shoulder. "I didn't mean to scare you."

She smiles but doesn't relax her arms.

They started without me. I was working and they decided to play. They had their hands on her while I was sending a message to our parents. I kick all of the thoughts from my mind and focus.

"You're a virgin?" I make a mental note that my brothers still have their pants on, and am eager to hear the answer from her sweet lips.

"I am, but they said you're all willing to teach me. That you'd be okay with this."

"I am." I point at my brothers. "And if you had waited until I was available, I wouldn't have recorded our sister's orgasm in a message to Mom and Dad."

"You recorded it?" Her eyes widen.

"I hung up as fast as I could. Hopefully the receiver didn't pick it up clearly."

"Can you unsend the message?" Aurora asks.

Shaking my head, I say, "It was a voicemail.

Big D offers a sad truth. "They'll probably think it's just some groupie in the background. They think all we do is have sex between concerts. That's what everybody thinks we do, but it pays the bills, so it's all good."

"It's not all good. This..." Rory motions to all of us, climbs off Jack's lap, and reaches for her dress. "We shouldn't be doing this."

"I think we did it quite well," Jack says.

"But look how close this came to a huge mistake. When we get to your hotel, I'll get a ride home and focus on my audition."

I clamp my hands around hers, holding the balled-up dress to her chest. "Slow down. I'm not about to be the only brother who didn't get a taste of you."

She sputters. "Um, well...no one *tasted* me. We were just getting started on some sex lessons."

"Good, then you still need a teacher."

She glances at each brother. No one objects.

"No one has to know. Consider them private lessons." It's unlikely I can keep that promise, and it pains me to even remotely lie to her. But for now, it's the truth. Gently tugging the dress, I'm able to slip it from her hands.

I had no idea a woman could be so perfect.

Jack stands behind her, slides his hands from her shoulders to her fingertips, then laces their hands together and moves them onto her belly.

Damn if my mind doesn't go straight to thoughts of her being full of my baby. She'd make the perfect mother. Is that what Jack's thinking too?

He moves their hands upward, caressing her breasts, going up to her neck into her hair. It's a tease. He's making her caress herself for me.

"You know you want her, Calvin. Teach this goddess how good your mouth will feel on her pussy."

I rake my hand through my hair, then let my gaze linger on her long eyelashes, the pale blue of her eyes, the look of hopefulness.

"Has anyone ever gone down on you, Sweetheart?" The possibility of going to Hell for putting my mouth on my stepsister's pussy isn't enough to stop me from dropping to my knees.

Everything blurs as her scent intoxicates me. I tease my thumb over her hot, wet, pink silky panties. "They've already got you wet. You smell so good, you're going to ruin me."

"I don't want to ruin you." Her fingers drag through my hair, ensuring my ruin.

I cup my hands in that sweet spot where her ass meets the top of her thigh. She's mine.

"Hold her," I say as I dive in.

Jack wraps his arms around her and lifts so I can strip her panties down.

But he doesn't set her down. He works his hands under her. The other brothers, on either side, each take one of her legs and splay her wide for me.

Holy fuck, I am definitely going to Hell. I kiss, then lick, then suck on her pretty, pink, untouched pussy. Her juices are the ambrosia to the gods. The buck of her hips ensures she's enjoying the lesson.

Being between her legs makes me feel like a god. And then she comes undone.

The world could cease to exist and I wouldn't care. I've claimed my sister.

Eleven

Jack

Heading into the last verse of our encore, Big D gives us a nod, letting us know that he'll take the improv before the last note. He segues into his solo, fingers flying over the keyboard, and my thoughts drift to earlier when I was holding Aurora against my body, Travis and Big D held her legs, and Calvin sank to his knees in front of her.

Each shake and whimper of her orgasm is ingrained in my soul.

Staying engaged with the audience is important, but not today. I turn my attention to the side of the stage where she's waiting. Did she hear me say that I love her before Calvin walked in on us?

She hasn't brought it up, but she also didn't go home. She signed up for more lessons and we've had one hell of a day with her.

It's still not enough. Until she commits to being ours, I fear she'll consider us temporary.

Can she see me as Jack, a guy who's completely enamored with her, and willing to throw everything away to claim her? Or does she just want Jack, the bad boy of The Rebels? Will letting down my façade help us grow closer, or drive her away?

Big D's going crazy on the keyboard, his signature move of turning around backward and still playing something that makes a little bit of musical sense.

I work my way to the side of the stage. Calvin's watching me, no doubt wondering what I'm up to. Slipping my bass strap from around my neck, I split my attention between Big D and Aurora.

When he gives the final nod, I bang out my cord, set my bass out of the way, and rush to Aurora.

"Aren't you supposed to stay out there?" She looks over my shoulder.

I lace my fingers with hers, bringing them up to her shoulders, and pin her against the wall.

"Show's over. Time to focus on the only thing that's been on my mind."

"Don't be silly."

I rock my hips into her. "Does that feel silly?"

She shakes her head. Even if she'd verbalized an answer, I wouldn't have been able to hear. The crowd's going wild. It was a high-energy performance. I'd wondered if the energy was from the crowd or just from me, knowing that Aurora was waiting for me, for us.

"I love you, Aurora." I lowered my mouth to her ear. "I need to make love to you."

Her response is hard to hear above the noise. "Is that my next lesson, make love? It sounds so polite. I thought you were supposed to be the bad boy."

My chest tightens. I won't force her to acknowledge my first statement. "I'll be whatever you want me to be."

Glancing over my shoulder, I confirm that the audience can't see us. Then I unleash my desire. Gripping her chin, turning her face to mine, I lock my lips on hers, channeling that bad boy energy.

"You want a bad boy, then you're going to get fucked right here." I need to get my dick inside of her. I need to make her scream. I need to make her feel good. I need to make her mine.

"Let me fuck you bare, Aurora." I lower a hand, shove her dress between her legs, and cup her sex without applying pressure.

She trails kisses over my shoulder.

"You have to consent."

Her hips are wiggling against my hand and she whimpers. "You have my consent, always and forever."

Pulling some petty sibling shit like 'no take-backs' would kill the bad boy vibe. I damn sure hope she meant it.

I'm about to be her first. I'm energized with how right this feels. With the energy of the crowd still screaming. Our brothers are feeding the applause, playing extra little riffs.

We work together to get her skirt up and her panties down.

"We're going to get caught." Her excitement over it surprises me.

"You like that, don't you? The thrill of the risk?" I lift her and press my tip against her wet pussy.

"Our brothers are going to be pissed." Her breaths come even faster and her cheeks flush.

"You're a naughty girl, trying to get me in trouble." I lock my eyes on hers and tilt my hips, forcing her virgin lips to spread for me.

She gasps, her expression pinches, then softens happily.

The rush is intense. I force myself to stop. "You okay? I'll be gentle."

"I want my first time to be memorable." She hooks her legs around me. "I want you to fuck me like we're about to get in trouble."

"I don't want to do that with you, Aurora, not for your first time."

She rocks her hips hard and fast against me. "Hurry, they're going to catch us."

Shit! My balls are ready to unload per her request, but I don't let them. Leaning into her, I pin her firmly against the wall. "If I'm going hard and fast, you have to keep your eyes open. I have to see that you're okay."

The amount of certainty in her baby blues is staggering. Where did my sister learn that? I fuck her as hard as I can, pounding her into the wall. Every sensation grows more intense. Louder. Clearer. The earth shakes underneath us.

Except that it really does, or at least the stage does. And the roar of the crowd is too close.

The clench of Aurora's pussy around my shaft snaps me back to a solitary focus—making her come.

Her fingernails dig into my shoulder as she cries out and falls limp against me. I don't want this to end, but something's wrong. Sharp commands from our security team direct us to leave the stage.

The audience must be out of control. This can't be happening. The only fuck my balls give is the one that involves Aurora. They pump surge after surge of my seed into her.

I lean to the side while my hips insist on finishing their primal function. The crowd is rushing the stage.

Bodyguards and security are in place, pushing them back, but there are too many audience members on stage to count.

If I can see them, they can see us. Fuck!

Some of them have their phones held high. This will be public soon.

Calvin's rounding the corner and Big D is right behind him. They look horrified when they see me pinning Aurora to the wall.

Twelve

Big D

What the hell? We're having an emergency and Jack's over here fucking Aurora?

Security personnel don't bat an eye, just add Jack carrying Aurora as they usher us backstage. There's too much chaos to stop.

Safely inside the tour bus, we all turn to Jack, who's set Aurora on the couch and is just now putting his dick back in his pants. That couldn't have been a comfortable run to safety.

The bus is in motion, carrying us away with a police escort. We're all supercharged with adrenaline, except Aurora. She's blissed out.

Rather than yell at Jack for claiming her without talking to the rest of us, I sit beside her and lean her body against mine. "Can I make you mine?"

My question perks her up. "Can I get on your lap to do it?"

"Sure thing. I'm just here to make you happy."

I've barely got my pants shoved to mid-thigh when she straddles me and drags her fingernails over my erection. It's an electric surge. Pre-cum spurts out and she swirls her fingers through it.

"Big D... I guess your name isn't just because you don't like being called Doug."

"I'll sure as hell take that compliment." I catch my brothers taking a look, but nothing comes of it since Aurora's ready.

Her hands are on my shoulders and my hands are around her waist.

"You want to lead the pace?" I ask.

Her mouth opens to answer but she interrupts her own response by teasing herself on my rock-hard cock. Wiggling her hips back and forth, she combines our wetness before sinking onto me.

The start-and-stop of her motion is sweet torture. Her warmth and tightness welcome me. I throb inside of her, barely holding off an orgasm.

She picks up the pace, her head lolls back, and I quietly nod and ask Calvin to strip her dress off of her while she's pleasing herself at my expense.

I'm not complaining. My little stepsister sure loves fucking as much as I do.

Calvin strips her bare, and her tits bounce in my face. I lean forward, catching her nipple with my tongue. It makes her shiver, which makes her pussy clench, which makes my dick twitch. Yeah, it's a hell of a chain reaction until her pussy doesn't stop clenching. Over and over again, she constricts around me.

I have to take over, pumping her on my cock as she loses her ability to focus. She comes so hard, she obliterates the road noise of the highway.

"I love you." And I'm helpless to resist. I shoot rope after rope of cum into her womb. Baby-making time. I'm a bastard for wanting that. We all are.

When I regain my composure, I slide her off of my cock, turning her sideways on my lap, and cradle her against me. "You better rest. From what I saw, you took it pretty hard with Jack, and you didn't go easy on yourself with me."

Of course, Travis and Calvin might disagree, but they nod understanding.

I hate that I'll have to let her go at some point, but I hold on for now. Much like I hold on to the hope of getting her pregnant. She's bound to hit me with a wrecking ball at any moment and say that she's on birth control. For now... Hope breeds eternal...or something like that.

Travis disappears for a second, then comes back with a washcloth. He sits at her feet, rests his hand on her knees. "Let me clean you up."

He eases her legs apart, then tenderly cares for her with the washcloth. The warm water drips on me and it feels damn good, but I know better than to ask him to clean me up. Even if Aurora was offering, I wouldn't want her to. I want to bask in her scent for eternity.

He's paying a little too much attention, so I tell him, "Fuck off. Let her rest."

She falls asleep in my arms. It's the sweetest thing that's ever happened. I'm usually up for a rowdy, good time, but it turns out this tops everything. Might mean I actually have a tender side.

And the way my heart feels, I think I'm getting set up for the biggest adventure of my life. I kiss Aurora on the head as she stirs. "Sorry, I didn't mean to wake you."

"I wasn't really sleeping."

"You need to travel with us. We can have this all the time. You can travel the world with us."

Calvin says, "If we do the world tour. If not, just stay with us."

She squirms to sit upright against me. "If I get the part, I'll have rehearsals. I can't be on the road." She lays out the plan, the rehearsal schedule, and the performance dates. "In fact, I should do some vocal work." She pushes off of me and walks toward the back of the tour bus.

But Travis, drumsticks in hand, swings them around her waist and locks her in with his other hand. "Take a break. Just for today."

Thirteen

Aurora

Why do I love him forcing me to stop? Why am I so turned on by being restrained?

The drumsticks pressed low across my belly and hip bones... I like resisting against them. As I try to step farther, he pulls tighter.

"Where are you going? Don't let our talk about tours make you think you have to practice," he says with his arms wrapped around me.

I want him to restrain me more, and in different ways. I wrap my hands around the drumsticks. Over my shoulder, I say, "Can I see these?"

"Sure." He lets me take the sticks. I spin around and kiss the ends of them.

"You want them back?" The tour bus is big, but only so big, so I don't have much of a plan to run away with them. But we're near the front and I want to be chased.

His eyes narrow. "You can keep them."

I drag the drumsticks down my neck, through my cleavage, and stop on my belly. "Are you sure you don't want them?" I step away tauntingly.

"On second thought..." He steps closer, eyeing me questioningly.

I scurry a few feet toward the back of the bus, but he catches me before I get to the door that I had hoped to be able to try to close between us.

His arms wrap around me. The security that washes over me is so wrong. I shouldn't want any of this. But I do. And I'm going to accept it.

He takes the sticks from my hands and he presses them between my legs. The angle he has them at catches my clit, causing me to shudder. I squirm away but he catches me from behind, grips my wrist firmly, turning me into his chest, and pinning both of my hands behind me. His huge paw is able to grip both of my wrists and the drumsticks.

"Are you taunting me?"

"Are you going to punish me?" I bat my eyelashes at him, hoping he'll continue with our little game. He strides forward, forcing me back until we pass through the doorway.

He turns me, backing me against a desk. "Maybe it's not so bad Calvin insisted on having this in the bus."

I glance over my shoulder, and thankfully the top is clear.

He leans me back, then holds both of my hands in front of my stomach with one hand while he unzips his pants with the other. He helps me get my feet onto the desk, which is much more comfortable than when my legs were dangling.

Then he leans into my legs and fucks me hard. A hint of light enters his dark eyes as we drive each other to climax.

Fourteen

Travis

My heart fails to beat as my brothers and I pile into the SUV in a mad dash to get to Aurora's audition. We want to celebrate with her afterward, even though she won't be notified right away. We know she deserves the part.

The question is if she wants us there. It's the thing keeping all of us silent as Calvin drives.

I was pissed when we woke up in the hotel this morning and she'd snuck out. I've never had sex so good it left me basically unconscious.

She left a cute little note with hearts on it saying she didn't want to bother us.

We'd promised to get her to the audition, but apparently she had a friend come pick her up. My lungs barely take air. She had to plan ahead to leave us.

The drive gives me time to get lost in the memory of making love to her. She liked being controlled. She liked being restrained. I'm not nearly done exploring that.

184

I rub my hand over my mouth. Her lingering scent serves as a reminder of what we've done.

She's a sexual goddess beast. That may not have been a thing before, but now, it's alive and well in Aurora.

My chest has phantom vibrations as I recall our second round of sex. She wanted my hand over her mouth to keep her from making too much noise in the hotel room. Her head thrashing side to side made it extra fun. She had me throw her on the bed, something she'd seen in a movie. Then she wanted me to force her to stay before she could get up. She really gets off on being controlled.

My cock nearly splits through the leather of my pants, it swells so hard and fast. I wonder if she'll be up for some CNC, if she's even heard of consensual non-consent. Would that push a limit? I'd sure as fuck like to find out.

I'll talk to her after the celebration. *Celebration*...that's fucked. I'm ecstatic that she's pursuing her dreams, but they're in conflict with our schedule. We have obligations to a lot of workers that support us. We'd be nothing without them.

But I'm nothing without Aurora.

We keep rockstar personas in public, but we're businessmen behind the scenes. None of that will be helped by shacking up with our sister. More fucking conflict.

I think we're just a behind-the-scenes thing to her, anyway. She might be wise. Our parents already despise us being wild rock stars with no morals. If they find out we're fucking our stepsister, they might never speak to us again.

The same might be representative of how the public would react.

Asking Aurora to suffer that judgment isn't fair. But living without her... That's it. That's the strange tangle inside my chest. I can deny what it is I want, but it's the nagging feeling that maybe I don't have to be alone in this world.

I mean, I'm never alone. I've got my brothers. I've got the band. But I've never connected with a woman. Aurora gets me. I don't even have to pretend to be broody.

That's what I want out of life...my sister.

Can we make it work? Can we be enough for her? She's so much. She's so full of life. So young. Damn. I've got ten years on her, and Calvin even more. Why can't I let this go?

"We've got a helluva mess on our hands. Is this thing with Aurora real?"

"What the fuck? You don't know if this is real? What do you think, it's just playtime?" Jack doesn't get where I'm coming from.

"It's real to me. Is that where we all stand?"

They all speak over each other, not giving space as they clamor to admit they've all caught feelings for her.

I try to steer the conversation. "Do we want to explore the cost of a relationship with Aurora, explain that it could cost her the relationship she has with our parents? She hasn't had time to come to terms with it like we have."

"Maybe if she hooks up with us, our parents will come around." Big D has to be joking.

"You've got to be kidding me," Jack says. "It would only be worse."

"Just trying to lighten the mood."

"We're a fucking thing, she just doesn't understand that yet." Calvin ends the discussion as he turns into the theater parking lot.

Our celebrity status and a promise to stay out of sight get us in the back door. Aurora's singing her heart out. She has the voice of an angel. She has everything of an angel.

I'm going to have to choose between being there for my brothers and the band, or being there for Aurora. Technically, the drummer's a pretty easy band member to swap out. Can I use that to my advantage?

I can focus on my personal work, turn it into something. Time to figure out if there's a market for Viking Fusion.

She runs through some spoken lines, sings a piece of the director's choosing, and does it well, then wraps up.

The director thanks her, and Calvin motions for us to step outside so we don't end up causing a scene if she catches us backstage. The four of us are leaning against the brick wall behind the auditorium when the door opens.

It's the sharp inhale of a sob, then the motion of her hand across her eyes, and the heave of her chest that wreck me. Shit. They're not happy tears. What's wrong? I rush to her.

"He asked if I could bring my brothers in to do a Master Class on stage presence."

I pull her into my chest. "We'll do it, but only if you want."

"No, don't interfere. Nothing at all from you guys. It makes me angry that he asked before giving me the part."

"If he wants us, he should reach out to our manager. Your audition is your space. I'm sorry people try to use you."

"It's not your fault."

I hold her tighter. "Now, explain why you left this morning. We worried—"

"I'm sorry, it was nerves. I thought...well, that if you were there, your presence would impact me. It happened anyway."

"I can't help that he's an ass, but I might be able to help with some of your anger."

"How?"

"It involves sex."

"What are we waiting for?"

"It's controversial to some people. It's called consensual non-consent. We'd agree on—"

"You mean CNC." Her eyes light up.

Fuck. She truly is an angel.

Fifteen

Aurora

I sang *Jingle Bells* while straightening the sheets of music on the coffee table. *Rudolph* and *Frosty* while spreading melted chocolate in the molds for hot chocolate bombs. And *Baby, It's Cold Outside* while strolling through their huge house familiarizing myself with the two-story layout.

Imagine the fun we could have as a family singing Christmas carols. Stopping by the fireplace, I sing *Chestnuts Roasting on an Open Fire*, although I don't think that's the actual name of it. The tiny tots with eyes aglow...I rub a hand on my belly. I could be pregnant. I want to be pregnant.

I love kids, but have I done something foolish? And not just me...my brothers never asked if I was on birth control. How did I go from thinking one night with them would be enough, to a few lessons, to anxiously awaiting CNC play?

I'm doing everything I can to act normal, including singing every Christmas carol I know while I wait for my brothers to make their move.

When he brought up CNC, I just about passed out. I've read about it as a safe way to act out what would normally be a terrible thing. Acting is the key. Everyone understands that I won't ever actually be in danger, but it's fair game to get aggressive.

We decided on the classic, *red*, as a safe word.

Jack asked about what to do if my mouth was full. We agreed that I would tap them with an arm or leg or tap the ground three times. Of course, that means they can't tie up my arms and legs and fill my mouth up at the same time, which I'm a little bummed about, but we'll do that in a different session.

The anticipation is killing me, but Travis insisted that I not know when to expect them to come for me. It'll be a better adrenaline surge.

We worked out a loose scenario and the guys are honing details amongst themselves.

Running out of classic Christmas carols, I break into Gwen Stefani and Blake Shelton's *You Make It Feel Like Christmas*.

I pull up the sheets on Jack's bed, wondering how many women he's had in here. Has he played this game before? What do I really know? I feel like I'm losing my heart to my brothers without seeing how it will ever work.

I've almost convinced our parents to come into town for Christmas, but a sexual relationship between us siblings would destroy them. It's too soon to worry about saying anything anyway. If our parents agree to dinner with all of us, we'll act normal. If I even know what that is anymore.

I fluff the pillows, then head downstairs to the kitchen. I love the open-concept home, with almost entire glass walls. So light and free in the middle of several gated acres. I don't have to flip the overhead lights on because of all the sunlight.

We confirmed that I'm fine if all of us end up together, but that I'm only okay with two of my holes being filled right now. One of those is my mouth. We'll work on the other hole a different time.

I handwash the single cup in the sink, dry it, and put it away.

Closing the cabinet, I turn toward the sink and stumble backward. Through the window, I see Calvin standing outside at the picnic table, arms folded and one ankle crossed over the other. Surely I would have noticed if he was there earlier.

When we were hanging out talking about our favorite shows, I told them how hot it was in *Good Girls* when Rio watches Beth through the kitchen window. Is that what they're doing?

Maybe. Maybe not. But the scene has begun. My heart races and I turn the water on to pretend wash my hands.

Footsteps approach from behind. I can barely breathe.

Calvin's watching but he won't have that great of a view since he can only see me from the waist up. I presume I'm about to get railed at the kitchen sink. Or not, if I resist.

"Is someone," I start to say looking over my shoulder and Travis closes in on me, his hips pinning me hard against the kitchen counter, his hands on either side.

"Hey, neighbor. Thought I'd come over and we could have some fun."

He's my neighbor, okay. How do I want to play this?

I'm so excited to be taken by my brothers again that it shocks me when Travis lifts one of his hands and whispers in my ear, "Run."

Despite all of my acting training, all of my improv sessions, all of my desire to do this... I freeze.

He leans away, and I'm trying to gather myself to do what he said, and a sharp slap on my ass is exactly the incentive I needed.

Every single muscle in my body tightens, for a split second before I sprint to the other side of the kitchen island. I grab the edge and stare him down. I hope I do this right. This is my chance to get aggressive and process my frustrations, but the promise of sex did that already.

I do love a chance to act, though. I cautiously lift one hand and say with a shaky voice, "I didn't let you in."

"You left the door unlocked." He rounds the island, and I don't freeze this time.

I bolt. He knows his house better than I do, but I weave through the long living room, around the couch, then the end table, trying to keep a piece of furniture between us at all times.

He slaps a hand on the back of the couch and launches himself over it.

I scream as he grabs my arm. Yanking with all my might, I slip away, positioning myself behind a plush chair.

"Leave her alone. I'm calling the police." Big D's voice from down the hall indicates he's on my side. Interesting.

"You want to call the cops? You'll have to come get your cell phone." Travis lunges toward the coffee table and grabs the phone Big D is heading for. "If she sucks my cock just right, I'll dial the number for you."

I'm tempted to drop to my knees, but movement out the back of the house draws my attention. Calvin has moved closer. He's on the back porch, his hands on an Adirondack chair, and he's smirking. Christ, that's seductive.

He lifts one hand and motions with his fingers for me to come outside. I doubt he's a good guy in this scenario.

Travis circles the far side of the chair, and I plan an escape, darting toward the front door. I throw it open and Jack steps out from behind a bush, rapidly approaching the door. The fire in his eyes is to die for.

But crap. There are so many of them. I detour to the stairs, grabbing the spindles so I don't overshoot. Travis's hand clamps over one of mine, his body presses into me from behind and my cheek hits our hands. Then he slaps my other hand back on the spindle.

Jack circles around us and runs onto the stairs, resting one knee on a higher step as he reaches over the rail and grabs my hair, forcing me to face his crotch.

"Hold this hand," Travis says to Jack, who complies, keeping me in place. Travis uses his now free hand to lift my skirt and promptly bites my ass.

"Help me, Doug!" I scream, hoping I read his role correctly.

"He can't help. You're ours now," Jack says while I hear a zipper being lowered behind me, followed by Travis shoving his pants down.

My eyes dart down to the outline of Jack's long, cock against his jeans. My panties are officially drenched.

"You want a closer look at my cock?"

"You can't make me." The crazy thing is I want them to make me. I've never been so aroused in my entire life.

"Leave my wife alone." Big D rushes in from the side, but Calvin knocks him into the wall.

That was rough. But he said *wife* and I can't get past it. My heart is about to explode. My pussy quivers at the thought of being married to them. The dream, the distant reality.

"Sit down and watch your wife take a real man's cock." That's Calvin slinging Doug into a chair. Then Calvin pulls his phone out of his pocket. "I'll make sure the neighbors can't hear."

Seconds later, Springsteen's *Santa Claus is Coming to Town* fills the house.

Jack lets go of my hair and Travis has taken control of both of my hands again. Jack strips his shirt then the rest of his clothes. His erection slaps his abs.

He positions himself on the stair so his cock is in my face and re-grabs my hair to make sure I see it. God, he's a work of art.

Travis slides his cock back and forth underneath me as Jack fists his cock, positions it between the spindles, and slaps it against my face, rubbing the tip over my lips. The salty pre-cum teases my tongue, the scent infiltrates my nose. I try to turn away but he won't let me.

I struggle but it's useless.

"Take a good look. When I'm done with your mouth, I'll flip you around and sink balls-deep into your cunt. Now open up like a good girl."

Without thinking, without resisting, I do. Dang it.

Jack slides in and out. Our hands cushion my face from the wooden spindles. I try not to moan in pleasure. My acting skills are getting a workout.

"Don't you dare move your hand." Travis waits for me to mumble agreement around Jack's cock before releasing one of my hands.

In one swift motion, he's using it to shove his cock into me. Two at a time. I love this. And I don't want to break anyone's cock, which I guess could happen, so I don't resist.

"I told you we'd have fun." Travis is right. The game is over. I'm not resisting. I'm loving every minute of their attention.

Even poor fake husband Doug, who's forced to watch instead of participate.

I moan and cry against Jack's shaft.

"Look how hot your wife is, getting double-teamed."

I'm confused by a scream from the front door while Calvin's bossing Doug.

"Stop that."

Oh no, it's my mom.

"Stop it right now." Our dad is with her.

Everyone's startled. Travis pulls back. The absence of Jack's cock in my mouth and Travis's from my pussy leave me abandoned and vulnerable. And yet they're both right here as shocked and probably embarrassed as I am. Humiliated.

Cold air graces my ass briefly before Travis pulls my skirt down. I force my body to stand. I don't want to turn around, but what good will it do to stay turned away?

The loud music stops abruptly. I turn to face the figurative music with my brothers.

"Aurora!" my mom shrieks, the level of horror in her voice etching itself into my memory.

Sixteen

Aurora

"Come with us young lady," our father says, reaching his hand out. My mother's already outside.

Jack pulls his jeans on, forgoing his underwear. "She doesn't have to go anywhere."

"It's okay, Jack. I'll go." I'll do whatever it takes to make this end.

Travis zips his pants, stands at my side, and speaks to our father. "She doesn't need saving. We're all adults."

Big D pipes in, "How the hell did you get in?"

"Calvin gave us the gate code, said we're always welcome."

Calvin paces away from us. "That was...over a year ago."

"We didn't realize we weren't welcome anymore. Your text said you wanted to see us. Take a good look. Now, we've got to get Aurora out of here before you corrupt her any more."

My four brothers try to intervene, but they're fired up. Letting them argue will only drive a bigger wedge in our family. I calmly say, "Let me handle this."

Then I scramble to figure out how as my parents drive me to their hotel. The drive is silent with the exception of Dad's loud, nostril-flaring breaths.

My phone keeps buzzing. The guys let me know I don't have to do this alone. Then a message from Cindy: *Having celebs in the family can suck*

She attached a video. I turn my volume down then play it. Lovely—footage from when the crowd rushed the stage after the concert. It's hard to make out, but in the background, my legs are wrapped around Jack. My face is nuzzled into his neck.

At least our parents don't use any social media.

When we finally get up to the room Dad paces, Mom sits in one chair and I take the other. Dad kicks off the inevitable. "You're young and impressionable."

"I'm an adult. I was as much a part of instigating it as they were. I gave my consent. We love each other. You don't understand what you interrupted." The more rapid-fire defensive statements I make, the flatter they fall.

"Oh, you love each other? Did they tell you that?" Dad asks.

Their proclamations streak through my mind.

He shakes his head. "And you believed them?"

I shrink into the cushions of the chair a little bit more.

"I never thought the four of them would stoop this low, especially Calvin."

My mom's voice is softer, and instead of anger, her words bear hurt. "Don't get tangled up in their world, honey. They make a lot of money and think that means they're successful, but they've thrown away their morals."

Dad interjects, "How did your last audition go?"

This question, on its own, could have a lot of different connotations. Coming from him, it pours alcohol straight into the wound.

He barely pauses. "Okay. Judging by your face, it didn't go well."

My face? Does he not understand what I'm going through? It doesn't matter if they outright say they're disgusted that they caught me having sex with my brothers.

He keeps going. "It might be time you get a real job. You've been disillusioned by your brothers that you can be a celebrity. But fame is fickle. Accounting...that's where it's at. A good, steady job."

"Yes," Mom says. "We tried to get your brothers to get real jobs, but they insisted on this music thing. They had a lot of really hard years. You were too young to realize how poor they were up until the last couple of years. We don't want that for you."

It's probably best if I let them speak their minds, but a ball of frustration grows inside of me. I wait as she purses her lips and takes in more air before continuing her monologue.

"And the fornication, you could end up pregnant."

My belly tightens. Now we're back on that topic. Not good.

"Whatever that was, Aurora, it's not normal. You have to value yourself. If we hadn't—"

"I get it. You don't approve of them. You don't approve of their music, but you don't even understand it, and you don't approve of my dreams, but that doesn't mean I don't have a right to explore them. And do even you realize what a big deal my brothers are?"

"Do you realize what a big deal incest is, honey?"

I can't believe Mom said that. Pointing out that it's not incest won't help.

"Honey, if people find out you've done that, you'll never be respected. It might even be hard to get a job as an accountant."

Too late for that warning, since the video surfaced. And why are my parents so convinced I should be an accountant? Sometimes I think Cindy should be their child instead of me. She's working on getting her accounting degree.

"That's my risk to take. I don't want to sit at a desk and look at numbers all day. I thrive on creativity. I want to inspire creativity in others. And I'll work whatever minimum wage jobs I have to while I establish myself. I get to make that choice. I get to pursue my dream. You don't get to stand in my way. They don't get to stand in my way. Nobody gets to tell me how to live my life."

I rush out the door, tears streaming down my face.

My words are much stronger than my soul, which is now crushed. Pieces of it fall with each teardrop as I rush to the elevator. I pull out my phone and open the rideshare app.

I need time alone. That's weird. I usually want to be with people. Travis is the loner of the family. Maybe I can learn from him. Time to go sit with myself.

Seventeen

Calvin

Of all the times I've told my parents I'd like to see them... It's not their fault. Any time in the last few days would have been risky.

Embracing reality doesn't help.

I wouldn't have thought they could think less of us, but now Rory's involved. Why the hell didn't she let us help her? How can I protect her from society's judgment if I can't control my own home?

Hating the answer, I slam my fist into the wall. My fingers ache as I rub them. Wouldn't be a smart move to break my fingers while we're on tour. Except that without a lead guitar, we could cancel. No. I'll do that of my own choosing if needed, not because I'm a dumbass who can't control my reactions.

Which reminds me that I need to think with my head. Rory wants to act, wants to have her own life, and wants to run a children's theater. That will mean she can't be on the road with us. I can't make her do it my way.

Fuck. If I want to show her that I respect her, I have to actually respect her. She deserves to be happy, even if it's not with my dick inside of her. Going on the world tour could be just what we need to give her space. How fast can our tour manager get venues booked?

I call my brothers into the living room.

"There's only one way I can see this working."

"All right, give it a go," Big D says.

"It's not going to work with Aurora."

They all rear up, but I motion for them to hear me out. "That horror on Mom and Dad's faces, we'll experience it elsewhere. Rory will experience it elsewhere. It's not something society's ready to accept. It's not going to advance her career."

Travis is sitting in the oversized chair Rory hid behind during our CNC play. He'd look like a fucking king if we hadn't just been destroyed. He leans forward. "So you're giving up on her?"

"Not giving up."

Jack stands in front of the couch and throws his arms out to the sides. "Sure sounds like it."

"I'm not giving up. I'm using logic and reason."

"How is your heart not in shambles?" Travis is furious.

"It is."

"Not if you can still think. I'm done with you and this fucking band. I'll do whatever it takes to be with her."

"I'm not thinking of us. I'm thinking of her. She wants to work with kids. How will she get people to trust her with their children if she's fucking her four brothers? Can you engage your brain enough to process that?"

"How can you feel—" Big D steps too close to me and I shove him back.

"This feels like absolute shit. She didn't even want us talking to Mom and Dad. She wanted to do it her own way because we always fuck things up for her. Let's all keep our dicks in our pants and not fuck her career up any more than we already have."

Eighteen

Travis

Calvin's trying to do the right thing, but the arrogant prick is still missing the point.

I say, "You guys are forgetting something pretty damn important."

Everybody looks at me.

"She wants to be heard and seen. She wants to be acknowledged for herself. Let her make the decision."

Our phones all buzz at the same time. Please let it be Aurora. We've texted her but gotten nothing back.

It's Mom: *Aurora left. Please let me know if she reaches out to you. I need to know that she's safe.*

At least there's a tinge of humanity in that woman.

None of us bother texting back. It would just open the door to criticism.

I usually sit back and let Calvin run the show. Sometimes Jack leads us on crazy adventures, or Doug charms us into shit. But this time it's too important. "We have to find her."

Jack volunteers, "I'll check her apartment."

Doug's on his phone. "I'm checking social media."

Calvin says, "I'll track down her friends."

We all head our different directions.

Aurora would be pissed that I use my celebrity to get into the otherwise closed children's theater. At least my intent is good. The second the door opens, the haunting words of my own song float around me. Some of the pronunciations are wrong, but it's unmistakable.

Have I lost my mind? I haven't shared that song with anyone.

I rush inside and stop short. I'm not hallucinating. It's Aurora.

I watch and listen from the back of the stage. A single spotlight shines on her. She's front and center, singing to a dark, empty auditorium, reading the music from her phone.

She's bringing it to life, tapping the drum beat on her thigh. Does she understand the words she's singing? The meaning? It's about devoting your entire soul to a person, your entire existence to serving that person. The person that you would travel to the ends of the earth for.

I text my brothers and let them know where she is. I don't disturb her. It's a little self-serving, hearing her sing my song. My fingers join her in tapping the drumbeats.

Aurora's singing has always been beautiful, but she might have perfect pitch. As the piece continues, I hum the baseline and I'm stoked over how haunting it sounds, how perfect we blend.

"Hey, Travis, I thought Aurora came alone," a man's voice says from my side. Dammit, there's where my celebrity gets me in trouble. It's a stagehand who's carrying a bundle of cables. I wave and he moves on.

Aurora's angelic tones float into the catwalk as she spins around. "I'm sorry, I took a picture of your song. I was singing it without permission."

I step out from the shadows. "You have my consent, always and forever."

"It's gorgeous, with an artistic simplicity. The kids would love performing something like this."

"Then let's do it with the kids. But I wrote it for you." I cross the stage and stop at the edge of the spotlight. My eyes drift to her belly. "Don't you think they're a little young?" My effort to make a joke is buried under uncertainty.

She grips her phone nervously at her waist. I reach into her spotlight, take her hands, and bring them to my lips.

"What if I am?" she whispers.

I step closer, covering her hands with mine. "I love you and I think that you are. We'll figure it out with you. Just don't shut us out."

"Deal, as long as you don't refer to the possible pregnancy in the plural again."

"Did I do that?" I mock disbelief.

"*They're* a little young?"

I wrap her in a hug, frustrated that my brothers arrive.

She pulls away. "What are you all doing here?"

"We were trying to find you. We didn't like the way that ended. How'd it go with the parents?" Doug asks.

"Exactly as you would think."

Doug exhales loudly. "First of all, we're sorry. And don't bother with telling us an apology's not necessary. Second of all, I love you, and—"

We cut him off as we talk over each other, vying for her to hear each of us express our love.

"Okay, okay, I get it...but our parents." She's young, hasn't even lived on her own for a year. It's a fair concern.

"Our parents have a lot of growing up to do. But that's what we want to ask you. We're willing to make this real. To be here for you, to have a relationship, for always and forever. But we need to know if that's what you want."

"Well, Travis says I'm pregnant, so we might not have a choice."

"Whoa." Calvin rests his hand on her shoulder. "You always have a choice. We're not forcing you into anything. But we hope you'll choose us."

"And there's one other thing you still have to choose." Big D looks proud of whatever he's scheming.

"*Still?*"

"Yeah, you haven't told us which position you prefer."

Nineteen

Big D

Not only did Aurora choose all of the positions, she chose all of us.

That sparked us to make some decisions pretty fast. No world tour, especially since she's probably pregnant. She agreed to pee on the stick today, but has already moved in. And adding her to our band, we're exploring Travis's Viking stuff.

I'm at my home keyboard, making sure I've memorized the Viking piece we're about to head to the stage to try out when my phone dings.

"I got the new logo back from the designer," I call out and wait while my siblings head over. Aurora doesn't know the logo's a joke. And I didn't expect the designer to turn it around by Christmas.

"A new logo?" She studies my phone screen. "You changed The Rebels to The Revels?"

Jack says, "It seems fitting since we're doing a lot more celebrating than rebelling these days."

Calvin continues the joke. "The oversized V in the Viking font sets our new tone."

I pull her onto my lap, struggling to sound serious. "Symbolic of our sister giving us her V-card."

She slaps her hands over her mouth and blushes. "Absolutely not."

"But you're our inspiration." Travis's sincerity shines through.

She slides her hands over her face, takes a few deep breaths, then says, "Since we're honest...I have to admit, I like it."

"Really?" I hope she does. It came out better than I expected.

"Yeah, it's—"

"We did it as a joke," I clarify.

"But it's great."

"It's us," Travis says. He's right.

Hugs ensue, as they often do, then Calvin reminds us, "We can't keep the stagehands away from their families too long on Christmas Eve."

When Aurora shared a Viking demo we threw together with her co-workers at the theater, they insisted we try it out on stage.

"They aren't expecting us for one more hour." I kiss Aurora's neck, sending shivers through her.

"Time for a quickie?" Jack asks.

"As long as there's time for me to clean up." She strides across the room, tossing clothes as she heads to the Christmas tree she insisted we put up, tinsel and all.

Calvin throws a blanket on the carpet then gets rid of his own clothes. She drops to her knees, leans forward, stretching her hands out as she lowers herself to the blanket. Her ass looks great in the twinkling lights of the Christmas tree, but I think it looks great everywhere.

She looks great everywhere, no additional sparkle needed.

Rolling onto her back, she smiles up at us. We drop to our knees around her, everyone content with where they are. I'm the lucky one at her feet. After kissing my way up her legs, I lavish my love on her with my mouth, then bury my cock inside of her.

Jack has his cock in her mouth, getting the benefit of her moans vibrating on his shaft. Calvin and Travis cover her body with their attention.

Watching Aurora surrender so freely to all of us while she comes on my cock fills my heart and soul with more joy than I thought was possible. And watching her take each of my brothers in turn solidifies how intensely I needed this...a family that truly loves each other.

Calvin makes sure that we are cleaned up, get to the theater, and finish our setup, even adding Viking face paint, on time. Everyone knows their role.

Travis starts with a monotone hum amidst total darkness. Aurora joins softly, her voice floating above his in a perfect octave. They build over a long, slow crescendo, before Travis adds the beat, increasing the tempo.

I sneak in on the keyboard, sliding the volume up slowly. We want it to grow into the audience's awareness. Then Jack hits a single note on his bass, letting it fade before repeating it.

Everything builds to the big entry with Aurora shifting to the chant and Calvin coming in on lead guitar. The stagehands time the spotlight perfectly, shining it on her.

The rest of us linger in the dark background; we're incidentals, put on this earth to nurture her.

When we wrap up the set, Jack disappears briefly then comes back without the face paint.

He greets Aurora with a hug. "Let's get home to celebrate Christmas."

"You cleaned up awful fast," she says.

"I'm only that guy on stage. I'm not the bad boy. I'm not a Viking whatever. I'm yours, and I want to make sure you see that."

"I do, Jack. I see the real you. I also know what you're really in a hurry for."

We've waited for this day. We put it on the calendar and promised not to bug Aurora until today came. We head straight to the store and let her go inside and get the pregnancy test of her choosing. Then Calvin drives us home and we wait anxiously while she pees on that little stick.

It's agony waiting, but when the little pink plus shows up, I watch her expression.

A smile. Fuck yeah!

"Dibs on the kids calling me Pappy." I'm laughing so hard I can barely finish the line.

"Have you been waiting this whole time to say that?" Calvin doesn't appreciate the humor."

"Yep, because it means I got her pregnant."

"You?" she asks.

"A guy can dream." And thank goodness I did. She's ours forever and she's truly happy about it.

Epilogue

Aurora

Staring at the heavy curtain on the stage, I'm tickled by all of the buzz around me in the audience. Parents are eager to see their children perform. I've achieved my dream with the help of my brothers, not in spite of them.

They bought out the theater, allowing the current director an easy, early retirement. And with all of our changes, the guys finished out the shows they were committed to and helped me put on our first children's theater performance.

It's even more nerve-wracking than I expected, but they made me promise to rest and trust that they could handle showtime, since the twins have been giving my belly a workout.

My brothers were theater kids growing up. They remember the fun. And they've spent the last several months brushing up on the details.

I rub my hand over my giant belly. This very well could be one of my last outings.

"Is the baby kicking?" my mom asks. "It's not time, is it?"

My dad winks. "I'm eager to meet the grandkids, but I don't think the show can go on if your whole family has to head to the hospital."

My whole family...my heart melts. I wasn't sure if we'd ever get to this day. Our parents couldn't understand how we could be attracted to each other. My brothers are older, and all of them sharing one woman?

I understand it sounds weird, but it's us.

Once our parents saw that we were dedicated to each other and that we would risk losing them before we would risk losing our crazy ensemble, they had to make a choice.

"Not time to go yet, Dad." I pat his leg.

"This is going to be amazing," Dad says.

"The guys have to put on the show before we give accolades."

And they do. The show is a stellar success. The guys are a little ragged, but we meet backstage afterward.

Travis emceed the evening, no more hiding behind his drums being dark and broody. He had the crowd lit up before the show even started.

Calvin flicks a piece of glitter off his phone as he shows us a picture of his handiwork. He fixed a tutu with a stapler. Very clever. He realizes the glitter is stuck to his fingertip, wipes it on my cheek, and winks. I do love to sparkle.

And Big Doug, as he's called by the kids, did a fabulous job on keys for the musical numbers, even seamlessly helping the kid who mixed up his lyrics get back on track.

I'm doubled over my belly laughing as Jack wraps up about one of the little boys who came crying to him that someone had stepped on his kazoo. Jack saved the day with duct tape.

They're going to make great dads. And maybe sooner rather than later.

Intense pain shoots through my midsection. I've been having Braxton Hicks, but this is more intense.

Travis rubs my back. "And we couldn't have done any of this without Aurora. Shall we go celebrate?"

I lift up and meet his eyes. "Sorry to force a change of plans, but we better go to the hospital."

My mom laughs. "Honey, you always know how to steal the show."

The guys help me into the SUV and our parents follow us to the hospital.

Between contractions, I say, "You guys did amazing tonight."

Calvin meets my eyes in the rear-view mirror. "We never could have done that without you. Love you, Aurora."

And we live happily ever after!

If you'd like to read a deleted scene where the brothers agonize over what to do about Aurora, I have another BONUS SCENE by signing up for my newsletter.

https://SylvieHaas.com

Sugarplums and Submission

A Stepbrother Reverse Harem Romance

Sylvie Haas

Blurb

My sinfully gorgeous, muscular, hockey-playing stepbrothers are in trouble. They misbehaved a little too much and their coach insists they do damage control to clean up their reputations.

I'd normally be on board with that.

But tonight, my plan is to auction myself at the Christmas Cherry Auction to take care of a rather private problem.

One that stepbrothers shouldn't solve.

So when my stepbrothers decide that their good deed will be a million dollar donation to charity and that they'll make it by winning me, my plan is ruined.

I'm not normally one to pivot gracefully, but they make a secret offer I can't resist.

Are they setting me up for the wildest time of my life, or smashing a wrecking ball into my carefully structured plan?

If you love dirty-talking men who plan on pleasing their stepsister, don't miss this year's Christmas Cherry Auction!

One

Cindy

Gripping the auction program with both hands, I take deep breaths as I re-read the order. I was supposed to be second out of three. But with a last-minute addition, we have a fourth, Wendy. Offering a forced smile at her as Aurora quickly helps her with makeup and body glitter, I tamp down my anxiety over the change.

Why would Wendy run away from her own wedding? So many plans scattered to the wind. Not just the ceremony and reception, but the entire rest of her life. And out of all of the places she could run to, why an auction at a sex club?

Surely she didn't show up here wanting to donate four hours of her time doing holiday prep for the winner. Which means...she must need to clinch destroying her wedding by selling her virginity.

Butterflies migrate through my stomach at the thought of making such a rash decision.

Give me a plan and I'll carry it out, but I'm not your girl when it's time to pivot.

The emcee announces that Bianca's been sold and the crowd gets extra loud. Not just cheering, but demands that I can't quite make out. In a giant blur, Aurora's rockstar brothers insist that she go next because they have a concert to get back to.

I'm being asked to carry Bianca's bag to her since she's being carried to the parking lot. This can't be happening. All I can do is take orders. If I'd been able to think, I would have grabbed my stuff and left when I took her bag outside.

A wilder version of me could have jumped on the back of one of the motorcycles that pulled in and told the beefy rider to cart me away.

I should have left, but somehow I've made my way back to the prep area beside the stage.

I could still leave. I could grab my phone, open the rideshare app, and have a car here to take me home in minutes...if I could move.

But I can't. I'm totally caught in my head.

Another change of plans starts palpitations in my heart. The motorcycle gang that arrived when I carried Bianca's bag out is here for Wendy...her stepbrothers are in it.

Can the world spiral out of control any faster? She's frantic that her brothers are here. I'm fretting over the fact that mine aren't.

My stomach has that weird feeling like it can't quite find where it belongs in my body. My legs aren't convinced they can hold me up much longer. And humiliation might be the most likely result this evening when I'm the only one whose stepbrothers don't show up.

I'm also the only one of us who's admitted she has a thing for her stepbrothers. That was two years ago, but my friends all know. Ever since then, I've tried to hide behind the fact that every female would like to take a spin on my brothers' Zambonis.

Meanwhile, Aurora's brothers are making quick work of winning her.

I refocus on my goal for the evening: have sex with one or more men who will get it right. And with full diligence, I've done my homework, reading about sex and positions. I don't need a relationship. In fact, a relationship with a group of guys sounds complicated.

Especially with my stepbrothers.

They travel with their hockey team. I prefer my routine. I can't get lost in the whimsy of a taboo relationship. I just need one night.

Aurora makes her way backstage to grab her stuff and eliminates any chance I can think someone didn't notice all of the stepbrothers. She asks, "Any chance yours are showing up?"

"If I could only be so lucky." I wouldn't be the only woman farming herself out to a stranger.

"So if your brothers showed up and bought you, that would make you happy?" Wendy looks at me expectantly.

"You know who they are, don't you?"

Her nervousness eases. "The Tri-anything hockey gods."

I wish their nickname didn't make my lady bits tingle. My shrug almost appears casual. "If they bought me, they'd probably just take me home to Mom and Dad and tell them I got loose and went to an auction at a sex club."

She laughs, but my anxiety level rises. My Friday evening shift at Santa's photo booth in the mall calls to me. Why did I deviate from my schedule? I rub my thumb over the dandelion tattoo on the inside of my forearm. It's not enough to calm my nerves.

Too many unknowns. When it's not the holiday season, jigsaw puzzles are my Friday evening routine. There is one right answer for each piece, and when you find all of the right answers, you create a beautiful picture. My fingers itch to run around the edge of the innies and outies of a piece while scanning the table, looking for the exact right placement.

Wendy grabs an empty cup. "You don't look so good. Are you going to throw up?"

"I don't think so."

"Are you thinking of backing out? I certainly get it."

Should I be taking action like she did, running from her own wedding? Is the auction a mistake? Maybe my first time for sex should be more organic. If only the right answer would simply click into place.

"Aurora warned me that if you got cold feet, I was supposed to remind you to look at your tattoo."

"She told you about that?" I look around. How did I miss Aurora leaving?

"Just said to remind you."

"Thanks." I read the words under my dandelion tattoo: *The flower is no less beautiful if the seed is planted by the wind.*

It's usually enough to settle me when my schedule is disrupted. Not tonight. It reminds me of my brothers. They didn't appreciate the beauty of the intact dandelion. I couldn't appreciate the randomness of the seeds blowing away.

"Next up, Cindy. Let's have a round of applause to welcome her to the stage." The call of my name over the PA draws my attention to the curtain separating me from the stage. I can follow directions, I'm good at that. Directions take away decision making, and sometimes even responsibility.

That's why I'm studying to be an accountant. Numbers just fall into place. And if they don't, you fix the problem. They're not difficult like people. Which leads me back to tonight's goal, and not wanting to be a virgin spinster someday.

I start my mental checklist, walk on stage, shake hands with Jefferson, put on a big smile, turn to the audience, pretend to scan the room, and pray that I get bid on...and not just for four hours of holiday help.

Roxy, Maggie, Isadora, Sasha, and Jade. I channel the names of the women who all got married as a result of last year's

SYLVIE HAAS

auction. I don't need to get married; I just need to get laid so I can check that off my list.

The *yip* type sounds the auction helpers make each time someone increases the bid piques my curiosity. I let my eyes fall on the next bidder paddle. The man holding it is none other than Adrian, one of my stepbrothers. Shivers run through my body. Sitting next to him is Ballz, the nickname for our brother Balthazar. But where's Jeff? The three of them are practically inseparable.

How did I not see them sooner? The baseball caps on the table are the likely answer. When I looked around earlier, all I saw was the top of baseball caps and guys playing with their phones.

I glance to the side of the stage. Wendy is jumping up and down excitedly and has her fists balled in front of her mouth. It's a nice vote of confidence, but there's a real possibility they'll send me home. My entire evening would be undermined.

"One million," Jeff calls out, bringing a halt to the other paddles that were being raised.

Dollars? What? Wasn't the last bid one hundred thousand?

No one will be able to outbid them. I'm poised on the fence between total humiliation and a fantasy coming true.

"Going, going...gone, for one million dollars!"

Ballz jumps from his seat and runs to the stage. I rub my thumb over my tattoo. No more changes of plans. I point him to the payment table, reminding him of the proper order. "I'm staying here until the end. The time I owe you doesn't start until this is over."

I want to be here for Wendy, but I'm also nervous. I don't want them to take me home to Mom and Dad.

Two

Ballz

Waiting for the auction to end to claim my stepsister has my balls in a bind. But when she gets her head set on something, it better happen. If I want any chance of *claiming* her, I won't stress her out.

It's a risky longshot anyway. Coming here was supposed to be a fun, public way to make a huge donation to the woman's shelter and then let whoever we won off the hook...a publicity stunt to satisfy our probation.

But we bought our stepsister, and I know exactly what I want to do with her. Adrian's having the same thoughts as me.

Jeff couldn't come because he's at his anger management class. We'll have to talk to him about how to handle winning Cindy.

Three leather-and-denim clad bikers storm the stage after winning Wendy, who wasn't even in the auction program. I've caught a hint that she's their stepsister, and the first two girls were bought by their stepbrothers.

The bikers start barking orders for everyone to clear out. I rush onto the stage and past the curtain to find Cindy. If we weren't under strict orders to behave ourselves and repair our reputation, I'd have thrown Cindy over my shoulder and carried her into one of the rooms I saw Wendy's brothers looking at.

"As tempting as it is to stay, Coach will be pissed if we're caught in the middle of something."

"Yep, we did our good deed," Adrian says.

Cindy's expression falters.

"We're capable of good deeds. We don't always screw things up."

"Is your good deed mandated by the coach?" she asks.

"He just said to do something good. Make it public. Our million-dollar donation to the woman's shelter will take care of that."

"Right." Why the hell does she looks so unimpressed?

I grab her upper arm and guide her through the sex club. Looks like Wendy's about to have a boatload of fun with her brothers. Jealousy stirs inside of me.

"Slow down, Ballz." Damn. Even my sister calls me by my nickname. Admittedly, Balthazar is a bit of a mouthful. "If you wanted to do such a good deed, why couldn't you have asked me if I wanted to be a part of it?"

I stop and angle my head down to squarely look at her. I've denied myself that so far because of what she does to me. "You didn't want us to buy you?"

"It depends."

"We're going to take you home just like we're supposed to. Right, Adrian?" I hope I'm giving the answer she wants.

"Check."

She sighs. "Promise me you won't tell Mom and Dad I was here."

"I won't leak a word to them. But you need to be more careful. If a stranger had won you..." I scan the room, unable to bear the thought of any of these guys touching our sister.

"That was the plan."

"Sorry, sis. I know how you like your plans, but you may not have understood what people are actually winning."

She hesitates, studies her feet, and wrings her hands.

I wrap an arm around her shoulders and it's far too intimate. I hug her tighter to my side. "Sis, this auction has a reputation."

"I understand what cherry means."

One of the bikers carries Wendy past us. "You could toss her in a room, too."

I can't stand the thought of anyone seeing Cindy that way. Anyone but me and my brothers. And that can't happen publicly. Guiding her outside, I continue the conversation. "You wanted to be won for sex?"

"I'm not good at dating, so it seemed easier to skip ahead."

"That's so unlike you."

"I was worried it would never happen."

Adrian steps closer. "If you're willing, we could do that. I mean, as part of our good deed, we could teach you to *date*. Right, Ballz?"

For a second, I thought he was going to say we would fuck her. He's on to something with the dating.

"Who am I to deny my little sister? I'll happily help you practice dating." I'll figure out how to untangle it later if she learns from us and moves on.

"We can both help, different styles and all. And you know Jeff, he'll want in on it."

"What do you say we head back to our place to sort this out?" In my mind, I'm already balls deep in her. Tonight is not a time to earn my nickname. But I'm not sure how to hold myself back with her.

Three

Cindy

Conversation has been light and uncomfortable. Negotiating dates with my brothers is terrifying. I wish one of them would just toss me over his shoulder.

We've barely gotten drinks and sat on the couch when a door slams. Jeff's voice booms from the kitchen before we see him. He must have just come in from the garage. "Three more fucking meetings. Hopefully, I don't snap anyone's neck in the meantime."

Keys clatter onto the granite countertop.

"What the fuck are you doing here?"

I cringe at his harsh tone as he rounds the corner into the living room.

Ballz leaps to his feet. "Fuck off, dude. We won her in the auction."

Jeff throws his hands up in the air. "Wasn't your mission to go do a good deed and repair our reputation?"

He seems to make a deliberate motion of bringing his hands down in front of himself as he exhales.

"We donated a million to the woman's shelter on behalf of our sister."

Jeff avoids making eye contact with me. "The Christmas *Cherry* Auction. Rumors will fly."

"Rumors fly no matter what we do," Adrian says.

"And it turns out sis was hoping to gain some dating experience by whoever won her."

"Do you want this to blow up in our faces?" Jeff's eyes are cold and dark. His nostrils flare.

Hope must reside in my heart, because they both seem to sink. I should set up an online dating profile like everyone else. I don't need my brothers. "Never mind. It's too complicated. You're not the kind of guys I would date anyway."

Jeff steps closer as I stand, stopping me from putting my drink back in the kitchen. "How do you know?"

"Just look how complicated this already is." I try to sidestep him, but he blocks me. I crane my neck up.

"I mean, how do you know we aren't the kind of guys you would date?" The fresh linen scent of his cologne is certainly acceptable. The contours of his chest pressing against his t-shirt are a decidedly positive attribute. The way my body is begging him to scoop me up points at agreeableness.

Perhaps he could be my type. I give myself a mental shake. "I would date someone less obnoxious who doesn't need anger management classes."

"Don't judge."

"You had a good reason for beating the guy up?" I can't believe I brought that up, but I'm desperate for an exit plan.

"I did," he mutters as he lets me pass.

I grow a little bolder at the tiny victory. If I prod a little more, I should be able to bring this mess to a close and avoid embarrassing myself. "And the wild weekend that ruined the hotel room? Are you going to tell me that was for good reason, too?"

He stops me in the doorway. "That wasn't actually us."

"The hotel room was in your name."

"We paid for the whole fucking thing, and we know which friends we'll never invite back."

"All the more reason you need to practice dating with us," Ballz cuts in. "People can be deceptive."

Is he being protective? My heart is racing. My panties are soaked. My sunken heart beats in my chest again. I want this to happen.

Is my resolve really so weak that I've gone from trying to irritate them to exploring sexual desires in three easy steps? No. The plan was to get bought and have sex. I'm adhering to my plan with a minor detour that includes family. Perfect.

I pull out my phone and calculate how many minutes I get with each of them. I hold the phone up, displaying the math. "I get to go on an eighty-minute date with each of you."

Jeff grabs the phone from my hand.

Oh no! I don't want him to see what else is on my phone. I flail but can't reach high enough when he extends his arm upward. "Give it to me."

"Nope. We don't calculate times for dates."

"Fine. Give it back." I wrap my hands around his thick bicep and instead of pulling his arm down, my feet come off the ground.

"Why the fuss?" Jeff looks up at the screen, which thankfully still shows the calculator.

I let go, plopping onto the ground. "It's my phone."

Adrian and Ballz laugh at us.

"You afraid I'm going to do something to it?"

"No." My breathing is way too ragged to play it cool. I pull a stray strand of hair out of my mouth.

Jeff's breath hitches. "You're nervous."

"Yeah, I just agreed to date my brothers."

"Fake date," Jeff corrects.

"Yeah. Fake date my brothers." Which is even more dangerous, now that I've wrapped my hands around his arm. I'm even more aware of how thick and muscular he is. His body's hard in ways I want to touch a lot more of.

233

As he lowers my phone, his thumb taps the button that pulls up the open tabs.

"Stop it." I try elbowing him in the ribs.

He doesn't flinch. "Whoa! Little sis..."

Jeff and Adrian step closer. I don't have to see the screen to know what he sees. I was reading the Kama Sutra, studying The Tigress position, just in case.

My chest hurts. My cheeks heat. I try to downplay my humiliation. "It's educational. Not all of us get to practice on fans who throw themselves at us."

At some point, Ballz stepped behind me. His hands gently pull mine away from Jeff, who continues to explore my phone without permission. My entire body goes rigid as he taps on my eReader.

"Oh boys, we've got a problem on our hands. It seems little sis is into stepbrother romance."

Four

Adrian

Grabbing Cindy's phone from Jeff, I hand it back to her.

"Thanks." Her downturned eyes and quick click of buttons to turn the screen off tear at my heart.

I put an arm around her. "Stepsibling porn is one of the hottest things out there. You're not alone."

"What I'm reading has nothing to do with our dates."

Can I lighten the mood? "Damn shame. Then again, fucking my stepsister is exactly the opposite of what the coach is asking us to do right now."

"I don't want to get you in trouble. Even if we fake date, it can't be out in the open." Her voice wavers.

"But the date has to seem real. Like we should tuck your hair behind your ear?" My finger mimics my words. The energy rush from the tender contact sends electricity through me.

"I suppose so."

"But what if I trailed my finger under your chin, tipped your face up like this, and stared into your eyes?" It's unsettling how it feels like she sees through my façade. That's never happened before with anyone.

"That might straddle the line."

I pull her body into me. My erection throbs with the pressure. "Which line?"

"A dangerous one."

"Danger...you know that just tempts me."

She nods.

"And what if I leaned down and my lips lingered right here beside your ear? People would think I was whispering sweet nothings. What if they knew you were my sister?"

"They'd probably think it was inappropriate."

With the lightest touch, I trail my lips over her cheek, to her precious little pout. "Does it upset you that they wouldn't approve?"

She pulls away from our moment, dammit.

"It would be terrible if you got kicked off the team. This has to be completely private."

Pulling her back into me, I put my lips on hers. "What if you taste too good for me to contain myself?"

Five

Jeff

I know how Adrian dates women. He sees them. He wants them. He takes them. I'm going to end up with more court-mandated anger management sessions if he does that with Cindy.

I clap my hands together loud enough to startle everyone. "We need ground rules for how to fake date."

"We were doing fine without rules," Adrian says.

"She's your sister, not a cheap fling. Let's sleep on it, give Cindy a chance to decide what she wants." I turn to her. "I'll drive you home since I didn't see your car."

"What the hell?" Ballz says.

"Cindy likes her routines. She likes to think about decisions before she makes them. We shouldn't rush her into this."

My brothers are going to hate me if I actually pull off what I'm trying to do, but I can live with that.

"You're probably right," Cindy says.

I don't think she's aware that her hand brushes the exact path from her ear across her cheek onto her mouth that Adrian's lips took. My cock thickens. If any of us are dating her, I'm going first.

"Grab your stuff."

"We could all go," Adrian says.

"No."

My brothers try to argue, but she shuts them down.

"If you can't agree on little things like a ride home, then Jeff's right. Fake dating is dangerous. Just take me home."

"We'll talk in the morning," Ballz says and we all agree.

With her alone in my car, the first few turns take us toward our parents' house, then I make a left. Her head cocks to the side, then to the other.

"This isn't the way."

"I know."

"I thought you were taking me home."

"There's something I need to know first." The question has burned in my brain. Had she really been studying for tonight?

"And you have to take me somewhere to find out?"

"Were you seriously going to ask a stranger *date* you?"

"Yes."

"And by date, do you mean fuck?" Every protective hackle in my body is raised. The irony isn't lost on me that I'm livid over her being willing to fuck a stranger, after all I've done.

She lowers her head. Shit. I reach over and put my hand on her shoulder.

"I didn't mean for that to come out so harsh. I just don't want you to get hurt."

"You can let the protective big brother thing go."

"It's not that. I care about you." And I don't say more. I don't want to scare her off.

Pulling into the parking lot of an overlook with a beautiful view of the glistening lights of the city below, I hop out of the car, circle around to her side, open her door, then extend a hand. She sets her delicate fingers in mine and allows me to guide her out. I walk her to the edge, my arms wrapped around her from behind.

"Are we having a fake date?"

"We need to clear up what you consider dating, in light of what you were prepared for. I'm not usually the kind of guy who does long courtships and tender gestures."

"What do you mean?"

"I'm already holding you, showing you the beautiful city." I caress my hand up and down the fabric covering her arm. "Some couples wouldn't go past a long, lingering gaze on a first date. Maybe their fingers brush. Since you're saying you just want one date with each of us, it's going to be hard to take it slow."

I cup my fingers over hers. Then I allow my fingertips to spread her fingers as I lace our hands together. "Others would have a little more contact, but nothing too personal."

Then I spin her around. She's tangled in my arms, unable to get free, her body pressed into mine the way I want to start the evening, not end it. "Other dates are more aggressive, more demanding. Do you know which kind you want?"

I roll my hips into her.

"I..." She licks her lips, the moonlight glinting off her cheeks. "I think I want the aggressive one."

"I was afraid you were going to say that." Everything about this is wrong. She's so young. She doesn't deserve to be kept in the shadows. Pretending she doesn't mean anything will just build up more tension. I can't deal with more anger management classes.

"Afraid?"

I loosen my fingers from hers, drop a hand onto her ass and pick her up, loving the feel of her legs spreading around my waist. This isn't helping any. Which head am I using to decide that she's worth getting cut from the team?

Too many questions invade my brain.

"You don't want to do this?" She looks completely confused.

"I want to."

"I don't understand. The Tri-anything brothers needed to do a good deed, which was the huge donation. Why can't you do this one little good deed for me?"

That damn pout has my thoughts on lockdown. She's the only thing in my head.

"Fuck it. I'm taking you back to our place. We're going to figure this out tonight."

Six

Cindy

I trace my finger over the trail of tattooed dandelion seeds blowing across my arm as Jeff drives. Throwing caution to the wind was tonight's plan. Would it feel this dangerous if complete strangers bought me? How ironic is that concern?

Uncertainty swallows me as we walk into the house.

"I won," Adrian proclaims the second he sees me.

"Fuck off." Jeff recognizes something in the statement that I'm not aware of.

"So what was it? You weren't smooth enough to convince sis that you want to breed her?"

Breed? The word freezes the blood in my veins. Is this one of those brotherly razzings?

The more nanoseconds my brain has to process what he said, the more confusing reactions I identify in my body.

My lips part as if I'm panting for my brothers. I close my mouth.

My legs threaten to give out as if I want my brothers to catch me. I set a hand on the counter to steady myself.

My eyes are drawn to Adrian's parts that breed as if... I force my attention to the signed photograph of Wayne Gretzky, one of many pieces of sports memorabilia my brothers have amassed.

Ballz enters, breaking my line of sight to the photo. I can't bring myself to look at any of them until I understand if Jeff or any of them really want to breed me. I'm afraid they'll be able to tell how much that turns me on. The tingling between my legs and the ache in my core threaten to betray me.

I spy my phone on the counter. Since when am I so distracted I lose track of my phone?

The only thing that's certain to me right now is that I absolutely cannot have sex with my stepbrothers. Even thinking about it makes me crazy.

"Real cool, Adrian," Jeff says.

It's unclear to me if his sarcasm is rooted in being annoyed that Adrian totally made the breeding thing up, or that Adrian spoke a truth that was meant to be private.

Adrian is unfazed. "I didn't believe for a second you planned on taking her straight home. My bet was you'd kick off a date and end up back here."

Ballz says, "I was with him on the date, but I didn't think we'd see either of you again tonight. What's your plan?"

"We're back because we're starting tonight."

"That's what I'm talking about." Ballz fist pumps and steps close. "Let's get this party started. I could whip up something to eat, grill something if you're into that *men playing with fire* thing. Or just Netflix and chill." He rubs his hands together. "I'm ready."

Jeff shoves him back a step. "Ground rules first." He steps to a huge whiteboard on their living room wall. Tape has been applied to make it look like a hockey arena. Ballz erases the X's and arrows.

Eat, sleep, hockey. It's been their mantra since as far back as I can remember.

Ballz has a dry erase marker in the hand that's not erasing. "All right. I know my sis loves some rules. What's first?"

My rules? I thought Jeff was going to make them. They're staring at me. I'll start with the simple stuff we sort of established already. "Number one: nothing in public."

Ballz writes it on the board.

Adrian points a finger at the whiteboard. "Can you define public?"

"Public is public," Jeff says, "This isn't a fucking vocabulary lesson. Just keep it in the house."

"We're under house arrest for dating? Can't we at least go on the porch or in the yard?"

"For fuck's sake, since when are you a stickler for rules?" Jeff closes his eyes and takes a deep breath before continuing calmer.

"Keep it away from the perimeter of the property. Nothing visible to anyone outside of the four of us."

"No public ass grabs?" Adrian feigns disappointment and grabs Jeff's ass.

Jeff elbows Adrian. "Knock it off—"

Ballz interrupts. "Take your argument outta here. Cindy and I are trying to make a list."

He winks at me then write a 2 on the board.

Given how quickly things get out of control with them, I decide to run with my idea that I not cross the taboo line of having sex with my stepbrothers. Dating is the proper first step anyway.

I stare at Ballz's hand as it hovers in anticipation of my words. "No sex."

They all whip their heads to me. Adrian raises a hand. "Not to be the troublemaker, but could you define sex?"

"Yeah." Jeff joins him this time. "I thought you wanted sex."

"It would be weird to have sex since we're siblings, right? It's best if you just help me practice dating and the things that lead up to sex."

Ballz taunts, "I'm pretty sure I've seen Adrian go straight from hello to sex."

Adrian grimaces. "Always used a condom. Get my medical checkups regularly. I'm one hundred percent clean."

Jeff and Ballz are quick to explain the same in their own terms.

I nod, giving myself a second to unknot my stomach. Their experience is no secret. "Good to know. Can we move on to number three?"

Ballz writes the digit on the board.

"Eighty minutes," I remind them. The finite time will help keep things from escalating. I hope.

"That's not going to work." Jeff snatches the marker from Ballz's hand. "If we only get one date, it has to be open-ended."

"He's right. If things are going well, we wouldn't want to leave you hanging," Ballz says.

Adrian laughs. "I can see it now. We're sampling a beer flight, or maybe wine, while watching the sun set, we don't want to rush things because the moment is perfect, and just when I'm watching you bring the last glass to your lips, the timer goes off and I have to rip the glass from your hands. The date's over. I have to walk away."

"At least you could go wank off so you don't nut in your pants," Ballz teases, but as the laughter drifts away, the weight of them staring makes it hard to breathe.

And not in the way I expected. I love being the center of their attention. I just don't want to make decisions.

"Fine." My voice croaks. I clear my throat but can barely whisper past the secrets my tongue is eager to tell. "Have it your way, no limits."

He grabs a new marker and adds *No Limits* to number three.

My pulse pounds in my ears. Then he draws an arrow between the two words and adds *Time*.

A sinking feeling oppresses me. If I reached a hand out, I could wipe the word from the board.

"Anything else?" Ballz asks, breaking the spell.

"Not for me." I'm torn between what my gut tells me to do and what my gut fears. The room is silent. I look at each of them in turn.

Ballz steps closer. "You're in control."

Isn't that what I'm supposed to want? How can I turn control into surrender? I shake myself free from the dangerous spiral. "We should look at our calendars. My phone is in the kitchen."

I squeeze between Jeff and Adrian, but they're not far behind. Ballz puts his hand over mine as I grab my phone. Flutters race from my heart through my entire body. Every inch of my skin craves the warmth and command of his touch.

"I'm free tonight." His mouth is far too close to my ear.

"Mom and Dad are expecting me."

"Rule number three. No time limits. Let them know you won't make it home tonight."

Seven

Ballz

"I have to help a friend in the morning." Is Cindy trying to back out?

"Can you do it a different time?"

"No, she has to address a bunch of invitations for her stepmom."

"I'll drop you off." I don't have any plans to let her go before I have to.

She texts Mom and Dad that she's staying with a friend. When she sets her phone down, I hand her a cheese knife. Jeff and Adrian are crowding us.

"Hold on a second. There's one more rule we need to add." I go to the whiteboard, and add number four while everyone trickles in.

4. If it's not your date, you get the fuck out of the way.

"That's fair," Jeff says. "But who decided you get to go first?"

"Tell me you didn't make a move on her when you were in the car."

"Technically, I didn't."

I turn to Cindy, who I'd rather look at anyway. "Did he make a move after you left?"

"Technically, yes. Just not in the car."

Ready to get Cindy alone, I clarify with Jeff, "So, my man, it seems you could have had your date, but your shot went wide."

I make a shooing motion to my brothers then set my hand on Cindy's lower back while guiding her to the kitchen.

"Will I need to defend myself?" She studies the knife while I get cheese out of the fridge.

"I hope you won't want to." I wink, and her smile showers my heart with happiness. That's not how my dates usually start. Then again, I don't really go on dates. I just hang out.

Which brings up a question I haven't had to answer before... What do I do with these warm, fuzzy feelings being slap-shotted around my chest?

I'm finally on an actual date and it's the woman who wants it to end after one night. I'd rethink my entire life if I wasn't worried about maximizing every single second.

I know right here and now that Cindy is who I've been waiting for, and I have to fucking pretend it's not real. I step behind her, pressing my body against hers, and reach to the side to pull a merlot cheddar in front of us.

Her exaggerated breaths cause her back to press into me on each inhale. I unwrap the cheese but I'd rather be unwrapping her out of the cute fucking little red and white dress. A prick tease if I've ever seen one. Appropriate, since she's clarified we're not having sex.

Instantly, I hate myself for thinking that way.

I can't be bitter, even though I'm certain she planned on having sex with whoever won her in the auction...just not with her brothers.

Time to capitalize on my time alone with her, but since there's no time limit on the date, how long can I keep it going? Only until my brothers revolt.

"You okay if we do this together?" I caress my fingers over her forearm.

"Yeah," she says in the throatiest voice ever.

While I'm wrapping my fingers around her hand as she holds the knife, an image of a wedding cake flashes through my mind. I'm fucking riding that image. Together, we press the knife through the cheese, cutting one slice then another.

I lift a slice to her mouth and she giggles. "Wait."

Quickly grabbing the other piece, she spins around and raises it to my mouth. I brace my free hand on the counter. I press my hips into her, then angle my arm through hers to mimic the wedding cake feeding. "To us."

Her lips part and I'm tempted to throw the cheese to the side so I can taste her. But we're supposed to be showing her how dating works. Sort of. It's too fucked up.

She slips her arm from mine and finishes the small bite she took. "Aren't we supposed to do that with champagne?"

"I don't want you drunk, Baby."

Movement from the doorway catches my attention. "Hang on a second... All right, guys, we're not teenagers spying on each other. Go to your damn rooms."

"Yes, Dad," Adrian mocks in a mopey voice.

I'm definitely going to find a way to get more than one night with Cindy, but there's no way my brothers will let me do it until they've had their turn.

Refocusing on her, I ask. "Is there anything you want to do?"

She steps away. "It's weird, right? Us? This whole thing? It's too confusing."

"It doesn't have to be confusing. Do you have any rules like *no kissing on the first date*?"

"No."

"May I?"

She nods.

In one motion, I lift her, turn around, and set her on the empty counter behind us. Lacing my fingers into her silky hair, I cup my hand behind her head, ease my hip between her knees, and land my lips on hers.

She gasps around my lips then settles in, her lips soft against mine. I ease up, wanting to make sure she's okay, but she clasps her hands around my jaw, keeping me close.

I shift my hips, spreading her legs more, and rub a hand up and down her back. Her scent intoxicates me. The need to claim her is killing me. She'll ruin me if she sticks to the rules.

Coming up for air, I ask, "You good?"

She hesitates then nods.

I trail kisses down her neck and onto her shoulder, then wiggle her skirt out from under her bottom. That's not enough. I have to see her. Slowly inching the zipper down the back of her dress, I watch her eyes. They fucking sparkle. She's into this. My speed picks up dramatically because as much as I want to prolong this, I want everything I can get from this date.

With her help, she's stripped down to her red bra and panties. My desire grows exponentially, along with my cock. Why on Earth is my sister so fucking captivating?

I slide her forward until her legs are splayed wide and her sex is pressed against me.

"Wiggle your hips, Baby."

"What?"

I lower my hands to her hips and wiggle her side to side while holding her against me. Her breath hitches and her eyes flutter. "Let yourself go."

She wraps her arms around me, works her hips, and moans.

"That's so fucking hot, Baby. I want you to come."

She stops cold and lowers her gaze.

Shit. "Have you ever come before?"

She hesitates. I gently press my lips into her hair.

"It's okay if you haven't. I want to know where we're starting from."

"I have, just not with a guy."

I'll be her first. My insides are light, my heart is happy, like a kid on Christmas morning. Only a naughty kid, and I keep my cool. "Okay, then you know what you're going for. Mind if I help?"

I ease a hand between us. She's already soaked her panties.

"Oh my gosh. Yes. I like that."

"That's my girl."

I hope she comes as fast as she's winding up. I have to slide my hand between us to get her off my cock. I was going to come before her, and I'm not having that.

Her moans escalate and she bites her lower lip, trying to quiet herself.

"Let me hear how good you feel, Baby."

She manages to say, "But they might hear us."

"They want to." But not as much as I want them to.

"Are you sure?"

"We could listen to you orgasm all day."

Her eyes light up.

"You like that?" I settle my fingers into a relentless motion. Her eyes roll back. "I'll give you orgasms until you beg me to quit."

I can't deal with the fabric between my fingers and her pussy. I ease myself into her panties, into her wet curls, and between her sweet lips. It takes no time at all to pick up where I left off, and I send her plunging over the edge.

She cries out, her arms and legs wrap around me as her release shakes her body, then she falls limp. I hold her, basking in her scent, in being the first man to give her an orgasm, and in knowing I'm about to take her to bed, even if she refuses to have sex.

When she lifts her head, her cheeks are flushed and her hands go to my waistband. I let her unfasten the button and lower the zipper because it's hot as hell.

"I think I'm supposed return the favor?"

My cock presses outward against the opening in my jeans, the tip poking above the waistband of my underwear. I grab her hand and drag her thumb over the bead of pre-cum.

The touch, even guided by me, is almost too much. My balls pump a shot onto our fingers. Then I lift her hand to her lips. "Lick it."

Her cute little tongue darts out nervously at first, licking my pre-cum from her own finger. Then she smiles, licks mine, and sucks my finger into her mouth. My balls pull up so hard, they shove my heart into my throat.

I have to pull my hand away. She uses the opportunity to lower her hand but I catch her wrist and press her palm into my chest. "If you touch it, I'll come."

"Do you want to?" Her tone is so damn innocent.

"On you, yes."

"I've only read about what to do. I've never..."

"Just touch me. I'm that close." I shove my pants and underwear down, springing my cock free. She wraps her fingers around it and her eyes go wide.

I can't hold back. The intensity of the release blinds me. My seed surges out.

"Oh!" she screams.

I pry my eyes open to see white streaks splat up her body and onto her face as I come completely undone to her touch.

Eight

Cindy

My brothers have never been known for waking up early. I can't sleep late. I also can't wash my face with my favorite minty vanilla sugar scrub, grab my bathrobe, or warm my feet in my fuzzy slippers.

I grab a hockey jersey from on top of a dresser, and cautiously bring it to my nose. Being engulfed in their scent...priceless. Smelling like I'm wearing a shirt that's been sitting balled up and wet in a locker for a week...not so much.

It's clean. I slip it over my bare body and pad quietly to the living room with my phone. It strikes me as funny that I don't feel like I walk the same. Will it be obvious to people that I had at least five orgasms last night? And that I didn't give them to myself? Surely it's not as obvious as it feels.

Grabbing a blanket off the arm of a chair, I head to the couch that's near the Christmas tree. They went with all blue ornaments. It's either team spirit, or represents their love of ice, and snow, and cold weather. Maybe it's reminiscent of that. And all white lights, just like Mom and Dad always did.

My toe bumps a package under the tree. Soft and lightweight. I squat, squish the package, and smile that Dad's name is on the tag. Every year, they get Dad a team blanket. It's sweet that they've kept things the same.

On the couch, I curl my legs under me, tuck the blanket around myself, then start my Morning Pages. They help me clear my thoughts each day. Calmness settles over me that this piece of my routine can remain the same.

I open my app and start typing:

Why are orgasms given by stepbrothers so much better?!?! The floating feeling was surreal, perfect. I felt so safe in Balthazar's arms, his body securing me. That even if I floated free, I would be floating with him, on his command. And when Adrian called Ballz 'Dad'! My heart still flutters at that, but Jeff is more of a dad type than Ballz.

A shiver runs through me and I tug the blanket up over my shoulder, bringing my phone closer to my waist.

Tingles in my sex reawaken at the remembrance of Balthazar's mastery of me. I try not to think about all the women he learned on. I know he's experienced. I know that all the men that were at the auction last night were experienced. That was the goal. Know how good things can be. Give myself confidence for the future.

The future? What future? What does that even mean?

I go through my routine day after day. Up until now, the future meant more of the same and that was comforting. I'm no longer typing, just thinking.

I angle my arm so I can see my tattoo. Am I finally understanding the true meaning of my blowing wild, throwing caution to the wind and trusting that I will still be capable?

When Dad talked to me about that, I doubt he meant to let my brother give me orgasms.

I usually get through my three Morning Pages without interruption. I resume typing:

The path forward will not be the same as the path behind, even if I control all of the factors.

The question is, would I want to control all of the factors? The way Jeff spoke to me outside of his car, I wanted him to tell him me what to do. And I enjoyed Ballz taking control. I love giving myself to them. That's a revelation. My whole life is built around control, but what I really want is to let go.

People say you can have epiphanies writing morning pages. And I do have some profound moments, like when I realized I didn't enjoy crossword puzzles so I switched to word searches. That was a good call. But there, even a word search is like a command: find this word and circle it.

There's no real thinking, it's just doing. I like that.

Wanting my brothers, I mean my future sexual partners, to be in control... Is that normal? Is that some primal need?

And why is an orgasm given by someone else so much better? That's a silly question. Of course, it's better. Eating food cooked by someone else is better. Getting a head massage by someone else is better. We've all been to the hairdresser and experienced that.

I'm typing away:

Is it a mistake to date my brothers...fake date my brothers?!?! It's only making me want them more.

"Whatcha doin', Sweet Cheeks?" Adrian catapults himself over the couch, plopping beside me. I pull the blanket over my phone to keep the screen private. Don't need more reveals.

"I didn't expect you to be awake so soon."

"So what you were doing was...not expecting me to be awake? That means you were thinking about me."

"Don't flatter yourself by twisting my words. I do a thing called Morning Pages."

"What's that?" He tries to peek at my phone but I pull the blanket tighter.

"I write three pages and brain dump everything my mind processed overnight. It's a way of clearing the slate, deciding what I want to focus on each day."

"So, you keep a diary."

"It's not really a diary. Okay... I guess it sort of is a diary."

"All right." He walks across the room, grabs his phone from the charger, then comes back. "How do we do it?"

"Morning Pages?"

"Yeah. I want to do it with you."

"Why?"

"Let me into your world, Sweet Cheeks." His voice falters as he says Sweet Cheeks, as if he is forcing himself to use the distancing term.

I could use some distance. His blue eyes and dark eyelashes, award-winning smile, and the heat of his body pressed to my side are doing me in. "Lots of people do it, not just me."

"Do we get a writing prompt?"

"No."

"A game plan?"

"No. Just, write whatever's on your mind and don't stop until you fill three pages."

"And then do we swap them or something?"

"You don't ever share it with anyone. You can do it in notes in your phone or use the app like I do."

He has me help him find the app and installs it.

I turn sideways on the couch. "Let's sit back-to-back. I can't see what you're writing, you can't see what I'm writing."

His back is broad, like I'm leaning into a wall.

"You're breathing kind of hard back there, sis."

"Sorry, I guess I'm just catching my breath from you startling me."

Sitting in silence with him is beautiful but inside my head, I'm a wreck. I haven't even finished my pages when he leans his head back. I tuck my phone to my chest.

"Got my three pages done, Sweet Cheeks." His body shifts behind me and I turn to face him.

"You're really fast."

"That's what she said."

"Oh my gosh. Do you guys ever stop?"

"Sorry, that was bad, but I don't want to stop with you."

I purse my lips.

"Aw, crap. That didn't come out right. What I mean is that once our date starts, I'm not going to want it to stop."

He stares into my eyes so deeply, I think he can see my brain begging me to commit.

I lean in. My lips part. I want him to start. But he pecks me on the cheek, pulls away, and tucks the blanket around me. "Sit tight."

Talk about unmet expectations. "For what?"

"I'm making you a gourmet breakfast before you leave."

"I don't usually eat much in the morning."

"Don't worry. Gourmet was a stretch."

I hear the freezer open and plastic crinkle.

"Do you still eat Toaster Strudels?"

"Blueberry and cream cheese."

"I guess I'm not the only one who's a little set in her ways."

"Didn't say it was a bad thing, sis." There's a pause while he warms them, then he brings a single plate with the pastries piled on it.

He holds up an icing packet. "Do you want me to spread this on your pastry, or on your body?"

I reluctantly point at the strudel before realizing it doesn't have to be all or none. I grab the edge of the blanket and slide it off my shoulder. The oversized jersey has already exposed my skin. "A little taste for later?"

"Does this mean we're starting our date?"

His evil smirk is followed by a delicate strip of icing and his tongue. My body melts.

He pulls my arm free from the blanket and trails the sugar over it, licking upward until his mouth is on the jersey. He detours to nuzzle my breast. My nipples are so hard he can flick them with his tongue through the heavy fabric. He leans me back and spreads my leg.

"You were driving us crazy last night. Can I add an orgasm to your breakfast?" He hands me a pastry, then slides off the couch onto his knees.

Warm kisses trail up my thigh. The tingling that had already sprung to life fully grips me as his mouth closes on my sex. Ballz did this last night, but Adrian has a little scruff and it tickles in a rough sort of way.

I try to eat the pastry, but it might be dangerous to swallow and deal with him between my legs at the same time. I'm about to set it aside when he hits the sweet spot and my body spasms. I crush the strudel in my hand, making a terrible mess as wave after wave of release washes through me.

He seems to know exactly where and how to please me. I choke on my own saliva before getting hold of myself.

He sits on his heels with a sheepish grin. "Sorry, I forgot to ask what you normally do after your Morning Pages?"

"I take a shower."

A wicked grin crosses his face.

Nine

Jeff

Snowflakes warn of the impending storm, and if Cindy doesn't get back soon, her car won't make the drive. Did she lie to us that she'd come back to finish the dates after doing the invitations?

I'm going through my Tai chi motions on the back porch, which faces the sunset behind the mountain, when I rotate an arm back and angle my body to that side. Cindy is standing at the edge of the deck, her hands clasped in front of her Spandex-clad body. An overnight bag rests on the bench.

I relax my pose. All of the tension releasing this is supposed to do for me, recommended by my therapist in the anger management class, is replaced by another sense of tension—my need to be with her.

"What was that?" she asks.

"Every evening at sunset, if we're not on the ice, I do Tai chi."

"Is that what you did the other night?" She mimics the motion I'd been making by bringing her hands downward in front of her body and exhaling.

Realization hits. "Pulling Down the Heavens, that's Qigong, but yeah, same kind of thing. It's replenishing and it helps me process whatever I dealt with during the day. A lot of people do Tai chi in the morning, but I need it at the end. I would've skipped today if I knew you were coming. I would've come and picked you up. The storm's blowing in."

"I needed some time to think and I wanted to have my car here."

"Are you okay with our arrangement?"

"I'm here."

"That's not what I asked."

"It's good. But I'm worried I'll cause trouble between you three. And I want to have my car."

"Fair enough. Let's go inside."

"I want you to teach me what you were doing."

"It's nothing."

"It was beautiful."

"Then come on over."

She stands in front of me, looking up expectantly. She raises her hands similar to the pose I ended on. The last thing I want to do is continue my Tai chi, but it gets me close to her.

"Is there an order to how you do it?"

I move behind her and grip her arms. I saw the way she lit up when Ballz did that in the kitchen. Guiding her through a motion, I say, "I think you like when a guy takes control, don't you?"

"I think so."

"Okay." I continue taking her through simple motions. She's so receptive. I've never popped a boner during my sessions before, but there's always a first. Her ass grinds into my erection and goosebumps break out on her skin.

The peaceful snowfall with a backdrop of a sunset over the mountains can't quench the fire inside of me. I rub my hands up and down her bare arms.

"Why don't we get you inside so I can warm you up?"

Ten

Cindy

Jeff strides to the other end of the deck and grabs my stuff. I sneak a peek at the outline of his erection against his sweatpants. My sneak turns into a stare, or maybe a gawk.

He catches me.

"That's for you, love. My Love."

The nicknames make this feel real. "You guys are really good at pretending."

"Because it's not pretend with you." True, he wants sex with a virgin...nothing pretend there. That doesn't stop my stomach from getting all weird again. Why can't I keep myself in check?

"We're fake dating. Remember?" I say it out loud for my own benefit. I shake off my girlish dreams of a professional athlete or three choosing me, especially my stepbrothers. They have their pick of women. They did their good deed. They're just helping their little sister.

He checks if I need anything to eat or drink, and I don't, then he leads me down to the entertainment room. It's a multipurpose room with a theater on one end and a mini stage at the other, along with a pool table, a ping pong table, a dartboard, and a bar.

"What do you want to do?" He sits in one of the recliners and pats his lap.

Imagining him taking total control, I toy with saying, *I want you to tell me what to do, Daddy*. The statement chokes me even though I don't let it out. I clear my throat. "I don't know."

"Then come here, we'll figure it out." I love the command in his voice, the Daddy vibe. I love the thought of him telling me exactly what to do. I just don't know if that's normal. Does he want a more aggressive woman? One who will be as confident as he is? But *he* doesn't matter. What would other guys want?

"We've already established that you don't think you want the slow and tender type. Is there anything particular you want to explore?"

"I've liked everything so far."

"What did you like the most?"

Approaching from the side, I sit across him, while awkwardly trying to avoid putting my legs on the arm of the chair. "I liked you telling me to sit on your lap."

A single huff, a suggestive smile, and the firmness underneath me hint that I'm not the only one liking our contact. He wraps his hand around my legs and pulls them over the side of the chair, snuggling my body into his.

"You did, huh? You like being told what to do?"

I'm about to answer when he brushes my hair over my shoulder, grips me around the waist, and turns me to sit with my legs splayed over his lap. Yes, I like being told what to do. And, I like being shown, or handled, even more. And I love having his hard shaft between my legs.

Catching my breath, I answer. "I hate making decisions. That's why I have my routines. They take away decisions. Everything's orderly and expected. But this," I motion between us. "There's so much unknown. I just want you to walk me through it."

"Let me kiss you."

I giggle. It's not exactly what I meant, but I lean forward, eager for his kiss. His technique is more demanding than that of Ballz or Adrian. It's aggressive. Our tongues mesh in the sensual dance and I find my hips curling into him, begging for pleasure.

He surprises me by pulling back and gripping his hands on my upper arms.

"For someone who put no sex on the list, you sure seem like you want to ride my cock."

"I'm sorry."

"My Love, that's nothing to be sorry about. You're listening to your body. And so am I. Based on your little whimpers, you need an orgasm."

"Whimpers?" And why is that not embarrassing? I've never whimpered over anything.

"Yes, My Love. And I heard how many orgasms you had last night and this morning with our brothers. You're a greedy little girl."

"I'm sorry."

"Shhh." He puts a finger to my lips. "Don't apologize for letting people please you."

"Yes, Daddy."

His expression tightens. His eyes go dark.

Did I say that out loud? Shit! The tingling that's been prominent between my legs creeps over my entire body. What's happening? Did his cock just get even bigger and harder under me?

"My Love..." His tone is questioning but he doesn't finish.

I've either hit an all-time low or I leveled up. I have no idea which. I opt for innocence. "Did I do something wrong? You looked...mad."

"Mad...as in driven crazy for you, yes. I didn't expect you to call me Daddy. Did one of our brothers tell you to do that?"

He's not mad. Good. And his erection definitely got harder. I can grind on him even easier. I'm nearly shameless with him.

"They didn't tell me to call them anything. But you're so in control and demanding, and I guess it just slipped out."

"Say it again."

I roll my clit into his shaft as I lean forward to bring my mouth to his ear. I lick my lips, and I'm so close that my tongue catches the side of his ear. I'm rewarded with a twitch from his cock. I might officially be ruined as I whisper, "Daddy."

My entire body shakes in anticipation of his reaction. He moves his hand up my thigh, rubs his thumb over my sex, and my body welcomes the pleasure.

"Show Daddy how you like to come."

"Yes, Daddy." I slide my hands onto my sex, replacing his fingers. I miss his warmth and pressure, but with a few quick circles, I fall apart, shamelessly pleasuring myself in front of him...because he told me to.

With him, I'm confident and worthy and can let go of the reins.

"I can't believe you can be even more beautiful. Do you know what you do to me?"

"Tell me, Daddy?"

"You're sweet and innocent, smart and methodical. You drive me crazy with your processes, but you're serious and focused." He bucks his hips upward, making me shudder. "This is what you do to me. And when you play the sweet, innocent, you're a sexual vixen."

My body giggles in an effort to release energy. I'm too taken by his words. Too convinced.

"You think that's funny?"

"You might have exaggerated." And if I could record his deep voice uttering these things, I'd play it on a loop.

"They're true. Do you not understand how sexy you are?"

"Sexy isn't really something I do."

"My Love." He caresses my torso. "It's not something you do, it's something you are."

"Thank you, Daddy."

"Fuck... Do you trust me?"

"Yes." Why do I suspect that's the single most dangerous word I've ever spoken? I try to lighten his intensity. "But no butt stuff."

Now he laughs.

"Don't worry, I consider that sex, which you've clarified is off the table."

He pauses. He wants me to retract my no-sex rule, I can sense it. The words line up on my tongue. All I have to do is open my mouth and they'll grant his unstated wish.

I nod instead.

His jaw clenches but he lets his thought go, pointing past me. "You see that stage?"

I glance over my shoulder. "Yes."

"Get on it and strip for me."

Nervousness tosses my stomach around. It's only for him, not like Wendy's brothers ravishing her at the sex club. I can do this, although I'll have to resist the urge to remove each item methodically, fold it, and set it aside. "I've never stripped for anyone."

"What if Daddy goes first?" He staggers me with the offer.

My entire body vibrates with excitement. "I'd love that."

With ease, he tightens his grip on me, gets up, and returns me to the cushioned chair. He's reaching over his shoulders for the back of his shirt as he steps onto the stage. As he lifts, the expanse of his muscular back is the perfect pairing for the swell of his sweatpants over his firm ass.

He faces me and tosses his shirt into my eager hands. I clutch it to my chest, barely able to enjoy his bare chest before he shoves his sweatpants down.

I swallow hard when his cock springs free. It's even bigger than I assessed.

"Now it's your turn."

I scoot out of the chair, pausing for a kiss as we pass. There's no avoiding contact with his penis. I'd be fine if he ripped the clothes from my body and impaled me. Geez, the orgasms have gone to my head. But I'm ready to have sex—no plan, no routine, just wild, passionate sex.

Continuing onto the stage, I focus on the hunger in his eyes. Grabbing the bottom of my Spandex top, I pull it upward and let my breasts bounce free.

Motion in his lap grabs my attention. He fists his shaft and pre-cum squirts onto his stomach. He doesn't bother to wipe it.

"No." He shakes his head and I follow his gaze to my arms. I've crossed them over my breasts. He lets go of his shaft and motions for me to toss my top to him. Of course, I comply. He balls it in one hand.

"You only get this back if you're a good girl and do what Daddy told you to do."

The uncanny temptation to disobey is gone in a fleeting second. I tuck my thumbs into my waistband and shimmy the tight fabric over my hips, bending forward. His eyes drift to my waist.

"You wake up every primal need in me, My Love."

I smile, unsure how to respond.

He inhales deeply. "I want to make you mine."

"For a date?" I'm having too much trouble faking it.

"No." The corded muscles of his neck strain. His rugged jawline stresses. "You asked for a date but I can't give that to you."

"I don't understand."

With forced calmness, he unballs my top and smooths it over the arm of the recliner. "If you stay, I'm going to protect you, breed you, and make you mine. If that's not what you want, put your clothes back on and walk out of here."

That breeding thing again. I move my hands in front of my belly. Why does that turn me on? Is this all part of the dating practice—he's showing me how some guys are?

I know how my brothers are. They work hard, they play hard... I want him to play with me.

He motions to my top. I stare at the pink stripe on the seam. I think about the lack of consistency my brothers offer. I angle my arm to look at the dandelion seeds that have blown free. It's only in letting go that they can blossom into their own flower.

Am I going through with this? All I have to do is open my mouth and let the words roll off my tongue.

My lips part. The cool room air enters my mouth as I inhale. It gives me life as my body warms it. I let the same air carry my words in place of an exhale. "Well, Daddy, since I'm not in the mood to get dressed, what next?"

The only sign that we're not frozen in time is the pre-cum dripping down the side of his shaft. How far will he go?

"Look down and see how beautiful you are."

Surprisingly simple. I lower my gaze. My dusky nipples stand perky against my lighter skin. My curls match my black hair. The curves of my breasts, waist, and hips are truly beautiful now that I'm stopping to think about them. And my toenails that are painted bright red to match my manicure. I love that little bit of familiarity and order.

"Come sit on my lap."

With each step forward, I think about stopping. I think about protecting myself from the unknown. About adhering to my own rules About the broader judgement of society's rules.

Yet I push off the ball of my left foot and swing it forward, then do the same with my right, unable to stop myself.

I step wide to plant my feet on either side of his, set my hands on his shoulders, and bring my knees onto the chair to straddle his lap.

SYLVIE HAAS

That primal need that he mentioned... I feel it. The pull, the need, the desire. Raising up on my knees, I slide my curls up and down his shaft.

"My Love, are you submitting to me?" His voice has dropped an octave.

"Yes, Daddy."

"Daddies don't have to follow the rules." His tone has gone stern.

I swallow, giving myself a second to back out before answering, "I know."

His hands lift from the arms of the chair, travel delicately up my thighs, over my hips and waist, and stop to massage my breasts.

"I'm going to fuck you."

"Yes."

A deep chuckle comes before he says, "It wasn't a question."

He fists his cock and slaps it against my sex. My body shakes. Before I can figure out how to respond to his statement or his actions, he adds, "Make yourself come."

I lower a hand but he grabs my wrist and returns it to his shoulder.

"Make yourself come by rubbing against my cock."

My confusion must be apparent.

"Not sex, yet. Lean into me. Slide your wet pussy up and down me. I want to be able to watch you come on my cock this time because once I'm inside of you, I won't be able to think."

276

He helps steady me. My lips part around his shaft. Should that count as sex? He's right, I'm so wet, I slick him from top to bottom. My clit throbs with need. I pump myself faster and faster, tempted to scoot forward an inch and come down on his cock, but when I do, his fingers grip me hard and keep me off.

"Naughty girl." He loosens one grip and I'm about to get back to business when his hand comes down hard on my butt cheek. "Don't try to take my cock before you have permission."

I'm so shocked by the moment, by the intense sting, I can't move.

"Are you ready to be a good girl and come for me?"

"Yes."

"Yes, what?"

"Yes, Daddy." My sex aches to be filled. It's hard not to try again, but my orgasm is wound so tight, I need release more than I need air.

His tongue darts out and flicks one of my nipples. The added sensation is too much. I hold on for my life as my world is obliterated from within. My orgasm splinters everything I know to be true. I'm drifting through bliss.

The faint sensation of Jeff physically guiding me through the orgasm fades into the euphoria.

I don't know how long I've been collapsed on him when I gather myself. Sitting upright, I notice his shaft is still rock-hard between us.

He lifts me, angling his hips so that his cock prods at my entrance. I balance with my hands on his shoulders.

"Let me know if you need me to stop." He's holding me as if I'm weightless. He pushes downward, pressuring his tip into me. My lips spread around his broad head with the help of our combined wetness. His musky scent mixes with my sweeter one.

I've never been so addicted to something. He's inching into me. Our eyes are locked in complete silence as he helps my body do what it was meant to do: take his cock.

"I can't wait to fill you."

My sex is stretched, doing its best to accommodate him, but the thought of riding him bare, being full of his seed, makes my walls tighten around him.

"Oh fuck, My Love." He pumps himself into me. A different kind of orgasm builds. It's deeper, stronger—

"What the fuck is going on?" Balthazar's voice comes from the doorway.

"You're not supposed to interfere with a date." Daddy, or Jeff, speaks with absolute clarity while I process what's happening.

"You're not supposed to be fucking," Ballz responds. He's only wearing athletic shorts, no top, and he has a small towel. His chest, abs, and happy trail tempt me to ask him to join us. How would that work?

"The rules changed. Get out."

"If the rules changed, I'm watching." Ballz grabs a chair from the poker table, spins it around, and sets his arms over the back of it, facing us. "Don't mind me."

I don't know what to say. I don't know what to do. Ballz shows no shame in studying my body and the union between Jeff and me.

His tongue grazes his lower lip. "Does that pussy feel as good on your cock as it did on my face?"

My body takes control. My pussy tightens. Electricity shoots through me. I'm coming. Oh God. I pump myself up and down, helping the climax fully explode.

The orgasm takes over, turning me into a limp doll as Jeff takes over. His growl fills my soul while streams of cum fill me in other more dangerous ways. The sloppy sound of our mixed release, the warmth of it leaking out of me, and the tenderness with which he holds me while we exist in a bubble I don't ever want to pop.

Eleven

Ballz

Wrapping up my workout and jog on the treadmill, there's still no text from Cindy. I didn't think she was going to be gone this long. It's already evening. Maybe she's not coming back. Maybe this nagging feeling inside of me about wanting more is one-sided.

She got what she wanted. It doesn't seem like her to lie.

But now that I had a taste of her, I can't get her out of my head. And worse, the word around town is that the other auction winners are all getting pretty damn lucky. My competitive nature takes that extra hard. I don't want to be the one set of stepbrothers that gets dissed by their stepsister.

That's messed up, but it is what it is.

But Cindy—I can't believe that for the first time in my life, I'm thinking ahead, more than just the impulsive moment. I want a life with her. I want kids with her, even if it includes my brothers. Okay, that's my normal impulsive thinking.

And yet, I banged out a workout. I went for a five-mile run on the treadmill, and still, there's that sensation inside of me that I finally know what I want out of life.

I grab my towel, wipe the sweat off my face, and head to the kitchen. Moans trail up the stairs from the entertainment room. Jeff and Adrian must have opted for a porno. We're all in a bad place over Cindy.

I pause at the top of the stairwell. There's no music. There's always music, really bad music, in a porno—at least the shit they watch. I step closer, putting my hand against the wall as I lean forward to listen.

That's Cindy and Jeff.

What the hell? The only reason a woman sounds like that is if she's getting railed.

I take three steps down the stairs, telling myself that if they're on a date, I'm not supposed to interfere. I barrel down the stairs, rounding the corner into the room, and I stop as if I've hit a brick wall. She's riding his fucking cock, her titties bouncing, her head thrown back in ecstasy.

"What the fuck is going on?"

Jeff says, "You're not supposed to interfere with a date."

"You're not supposed to be fucking."

"The rules changed. Get out."

"If the rules changed, I'm watching." I grab a chair. "Don't mind me."

Cindy's body, completely naked in full room light, is even more gorgeous than I could imagine. Why the fuck is she breaking her own rule, though? Her pussy lips flared around Jeff's shaft look like heaven.

He may be inside of her, but I want her thinking of me. "Does that pussy feel as good on your cock as it did on my face?"

I resist the urge to rub one out along with them.

Her body barely moves when she cries out and rides Jeff. He takes over quickly. She's blissed out hard, barely catching her breath. It's beautiful and frustrating all at the same time.

I focus on her, memorizing every inch of her body until she recovers.

"So what's the deal? I respected the rules."

She angles her head to Jeff, who answers. "It just happened. She was ready to change the rules."

"You could have let Adrian and me know."

"That would have killed the moment, dude."

I rake my hand through my hair. I don't want Cindy to think I'm mad at her, but I kind of am. Nothing sinking inside of her wouldn't cure. I motion to the two of them. "Are the rules only changed for Jeff?"

"No." She doubles down on her answer by shaking her head.

"Turns out she's a bit submissive. Tell her what you want and she'll make your wish come true. Just be sure whatever you wish for, it's going to please her."

"On it." I'm swinging my leg over the chair as I stand, move forward, and carefully pull her off my brother's cock. I turn her petite body and she wraps herself around me. "So you like it when the guy takes control?"

"Yes."

"Then first order of business... Sit right here and let me eat your pussy."

Her smile is worth gold. I grab a corner of my towel that I hadn't wiped my face down with and gently wipe my brother's cum. Then I go down on her. I wish it was only her sweetness, but it is what it is.

I'll never get tired of her thighs clamping around me or the tangle of her fingers in my hair or the sound of her orgasm. But the slight rise and fall of her stomach as I watch her drift through the pleasure gives me hope with each rise that I can make it stay rounded.

As much as I want to sink inside of her pussy, I also want to give her a new experience. "Have you ever given a blowjob?"

"No. Do you want me to?"

Right, the submissive thing. I want to know, though. "Baby, I can assure you that I want you to, but I want you to answer this one. Does the thought of sucking on my cock excite you?"

"Yes."

"Then get on your knees." I change to a commanding tone and step back to give her room to comply. It also gives me a second to undress.

She looks up at me from under her lashes. "I don't know what to do."

"Open your mouth and keep your eyes on mine."

She does exactly as I say. I cup a hand around her head. "Such a good girl. Now suck my cock."

Twelve

Cindy

I must have been exhausted after sex and a blow job and countless orgasms. I wake up in a tangle of bodies and carefully slip away to the bathroom. The last couple days has been a blur.

We haven't officially talked about this being anything more than the guys doing their good deed to tidy up their reputation. I don't figure I can trust declarations made in the heat of passion.

Everything between us has been private. It will be good for me to get away from the house and process what this is and what I want.

What I want? I remind myself we're not a thing, we're a fling. Although I'd at least like to keep this as siblings with benefits. Perhaps every Tuesday night we could...I smile at my wild bed-head in the mirror. No need to limit fun to Tuesday nights.

Showering and dressing, I wonder if I'll be able to slip away to work before they wake up. It's weird having time and space to myself. I button my blouse, and when I look up, Jeff is in the doorway to the bathroom.

"You're actually going to go to work?"

"Every Monday at the accounting firm."

"Can you call in sick? We need to check in with each other."

"It's not necessary. I get it." I want to drift on the high a little longer before facing the reality I agreed to. I try to move past him, but he grabs my arm.

"Do you?"

"I do. Don't worry. I'm not going to get all needy." I throw the statement out, having heard friends mention it being a big concern.

He flinches and for a second his hand grips tighter around my arm, then he releases me. "Is that the way you want it?"

Is he messing with me? How can they repair their wild and crazy reputation their coach is mad about if they go public with me? In my fantasy about how to make this real like so many other groups have, their coach seemed more problematic than our parents.

"That's what I thought," he says. "You feel it too. There's something more here. Stay, and let's figure it out."

I consider the option, but it would just be walking down a foolish path. They burn through women almost as if on a schedule. For the first time ever, a thought of a schedule isn't comforting. I let that sink in. I'm fun, new, and taboo.

The answer is clear. "I have a life to get back to."

Jeff follows me to the kitchen. "Here's the deal. If you're done with us, you had your dates, you committed your four hours, you did everything you said you would, then we understand and respect that."

"We?"

"My brothers and I talked while you were in the shower."

"Okay."

"But if you want more, we have a plan. Think about it. The storm has blown in and by the end of the day, the roads are going to be messy. I don't want you driving in that car back here."

He's right. The roads up to their house can get sketchy.

"We finish practice and will leave the arena at seven. It's not far from the accounting firm. If you show up, we'll bring you back here. If you're done with us, drive straight home. We're siblings, nothing more. You have all day to think about it."

When I get to work, Wendy's there—not a total surprise since her brothers are part of the local motorcycle club that runs it. We've crossed paths, but I'm always working so we haven't chatted much.

What's surprising is that she's upset and all alone in a meeting room. I slip in.

"What's going on? Is everything okay with your brothers?" I'm not sure how to phrase it after what I just went through.

"I can't blame them."

"What happened?"

Her eyes flash a desperate plea. "Is it terrible to have sex with our stepbrothers?"

I wish I could answer definitively. My head's too much of a mess. "I took two wrong turns driving here. I might not be the best person to ask for advice." Sitting next to her, I take her hand. "Are you concerned about the act of sex, or is your heart the question?"

"Have you told your parents yet?" Her avoidance of the question makes the answer clear.

"No." I decide not to explain that my stepmom is oddly accepting of things. Didn't blink when her boys all wanted to be professional athletes. She's uber supportive, but I need boundaries to feel safe. My dad lets her run the show. I think some of my need for structure comes from their lack of providing it.

"My dad was upset that I walked out of my wedding, which he'd carefully crafted as a business deal. And when he found out I hooked up with my stepbrothers, he no longer had my virginity to offer." She tosses her hands up. "Who wants tarnished goods? He was so mad he wrote me out of the will and said I better hang up my roller skates and get a real job."

"There are so many things wrong with that. You're far from tarnished. You only do roller derby for fun. And who—" Her brothers file into the room. We wish each other well and I head to my desk.

Numbers, my safe haven. I turn my computer on, sharpen my pencil, position my sticky notes in their designated space, and open the account I'm working on.

I followed my routine. So why when I poise my fingers over the number pad, don't they spring into action? I stare at the digits. I stare at the columns. I stare at the rows.

Forcing my fingers to move, I input in a few numbers and watch the automatic calculations trickle through the page. Not even a hint of excitement.

As I enter more dollar amounts from the invoices I'm supposed to process, a bright red number populates a cell at the bottom of the screen. Oh no, what did I do?

I undo the last entry and hold my breath, waiting for the red number to turn black again. It changes, but is still red.

Shit! I scan the screen for the error but my mind drifts.

The number of ways I've been given orgasms since hooking up with my brothers is phenomenal. It's like I've been doing it wrong all this time. But it's more than sex. I enjoy how free they make me feel, like everything will be okay, and I don't have to worry about making decisions.

How ironic that I'm facing the biggest decision of my life. Or maybe I already made it. My hand slides off the keyboard onto my belly.

They took a risk with me. They're very adamant that they never have sex without a condom, yet that's not true with me. Every paternity claim that's come against them has been proven false. Do they really consider me special enough to chance making a baby? Or as they called it...to breed me?

My computer beeps with the alert for an invalid entry. Crap! I fumble to hit the backspace key enough times to remove the letters DADDY from the cell. Who gave my fingers permission to type that? I'm at work, not in fantasyland.

Pushing away from my desk, I stand, stretch, and breathe. It's not the top of the hour, when I normally do that, but I need it.

Daddy—or maybe I should call him Jeff for now—was right. We need to talk.

No more sex until we've sorted the obstacles. I don't have much to lose, but I don't want to be responsible for trouble with their coach. Hockey has been their entire lives. They love hockey, they love being athletes, they love being rich. What would they do otherwise?

I check my clock. I need to leave in thirty minutes if I'm going to get to the arena on time.

Returning to my seat, my computer, and my messed-up data, I have an immediate problem. I can't be an accountant if I'm not meticulous with other people's numbers. I dutifully scan the spreadsheet.

Going back through the few numbers I recalled entering, the glaring red number remains. What have I done? I try resetting the spreadsheet but it auto-saved my changes.

I slink to the meeting room, ashamed that I'm going to have to ask Wendy's brother to access a previous version of the file for me. I don't have high enough clearance. But I spin on my heels when I pop the door open and find them...dating.

Why didn't I knock? I'm a freaking mess ever since the auction. What if this is the universe pointing out the decision I should make as opposed to the decision I want to make?

Adjusting the backrest on my chair, I'm determined to prove I didn't have to sell my brain to have sex.

If I'm meant to be with my brothers, I'll fix the problem in time. If not...I'll have a broken heart to mend.

Thirteen

Adrian

"Adrian, focus on what you're doing before somebody gets hurt." Coach's patience is wearing thin. It's just practice but I've missed every shot, pissed off two teammates by crashing into them from behind, and had to have plays repeated to me.

I tear my gaze from the stands where Cindy is distinctly not sitting. Jeff said she's supposed to show up if she wants to continue the relationship. I skate to my place in line, purposefully catching Ballz with my elbow.

He shoves me into the Plexiglass surrounding the rink. "What the fuck, bro?"

I don't respond verbally, just shove back and skate past him. I'm seething with anger. Why didn't he bring me in on the discussion of her staying with us? I'd been in our swag room autographing photos for the children's hospital, trying to making use of my time while she was occupied. Nothing that couldn't wait.

Practice can't end soon enough, except she's not here. Her shift should have ended ten minutes ago, which gave her enough time to get to the arena. Every number change on the digital clock escalates my anger.

I turn my aggression to the ice, but temper it just enough so everyone just thinks I'm getting into the practice session.

Practice ends. She's still not here. We shower and change. She still hasn't shown. We head to the front doors. I didn't have any doubts she wanted to be with us until my dickhead brother scared her off this morning.

"Must be hard not to take it personal that you fucked her and now she's not coming back, Jeff," Ballz says.

I stop so fast, my bag swings forward. "Wait, you left that out. You fucked her? Like actual sex?"

Jeff raises his eyebrows, then continues to the front doors. "Best sex I've ever had. That tight virgin pussy, and her titties bouncing in my face. Her mouth hanging open as she moans. And you should have seen the way Ballz went balls deep down her throat."

"What the hell? The first time I follow the rules... You're joking." Except that I can see by the starry looks in their eyes that they aren't. "So you both had sex with her?"

"Well, I fully had sex and she dropped to her knees for Ballz and sucked his cock."

I check outside but her car's not here. "You bastards. Did you make her feel used?"

"She's totally dickmatized. You should have seen the way she—"

"Stop. That's our sister. I actually respect her and care about her. I was trying to show her how she deserves to be treated."

Jeff is less cocky. "I have something special with her, it's not just sex. She'll be back."

"After you two, I doubt it. Jeff, you always think you're such a big shot. Always in control. You never listen to anyone else. I'm surprised you even listened to her rules. Although, apparently you didn't. Do you even know how to please a woman?"

"She was pleased, all right."

"I'm being serious. And Ballz, you just dive into whatever. Did you just tell her, 'Suck my dick,' and forget to please her?"

I shove Ballz. He shoves me back. "I went down on her first."

"Don't tell me you let your dicks cause more trouble. I'm serious about benching you, or cutting you from the team if you're more interested in sex than hockey," Coach says, as he catches us arguing in the lobby.

We hang our heads like bad little boys and wait for him to leave.

"She's coming back," Jeff says quietly.

"Do you see her? What time did you say?" I look at my wrist, pretending I have a watch.

"Seven," Jeff says and we all turn to the digital clock at the end of the arena: 7:03.

I check my phone, nothing from Cindy. She's made her point.

"Fuck it. I'm out of here." I need to get her alone and undo whatever they screwed up.

Fourteen

Jeff

Adrian throws the door open and storms out. Ballz and I follow but Coach's voice calls out, "Balthazar. My office. Now."

"Can it wait?"

"Now," Coach says.

Logically, I should get out of here. I'm not the one in trouble, but something nags at me. I can't leave. I have to believe Cindy will be here. She felt everything, and I don't just mean sexually. The connection.

Or Adrian's right. I like to be in charge, to be right, and to be called Daddy. Maybe I saw what I wanted to see.

Repositioning the strap of my bag on my shoulder, I stare at the clock. If she shows up late, I sure as hell am not going to have her thinking we left at exactly seven. And if she shows up late...she should call. She should respect us and let us know where she is.

Except that's not the deal I laid out. It never crossed my mind she simply wouldn't show up.

Through the glass door, I study the snow collecting beside the road. It won't be safe for her to drive much longer.

Calming exercises aren't going to help. I get my blades out of my bag and lace them up, not bothering with the rest of my gear. I shove my phone into my back pocket and dump a bunch of biscuits onto the ice. I slap them out of sheer anger.

It grows with each shot. A few more seconds of not having her in my life. How the fuck did I fall so hard and fast for my sister?

"Jeff," her voice floats through my mind, although I'm surprised I don't conjure up, "Daddy." She fucking wrecked me.

"Jeff," Cindy says again. This time it's clearer. My stick halts midair as I'm about to slam another puck into the next state.

I spin toward her. "Do you have a fucking phone?" If my anger management therapist was here, he'd soften his voice and ask me to walk through my emotions. I don't need a fucking walk right now. I need answers.

She steps backward toward the door she just entered, but it's swinging open, causing her to stumble as she expected there to be something behind her.

Adrian catches her.

I skate toward them. "I thought you left, Adrian." Like I give a fuck, but I'm too wound up over Cindy to risk saying anything else to her. If she's too immature to let us know she'll be late when this much is on the line, I'll get my heart right off that roller coaster.

"I saw her driving in when I was leaving."

Cindy is flustered. "I must have left my phone at your house again. I was trying to get here, but I messed up a bunch of stuff at work and I was trying to fix it. Then I drove as fast as I could, but there was a car wreck and—"

I've made my way to them as Adrian cups his hand around her mouth from behind. Do I trust her?

"I want to say that you're here, that's the important thing," Adrian says, freeing his hand from her mouth. "But you guys had a fuckfest without me, and now you didn't show up until I left. Are you interested in all of us, or just..."

Adrian swallows and doesn't continue. It's hitting him hard that she might not want him. How did she do this to us? I practically choke on the possibility that she could choose one of us and the others would have to fuck off.

Cindy rubs a thumb over the forearm of her coat. I've seen her do that motion enough times to know that she's overthinking something. "Adrian, no one's ever done Morning Pages with me. That was really sweet, just existing—"

"Yeah, yeah," Ballz says loudly from out of sight down a hallway. "Don't let the auction thing blow up in our faces and go fucking our stepsister."

Fifteen

Cindy

Ballz's footsteps plod closer, and whoever he was talking to mumbles something I can't make out, although the tone is clearly irritated.

Adrian won't let me out. I'm trapped. Jeff is mad.

My gut sinks. I was about to say that I hadn't meant to slight Adrian. I love all three of them. But I can't jeopardize their place on the team.

Ballz stops short when he gets to the end of the hallway. "Cindy…"

I lunge for the next door, but Adrian grabs the handle.

"Please let me go. I'm sorry, this was all a mistake. I don't want your good deed to blow up in your face."

Ballz rushes closer. "That's just what Coach thinks. We can handle it."

"Can we? Jeff yelled at me for not calling. Adrian thought I was avoiding him. You're arguing with your coach. Everybody's mad, and I'm the reason."

"I'm sorry I yelled at you. Won't happen again," Jeff says.

"Same. I'll find a way to call if I'm late again. Sorry to upset you, Jeff."

He looms over me, tips my chin up, and says, "Did you forget who I am?"

A zing of excitement races through me. Can I say it in front of the other guys? Our eyes are locked and his jaw tenses. I go for it. "Sorry to upset you, Daddy."

"What the fuck? I missed that too." Adrian shoves Jeff out of the way and takes my hand. "I was jealous that I got left out. Respecting your rules was so important to me, I followed them."

I can't help but laugh. "I thought you'd be the first to break them."

"I planned on it. But I'll do anything for you, even follow the fucking rules."

"Fucking rules." Ballz cracks up.

Life is simpler with rules and routines, that's why I love them. I motion to all of us. "What are the rules for something like this?"

"We could make them up as we go," Adrian offers. "The most important thing to me is that you're taken care of. I never thought I'd say this, but if it means we have to share you, it works. I trust these guys more than anybody."

Jeff says, "Coach can't dictate who we date as long as we don't break any laws."

"You mean I wouldn't have to pick whose dating style I liked better?" A lightness washes over me.

They simultaneously offer a resounding, "No."

Adrian speaks over his brothers, "But I would like to break rule number two as soon as possible." He brushes his thumb over my cheek. "And number one if you're game?"

He nods toward the other end of the arena, but I'm not sure what he's indicating.

"Meaning?"

"The Zamboni room's technically public. What do you say we go break some rules?"

Jeff says, "Heads up... She'd rather you take charge."

Adrian looks at me, a huge smile crossing his face. "Is that true?"

"I did like it when Jeff and Ballz took control. But why the Zamboni room?"

"That damn machine has a magical allure. Maybe just because we've been told since we were kids to stay away from it. Can't resist temptation."

I shake my head. Tell Adrian he can't do something, and he'll make it his next goal. I'm torn between thinking I'm simply a taboo temptation and trusting the way I feel with them.

He scoops me up and carries me behind the scenes into the room with the big machine. "I really want to lay you out on a bed and adore every inch of your body, but it might be dangerous to drive with this hard of an erection. There's not enough blood left to keep my body functioning."

"It's kind of exciting coming back here."

"Oh, you're going to come back here, all right. I really want to get you up top, but I want my brothers in on this too. Let's christen this relationship."

"All of us? I think I'm going to like that."

Have all of the seeds blown off of my dandelion tattoo? Order or structure feel unnecessary with my brothers so close. Adrian wraps me in a hug and I'm lost in his kiss.

His hand lowers and pulls my skirt up, kneading my butt cheek. His big hand feels so good and protects me from the cold air. Another brother peels my panties down, and helps lift each foot out. I shudder at Adrian's palm on my bare butt. The sensation of each finger becomes more prominent, especially when he spins me around, wraps his arm around my waist, and slips it into my sex.

"Feels like you're ready." His statement drifts in one ear and out the other. I don't bother answering—just respond to his motions.

With his free hand, he pushes my back so that I bend over. His other fingers run circle after circle around my clit. Jeff strokes my hair then gets on his knees so he can capture my mouth in a kiss. An extra set of hands, must be Ballz, awkwardly helps me out of my coat then rewards me with caresses.

To be so adored and cared for, I submit to them. I cry out, my body quivers.

Then Adrian slides his cock into me. Nothing's ever felt so perfect, so right, so absolutely divine as being filled by my stepbrother. My next orgasm builds unbelievably fast.

"I fucking love you," Adrian declares. Is that the impending orgasm speaking? Is it the taboo element? Or is it real? I don't know, but I've never felt like this. That's all I needed; I fall apart in their arms once again.

An unfamiliar man's voice breaks into my consciousness. It's from the PA system. "What the fuck am I seeing on the security cameras?"

I can't stop the orgasm. Nature insists on finishing.

"Oh shit. That's Coach," Ballz says.

Adrian grips my hips tighter, thrusting harder and faster as my body begs him to release. He growls out his pleasure, obliterating whatever Coach's next words are. We shamelessly finish each other.

With my body still responding to every twitch of Adrian's cock, and his seed dripping down my legs, the guilt creeps in. What have I done? What are the repercussions?

Sixteen

Cindy

It's quickly sorted out that the security guard alerted the coach to the players having sex on site. It's not the first time, and Coach had asked to be notified rather than security dealing with the players.

How many security personnel saw? Did they pull out their cameras and film it? Worries build in my mind.

Adrian slides out of me, his cock still hard. Jeff reaches in his bag and hands me a rag while they close in around me, blocking the angle from the camera. If we hadn't been so impulsive, one of us would have thought about that.

"I'm sorry I got you in trouble."

"You didn't get us in trouble," Ballz says. "It's just something that happened. We got caught. Not a big deal."

"Your coach was just saying not to—"

"We'll promise not to have sex in the arena, explain that we got overly excited about our new fiancée."

His words steal the air from my lungs. "I'm...not..."

"It makes what we did a lot more redeemable," Ballz offers leadingly. "And I think we're all hoping you will be."

Fiancée? Married? The reality of their world comes crashing down on me. The visibility, the travel, and the loneliness I'll be stuck with when they're on the road. My routines will constantly be in flux.

Sex is an amazing thing. But as they wait anxiously for my response, I get cold feet, and not just because we're in an ice arena "I don't think I can live in the public eye. Eventually we'd have to go public with our relationship. I can't do it. I can't be with all of you. I need my routines. I need predictability in my life."

"We can give you that." Jeff offers a reassurance.

"No, you can't. Thank you for teaching me how to date. I need to go home now." I grab my purse.

"Get in my office, all three of you," Coach demands over the speaker.

I'm grateful he didn't say four.

"Repair that relationship before worrying about ours."

I push past the guys. They object and follow me, but I point the direction I think the coach's office is.

They relent, but Jeff says, "The roads will be getting bad. Go straight home."

He's right. I barely make it to our parents' house. They have a thing tonight, but their car is still in the garage. I park next to it, hoping they'll be occupied with getting ready for their date.

They aren't in the living room, and I make as little noise as possible putting the chain lock on the back door. It's a small deterrent in case my brothers come.

"Hey, Kiddo. We'll be leaving soon. Need anything?"

I help settle my nerves with a deep breath. A few more minutes, then I can break down.

"I'm fine." But I'm not. Dad still calls me Kiddo. I still live at home. It all seemed familiar and frugal, but I need to spread my wings.

I rush up to my room, hang my keys on their hook, sit on my bed, and stare out the window at the softly falling snow. It can be silent and beautiful, and yet the very same snow can turn into a deadly blizzard. Is it weird to think of that as a metaphor for me? I usually do my own thing quietly, careful not to disrupt anyone, but a few wrong moves and I can ruin my brothers' careers.

I pull up SmorgasSmut on my phone. If the Zamboni video is going to show up, it will be there. I'm in luck, but Aurora may not be. There are videos from her brothers' concert and I'm pretty sure Aurora is having sex with her brother in the background, too far away and blurry to tell much more than her blond hair, though. I send her a message in case they need to get in front of it.

Being in the public eye isn't a life I can handle.

There are too many emotions jumbled inside of me to be able to cry. I squeeze a pillow to my face and let out a half-hearted scream.

Hugging the pillow to my chest, I watch the snow again, but Jeff's car pulls into the driveway. Crap. I toss the pillow aside and rush onto the second-floor landing.

They're already banging on the door.

"Kiddo, can you get that?"

"It's the boys and they're mad at me. Please don't let them in."

"Don't be silly. If you guys had an argument, you need to work it out. You're not children anymore."

Fine time for Dad to come to that realization.

Seventeen

Cindy

I can't avoid the conversation forever. The easiest way to get my life back in order is to forget the past few days ever happened. Well, *forget* would be a stretch.

We have to keep our sibling relationship as siblings and our romantic relationships with other people.

I'm not the adventurous, impulsive spirit that Ballz is. I'm not the rule breaker like Adrian. And I don't take control of every situation the way Jeff does.

I'm the girl who loves her rules, and schedules, and everything being in its place, and making sense, and not rocking the boat. My brothers offer the exact opposite.

I want what's best, what's safest. Even if it comes at the sacrifice of those incredible orgasms. From them. Surely other men are capable of doing that. I also make a mental note to buy a vibrator with more features.

More banging on the door causes Dad to give up. "You kids."

I don't know what to say, certainly not to explain this is far from a childish argument. My fingers trace over my belly.

My stomach does a flip-flop and I worry it's a baby tumbling around. Not an actual baby, but the start of one. What if it's too late to walk away?

There's a schedule I'd like to keep: my next period, which should start in two weeks.

The guys have already spied me, and the second Dad unlocks the door, they storm inside.

"Slow down, boys. Check your attitudes."

My brothers stop respectfully but split their attention between Dad and me.

"Whatever argument you had, don't come in here ganging up on your sister. She's a lot younger. Be role models, or remember that you're not too big for me to tan your hide."

Mom steps behind Dad, who's closing the door.

Mom angles her head up to me. "And if this is another one of those arguments where you got upset because they messed up one of your schedules, remember to take a breath and be flexible."

Mom and Dad have been trying to help me battle my rigidity ever since I can remember. I feel like I'm eight again, and my brothers are in high school when they'd put my Barbie dolls in the wrong order just to get a rise out of me.

This is so much bigger. None of us give any indication of what's wrong.

"Okay," Mom says, looking between all of us. "Your dad and I are leaving. We should be out for about out three hours and by the time we get back, I expect this will be resolved."

"Yes, Mom," I say. The boys each kiss her cheek.

They motion for me to come downstairs. I'd resist, but it's safer to meet them in the living room than next to my bedroom. Moments later, I'm alone in the house, face-to-face with my three brothers.

"How did it go with your coach?"

"I promised him we'd follow the rules," Adrian says.

"We didn't call you our fiancée, if that's what you're asking." Jeff nailed that one.

"His big concern is that we don't run around getting into legal trouble," Ballz says.

Jeff continues, "He's pissed and threatened to bench us, but I used some of that Qigong shit to calm myself down. That was the clencher. It's the first time I didn't blow up at him. I promised the anger management sessions are working, and he wouldn't want to invest that much in grooming me into the fabulous player I am, then let another team reap the benefits."

"It was a beautiful moment seeing Jeff work him over," Adrian says.

Now for me to stand up for myself. "What a relief. So let's officially end this chaos. It would never work."

"Hold on. We can make it work. Look how many couples in town have already pulled it off." Adrian tries to take my hand, but I step back.

"We'd have to tell our parents."

"They'll come around. They've always been open to crazy ideas. They supported us being professional athletes. They've always said they just want us to be happy."

He's right. Their mom more so than my dad, but they're very supportive.

"So, are you game for playing house?" Ballz says, giving me a wink.

"I want to say no."

Jeff gets a sly smile. "Not allowed, My Love. You're going to let us ravish you."

"It's a terrible idea." My response is a mismatch of my brain trying to convince me to walk away, and my instinct telling me to submit to them. My future plans scatter to the wind when I think about my brothers. The love and security they offer encourages a freedom I've never embraced.

"That's my favorite kind of idea." Adrian strokes his fingers through my hair. My eyes fall shut. His lips warm mine. He nips my lower lip, then trails kisses down my neck, licking and nibbling. My head falls shamelessly to the side and Jeff tips my chin so he can kiss me.

My greedy body is eager for Ballz to join in, but a cork popping in the kitchen steals that possibility. The faint sound of glasses and pouring are in the background while I'm being stripped.

Adrian grips my ass, his fingers possessing me as he pulls my body into his. "I need to make love to you, Sweet Cheeks."

Jeff whispers in my ear, "Daddy's going to watch, see how good you look taking our brother's cock."

I expect a brotherly grumble to break out, but Ballz interrupts by offering drinks.

"Champagne?" I ask excitedly, seeing the flutes of bubbly golden liquid.

"You're too young for that. We promised Coach we wouldn't break any laws." Is he joking?

"To us." Ballz's toast is simple. We clink glasses and a sense of oneness solidifies.

I love it. The bubbles tickle my nose as I tip the glass to my lips. The liquid chills my lips. My tongue is ready for the bite.

What? "Sparkling cider?"

"Seriously, you're under age," Ballz says. "And I don't want to dull any of your senses, Baby. I want you fully present when I lick your pussy."

I'm about to talk over him, tell him that I've had alcohol before, but the thought of him between my legs halts my monologue.

And when he drops to his knees and carries out his action, I set my unfinished drink aside and tangle my fingers in his hair.

That insatiably, greedy beast inside of me holds him in just the right spot.

Adrian and Jeff strip. Their cocks are as different as they are. Adrian's is thicker; the head of Jeff's seems more strained. All beautiful, just like their muscular bodies.

How many deviations from my norm did it take for me to end up naked in a room with such perfection? I lose focus as Ballz works magic with his tongue. My body crumples forward, my fingers tightening in his hair to steady myself as my legs threaten to give out.

Jeff and Adrian hurry to either side. Support, caresses, kisses... How can I be doing this with three guys at once?

As reality slips from my grasp, I put my full trust in them. I submit to whatever they want to do to me. Then my mind goes blank.

Daddy is cradling me against his chest when I come to.

Adrian spreads a blanket on the floor then approaches us. His usual naughty smirk is replaced by a gentle smile. He brushes my hair out of my eyes. "We thought Ballz stole your soul for a minute there."

I smile and pucker my lips when his finger trails over them. It's the best I can do. I don't ever want this moment to end. My hands are curled in front of me. He takes one, spreads my fingers, then places my palm against his bare chest. He's naked too.

"Feel how nervous I am?"

His heart is pounding away. I lift my eyes from his smattering of chest hair over nicely rounded pecs, and meet his baby blues. He's nervous?

"I don't want you to think this is some passing fling. Jeff and Ballz and I had a chance to talk. You're our forever."

How can he know that? How can any of them?

He brushes his fingers over my forehead. "Don't worry. We'll take care of you. Let us show you how good we are together."

I nod, caught in the fantasy that this must be a dream.

Jeff carries me to the blanket, sets me down gently, and trails his hands away slowly, letting his fingertips hang on for the very last touch before he steps away for a drink. He surprises me by extending it to me and helping me raise on my elbows to take a sip.

The crisp, refreshing beverage helps pull me back to the moment.

Adrian commences kissing his way up my legs, over my hip bones and stomach, then captures my breast in his mouth.

My nipple is so sensitive, I startle when he flicks it with his tongue. The sudden movement bumps the flute in Jeff's hand, spilling it, but thankfully not breaking the glass.

"Oh no!" I start to get up, but Ballz scoots me out of the wet spot.

"The blanket's going to get a lot dirtier than that. We'll wash it."

Adrian spreads my thighs and settles his body over mine. The other two brothers lie on either side of me. Fingers mingle. Kisses come at me from all sides. And Adrian's tip presses into the wetness of my sex.

I bring my knees up, spreading my legs a little more to make room for him. He's thick and heavy over me. The musk of the three guys, all primed for sex, intoxicates me.

Adrian pushes inside, pausing while I catch my breath as I stretch around him. Each movement of his hips stimulates my clit. I'm gasping and moaning.

"Say you're ours," Adrian says between thrusts.

"I'm yours." Do I mean it? The words are out of my mouth before I can decide. I want to be theirs. And while I feel like this, I can't find a reason to object.

My core tightens unbearably. Will I implode if I don't climax soon? Ballz dry humps my leg from the side. Pre-cum slicks the movement of his shaft against me.

Jeff gets on his knees. "We're all going to come with you, My Love."

My eyes can't stay open, but as they flutter in my attempts to absorb the masculine perfection around me, I'm drooling over Jeff's meaty hand fisting his shaft.

"Submit to us, My Love."

Everything snowballs on me at once as the thrusting, their groans, and the scent of sex push my orgasm past the point of no return. Warmth fills my core as Adrian's entire body grows hard and he rears up with one hard thrust, growling with his release. Ballz's mouth falls slack beside my head; grunts parallel his release coating my side.

And Jeff, I wish I could focus. The intensity of his eyes staring down at me as cum splashes my face, the salty yumminess dripping into my mouth, and his hand resting on Adrian's shoulder, lock the moment in. I could get used to this.

They join me on the blanket, our heads near the Christmas tree, and we look up at it as we all come down from the high.

I may have fallen asleep for a moment.

Adrian stands, reaching a hand down. "Let me take you to the shower and clean you up."

"I'll put the blanket in the washer," Jeff says.

And Ballz heads to the kitchen to tidy up before joining us in the shower.

Cleaning up was just a lure to get me to the next place they intended to give me orgasms. I make a mental note that shower orgasms are extra swoony.

And when I beg for mercy, they help me dress and Adrian carries me to the couch, where I snuggle up on his lap with our brothers on either side.

Jeff trails a finger over my tattoo. "I remember when you were little and got mad at us for blowing the seeds off dandelions. Never thought I'd see the day when you embrace it."

Watching his finger, I decide to open up. "I hated all three of you for disturbing the delicate order nature created."

"But the saying, that's a cool way to think about it."

"Dad found me crying with the stem of a dandelion in my hands after one of you blew every single seed off of it. He talked to me about the seeds needing to scatter so they can bloom. And that whether I hand planted a seed or wind blew it, the flower would look the same. I tried to tidy up his lesson for the tattoo."

Jeff kisses my inked skin. "I love you, Cindy." The sincerity in his voice is soft and tender.

He sounds vulnerable, but before I can say anything, Ballz says, "I've never experienced anything like you. I love you. I love your little routines. I love how you carefully consider everything. Will you teach me?"

Then Adrian adds, "I definitely don't want to be left out of this one. I love you Cindy, like I've never loved anything else."

"Anything?" she asks.

"Well, you know I have loved hockey most of all."

"I just kind of thought you'd say any*one*."

"No one's ever topped hockey. I always felt alone, and now I have you. Move in with us. Travel with us. Let us take care of you."

What Ballz said is right. I have to consider everything. I need time to think about decisions. Do I need to think about this?

Eighteen

Adrian

The hesitation in Cindy's eyes catches me off guard as we profess our love for her. I've never felt so free, and yet being tied to one woman is what's going to give me that freedom. How can we convince her that this is right—life is better with her? We'd do anything to make her happy.

Did I fall prey to the guy mentality that sex makes everything okay? It's hard to imagine Cindy not feeling the connection.

We're snuggled on the couch, and she's sitting on my lap. Jeff wanted to be the one to hold her, but I needed that bond. I rub a hand on her shoulder, which is drawn up—the effects of her orgasms wearing off way too fast. "What can I do to relieve this tension?"

"I don't know. Everything is so... It's hard to explain."

Ballz asks, "Are we moving too fast? We tend to do that—think fast, act fast—it's why we're good at hockey. But we'll slow down for you."

He has a good point. Dialing things back a notch, I ask, "First things first. Relationships take work and that's what we're doing now, putting in the work to make you happy. So, in a magical world where everything is easy, is that something you'd want?"

She smiles and nods. "But this isn't magical—well, the sex is, but outside of that, it's the real world, with real problems."

"What's your biggest concern?" I hold her tighter.

"I love my accounting job and my friends and my routines. How would they fit into life with the three of you?"

I resist making a joke about getting bested by her work. It hurts too much to think that even with the three of us, we're not enough for her.

"Your routines...we can make that happen, find ways to replicate them anywhere. And you don't have to work."

"I enjoy my job, but I'd have to abandon it for weeks on end when you're travelling, or be home without you."

Jeff says, "Unless we quit the team."

"No, you can't quit. I know how much you love hockey."

"We could take a year off." I pivot from Jeff's extreme idea. He and Ballz agree, but not Cindy.

"I won't allow you to give up something you've worked your whole life for. Besides, there's not enough time for all the Tai chi or Qigong you'd need, if you couldn't hip check anyone."

"You're wise beyond your years, My Love."

"I've got it," Ballz says.

"Really? Mister act first, think second, has a plan?" Jeff teases him.

"I'm as shocked as you. What do you think about this? There are three of us. We could rotate so that one of us stays home each time the team travels. You'd never be alone, and it would give each of us individual time with you."

"Your coach would never allow that."

"If he's faced with losing all three of us, he'll have to negotiate. But if we make it to the playoffs, we all might have to go."

"If you make it to the playoffs, I'll be right there by your side." Her optimistic tone gives me hope.

Ballz says, "I'd prefer playoffs, but if taking a year off will prove our point, I'm in. Whatever makes it work so we can be here for Cindy."

"I'll present it to him," Jeff says.

Teamwork just might pull this off. "That's fine. You're skilled with the 'take it or leave it' mentality." It's the negotiations that sometimes lead to punches. That won't happen with Coach.

Jeff hops up, and in seconds, he has Coach on the phone as he strides out of the room.

It seems like no time at all has passed when Jeff comes back but his expression is unreadable.

"That was quick. Did he go for it, or fire us all?" I ask.

"He's pissed as hell. But I explained our need to keep our situation with our stepsister on the down-low for now, until we make this official and marry you." Jeff kneels in front of us and takes Cindy's hand. Is he going to—?

The door clicks open. My head whips to the grandfather clock in confusion as I process that our parents are home. Where did the time go?

Holding my little sister in my lap isn't as acceptable as it used to be. She's fidgeting to get away, but I hold her close

"What the hell is going on?" Dad says.

I whisper to Cindy, "This was going to happen sooner or later. Do you trust us?"

"Yes." Her barely audible answer is a monumental step toward having a relationship.

I nod at my brothers. We instinctively, simultaneously say, "All for one." It's something we do before games, a ritual about solidarity. And this game has the biggest stakes ever.

Jeff stands. As usual, he'll handle the conversation.

Dad tips his head up, sniffs the air, and his expression shifts from confusion to horror.

"It smells like a goddamn brothel in here."

Mom steps inside behind him and pinches her nose. "Whoa!"

Nineteen

Jeff

"There's something we need to tell you." I move to the end of the couch so Cindy won't be caught in the middle.

Then it occurs to me, she actually hasn't said she loves us. Fuck. I hope Cindy doesn't dash. That'd be my classic way of fucking things up, always taking control. I feel so deeply in my soul that this is right, I haven't even processed that she might not go for it.

My brain risks fizzling out as I glance at Cindy. "Ready to be on our team?"

She smiles nervously, glancing toward our parents. Her tiny nod has me wanting to whisk her away to fuck her, but first things first.

"You might want to sit down." I motion to the bar stools behind Mom and Dad. She scoots closer to Dad and puts her hands around his arm.

"What is it, dear?"

"We're in love with Cindy and the four of us are in a relationship. We wanted to tell you first. We hope we have your support."

Mom steps closer and points at the sofa. "Did you..." Her other hand covers her mouth. "On the sofa? Oh no." She runs around the bar into the kitchen and opens the cabinet under the sink. When she stands, she extends an arm overhead, and is waving a can of air freshener.

"Sorry, Mom. We'll be more careful in the future. The sofa's clean, though," Adrian says.

The hiss of the spray falters. She shakes the can. Another sputtering hiss. Empty. She glances around. "If the sofa's clean, where's the blanket? And why is the washing machine..."

Dad looks like he's about to vomit. "This isn't right. That's my blanket. Take it home with you. Burn it. I'm never—"

"Dad, stop." Cindy pops up from the couch, pointing to the dandelion tattoo. "The saying you gave me, '*The flower is no less beautiful if the seed is planted by the wind*', I'm finally starting to get it. You helped me see that being flexible can show me opportunities I would have missed."

"That's not..." Dad coughs and sputters before finishing his statement. "I meant for it to help with...smaller things."

"She's right, dear. This is a huge step, and imagine how supported she'll be by her three brothers."

"Have you lost your mind?"

"I'm hearing a lot of couples, or whatever you call group things, are working out these days. Even with stepsiblings. It's kind of cozy," Mom says.

Dad's having trouble with flexibility now. "But you're my little girl, and they're..."

Mom gets control. "Ground rules will help. Your father and I need our space. The only sex happening under this roof will be between him and me."

Ballz busts out laughing. "I think we're all damaged now, Mom."

"Good, then you understand my point. When you're under this roof, you're our children." She spins on her heels, throws the spray can out, and opens the pantry.

"I can live with that," I say, and everyone except Dad nods in agreement.

Mom steps out of the pantry, her arms full of baking supplies. "In lieu of air freshener, and in light of us all being together, let's go ahead with our Christmas sugarplum tradition."

Saying no to Mom isn't an option. My much-needed celebration with Cindy for announcing our relationship will have to wait. Blue balls commence.

"I'd love that," Cindy says with a huge smile. Then quietly, only to my brothers and me, she says, "I love you, all of you."

Damn her. I might drown in the backlog of cum my balls are prepping for her. It's too much. I grab her hand as she passes, and I try to sneak her away.

A firm hand lands on my shoulder. Dad strength. Dammit, how can he seem so old and be so strong? Worry races through me like I'm a teenager again, sneaking off to have sex, only this time it's more awkward than I ever imagined.

"If you want me to personally castrate you, keep right on going. Otherwise, get back in the kitchen and obey your mother."

Ballz and Adrian lose it. The whole room fills with laughter. I let Dad take Cindy's hand from me, and I sulk to the kitchen behind them. Mom smacks my shoulder with a wooden spoon, which decidedly stings, then we fall into our holiday tradition.

We all know our way around the kitchen, gathering the rest of the ingredients, getting the bowls and measuring scoops out.

It's a genuinely happy family moment. Most importantly to me, Cindy is happy as she meticulously measures each item. That's always been her role.

Conversation, laughter, memories, and before long, the scent of sweet sugarplums fills the air.

As usual, Adrian is the one to violate the sanctity of good, clean fun. He has two rolled sugarplums in his hand, and extends them to Balthazar. "Want to lick my balls?"

Everyone goes silent. I keep an eye on Dad because I think he's going to pass out. The timer dings and Mom silences it with one hand while she grabs a wooden spoon with the other.

Adrian pulls his arm back slowly, as if that will keep her from noticing.

She swats him on the shoulder then smiles. "You boys and your dirty jokes. At least you're not pretending that they're poop balls this year."

Epilogue

Cindy

"I don't think it's going to fit," Aurora says, trying to fasten the tiny buttons that run up the back of my wedding dress.

"It has to."

I'm sucking my tummy in as much as possible, but it increases my nausea. I'm on thin ice anyway with how long my anti-nausea medicine will last. A serious drawback to having a wedding early in a pregnancy.

I'm disheartened when Aurora tugs on the bodice then says, "You're breathing for five. We can't have you passing out. Let me try something else."

Her hands move up my back and start buttoning at the top. "Okay, we might have to leave a few around your waist undone, but with your veil, no one will notice."

I glance at my tattoo. This is one of those times I really need the reminder. *The flower is no less beautiful if the seed is planted by the wind.* I smile at Aurora in the mirror. "The wedding is no less perfect if the buttons aren't fastened all the way."

"You know your brothers are just going to rip the dress off of you anyway. This way there will be a few less buttons rolling around."

"I'm going to be the one rolling around soon. I can't believe they knocked me up with quadruplets."

"I thought I had it bad with twins. I can't believe how fast your belly's growing. We put the wedding together in no time and you're already showing."

"When we get together to hang out, it's going to look like we run a daycare."

"Except the kids will be our own." She steps away from me and pulls the veil over my back.

"Promise it doesn't look weird?"

"You're beautiful. And if a few buttons are the biggest thing that goes wrong today, then you've practically pulled off the perfect wedding."

The perfect wedding. Yes. In my mind, that's what I *need*. I don't like that something's already gone wrong.

The Justice of the Peace has been warned not to do any improvisation, just read exactly what we gave him, and do everything in exactly the prescribed order.

Aurora guides me to our staging area, where I'm hidden from the guests. She's by my side until her music cue sends her away, arm-in-arm with one of the dashing groomsmen.

My Dad smiles warmly and steps close when we're the only two left. His voice is low. "The flower is no less beautiful if the seed is planted by the wind. It turns out, I had a lot to learn about being flexible too. Thank you for teaching me."

My hand clutches his forearm, and he pats it gently when the Wedding March starts.

"That's our cue," he says.

Everyone stands as I come into view. I'm met with smiles from more friends and family than I expected would be happy to celebrate our unusual marriage. Everything's going as planned. My vows are memorized. Jeff, Adrian, and Ballz, look absolutely stunning in their custom tuxes. Nothing in stock fit their broad, muscular shoulders and trim waists.

But the smiles that light up their faces when they see me is the most heart-warming thing I've ever experienced.

Or wait. Maybe that's heartburn. My father lifts my veil, takes his seat, and the vows start. Now I can't tell if I'm having morning sickness or regular wedding nerves. Or both.

Nausea builds inside of me. I had the wedding planner put a floral display next to me, and an empty bucket behind it, just in case.

I glance down. It's in place. I let my gaze linger on the gorgeous gardenias, lilies, and roses—traditional beauty, but my heart is full when I spy the dandelions sprinkled through the arrangement.

Jeff begins his vows. I meet his gaze, take a deep breath, and my stomach settles a little.

But as I exhale, I realize my body fooled me. It's all happening too fast. I can't get my bouquet out of my hands. No bucket, no humility, no restraint.

Jeff is directly in my line of fire as the full force of four babies expels the dry bagel, banana, and medicine I'd counted on holding me through the ceremony.

My guys circle around me, Ballz getting the bucket to my face about a gallon of vomit too late.

Mom rushes forward with a tissue. "Oh dear."

I consider the understatement as Jeff takes my bouquet, more worried more about me than his tux. Have I ruined everything? My big day will be memorable for all the wrong reasons. Somehow, I leaned forward enough not to get vomit on my mermaid-style dress.

Adrian steps forward, takes the soiled tissue from me, and offer his pocket square to wipe my hands. "You never really liked being the center of attention. And Jeff's going to need to take his pants off. Would it be preferable to you for us to have everyone move on to the reception while we finish up privately?"

"That might be best."

Aurora offers a glass of water and nudges Ballz to keep the bucket handy. "Maybe just swish and spit."

Adrian announces to the guests, "I can assure you that all is well, but we're going to finish the ceremony privately. Would you please head to the reception hall where we'll meet you shortly."

Jeff strips his shoes, socks, and pants off, without a care in the world that we're not entirely alone yet. "So, where were we?"

"You were reciting your vows." I grimace.

"And they made her barf. Ballz harasses Jeff.

My time is limited before I'm sick again, so I regroup them. "I thought your vows were beautiful..." Then I decide to run with the fun. "But you got a little too sappy and grossed out the kids."

Ballz takes my hands. "Tell them to suck it up, Baby, because here I go." His expression turns serious. "My beautiful dandelion. I fell in love with you and your love of order, thinking you were perfect just the way you were. Then you showed me that your beauty could grow exponentially by letting yourself blow free. Today, I vow to support you and my brothers and our children wherever the wind blows us, because there's nothing more gratifying than watching you bloom."

And we live happily ever after!

Would you like a little more **Sugarplums and Submission**?

You know the routine... If you'd like to read a bonus scene where Cindy tries to set rules on picking baby names, grab this BONUS SCENE by signing up for my newsletter.

https://SylvieHaas.com

Ribbons and Role Play

A Stepbrother Reverse Harem Romance

Sylvie Haas

Blurb

Running away from my own wedding is bound to irritate everyone involved, but for once, I'm sticking up for myself.

But where to run?

On a wild hair, I head straight to the Christmas Cherry Auction.

What I don't realize is that my motorcycle club stepbrothers aren't far behind!

How much family strife am I willing to cause?

If you love dirty-talking men who know how to please their stepsister, don't miss this year's Christmas Cherry Auction!

One

Knight

The uptight, pompous prick standing at the front of the church has no idea I'm about to risk everything to ruin his day.

Neither does my little stepsister he's about to marry.

And neither does his friend, my stepdad, who's sitting to my immediate left.

Holding the jacket of my tux open, I retrieve the piece of paper that changed my path. I haven't even told my brothers about my plan—because it wasn't exactly a plan. It was a wild idea presented to me as a fortune in a cookie.

I roll my shoulders, trying to get comfortable in the required attire. My two brothers and I are more comfortable straddling a Harley than perching in a pew.

Angling my head over my shoulder to stretch my neck, I wonder if this is the wedding Wendy always dreamed of or did our parents decide. Giant, identical bundles of flowers at the end of each pew, a red carpet, and a string quartet are more of my parents' signature.

The quartet shifts to something less...classic. An instrumental version of a pop song, possibly. At least it's from this century.

Everyone shifts their attention to the back of the room. The first bridesmaid and groomsman couple start their slow walk to the front. He's as old and stuffy as the groom, who's as old as our dad. She's young and vibrant, with streaks of blue in her hair. I recognize her as one of Wendy's roller derby teammates. That blue hair is the first sign Wendy has anything to do with this formal wedding.

The whole thing—minus the blue hair—reeks of our stepdad. Always pompous and posturing. If he didn't make my mom immensely happy, I wouldn't give him the time of day.

I rub my thumb over the long, rectangular fortune and exhale hard. I'll be judged for choosing now to stand up for my stepsister. But wrecking her wedding will be minor compared to what else I want to do.

The fucker standing at the front of the church started dating her when she was seventeen and proposed to her on her eighteenth birthday. Something doesn't add up.

Not just because my sister makes my cock hard. Not just because she's marrying someone I don't trust. And not just because a tiny piece of paper convinced me to say what I've kept secret.

It's getting hot. I glance at my fist that's concealing the piece of paper. If I sweat enough to dissolve the fortune, should I forever hold my peace? I run a finger around my collar.

The second bridesmaid and groomsman enter. Add one more stuffy old dude to the room. And a pin-up girl. I recognize her from the roller derby team, too.

Wendy's a free spirit, full of zest and zeal—and other words I only think of in relation to her. Why would she commit to a man who looks like he ran out of wild oats before she was even born?

Relaxing my fingers slightly, I confirm the ink remains on the paper: *Claim your destiny with your heart, and the important things will fall into place.*

Why do these things have to be so vague?

Our stepdad stands and crosses in front of me to the side of the church. I lean forward, looking past my brothers. One of the bridesmaids has signaled Dad over. Why isn't she in back with Wendy? Her expression indicates she got shit duty to tell him that some piece of minutia didn't go as planned.

Instead of having a bridezilla at this wedding, the Father Of the Bride is the one to watch for. Would that make him FOBzilla?

The sternness in Dad's expression crushes the humor. My brother, Nova, is closest. His head whips toward us, his face has gone white, and he instantly leans his mouth to Axel's ear.

Axel quickly turns to me and whispers, "Wendy ran."

Did she just save me from having to wreck her wedding? That's not right. I should be saving her. But Nova...this hits him hard. He never speaks of it, but he was jilted years ago, and had another serious relationship go south before that.

We lean close to one another. "What do you mean, *ran*?"

"From what the chick said, Wendy signaled for the ceremony to start, then rushed back into the changing room. The procession continued, but this chick was last, so she went to check on Wendy, who was tearing off her dress. She said not to follow her, then left."

"Naked?" My cock is shamelessly hard.

"That's what you're focusing on?" Axel, our youngest brother, says.

We all look at Mr. Cooper as he returns to his seat next to me.

"We have a problem. Come with me." He stands, faces the attendees, and with complete stoicism says, "Please remain seated."

He ushers us and our mom down a side hallway. His expression has shifted from stoic to worried. The man actually cares that his daughter freaked out. He might be human after all. "One of the bridesmaids just informed me that Wendy took off."

Dad's barely finished the statement when Nova says, "We'll look for her. We can get the whole motorcycle club to help." He's regained color and jumps into action to smooth things out. How far down did he shove the pain of his two failed relationships?

Mentioning the MC around Mr. Cooper is generally a bad idea. But for once, Dad looks relieved.

"Do it. She doesn't realize what's good for her."

"Good for her?" Axel asks.

"I worked hard to make this wedding happen. We only have until Christmas to lock down the marriage, and she runs out? She's too young to know what's good for her, for her future, for the legacy I'm building."

The wedding is a business deal? Everything clicks into place. Axel's wheels are turning and Nova mutters, "Fuck." He's always stepping in to keep the peace because he avoids conflict like the plague. Will this new information change his desire to help? We've never talked about our stepsister in anything but family terms. Not as a commodity. And definitely not as a sexual entity—which is the second bomb that will be dropped today.

I have no doubt what needs to be done. I extend my hand to assure Dad that we'll find our sister, and the paper I'm holding catches his attention. He reaches for it. Shit.

It's too private to let anyone see, even though they wouldn't understand. Yanking my hand away, a ripping sound lets me know I wasn't fast enough. Half of the fortune is in his hands.

I snatch it from him too late.

"Was that from a fortune cookie? Is that where you get your advice on *destiny*?"

I shove the pieces into my jacket pocket as he shakes his head. My brothers look at me curiously.

Our stepdad continues, "Don't look for answers on a whimsical piece of paper. Try manning up and doing the hard things."

Exactly what I was about to do, but that's irrelevant now. "We'll find Wendy, Sir."

What I don't tell him is that I have no intention of bringing her back to this business deal. I can't imagine a worse life for Wendy than to be confined by a loveless marriage. She's a beautiful soul, a creative spirit, and I'll make sure she knows that when I find her.

Axel rushes ahead and confirms that Wendy's car is gone. It had been suspicious that she insisted on driving herself to the wedding. My brothers and I head outside while Dad handles the guests.

Nova says, "I texted the MC."

We make a game plan, fire up our bikes, and roll out. Thanks to technology, we stay updated on any texts about Wendy without having to stop and check our phones.

Mom and Dad had been irritated that Wendy wanted our father seated when the ceremony started instead of him walking her down the aisle. I'd attributed it to my spirited, yet slightly stubborn sister doing things their own way. Now I wonder if it was part of her exit plan.

It doesn't take long for a message to come through that one of our MC brothers spotted Wendy's car. What I'm not prepared for is that she pulled into the Aubergine Affair, a sex club that's hosting the Christmas Cherry Auction tonight. I heard about last year's auction. All of the women ended up in reverse harems.

My heart races. If she plans to auction herself, she better be prepared for me to win.

My brothers and I get there in record time, arriving one right after another.

As we're striding toward the door, I fill them in. "I'm going to buy her. I'm going to fuck her. I'll explain later."

Axel clenches his fist. "I'm in. I'll buy her with you."

Before I can clarify if he also wants the other half of what I proposed, Nova looks at us as if we've lost our minds. "Joking?"

I bark out, "Nope."

Axel answers quickly. "Me either."

"That's not right. Dad will be pissed."

We're almost to the door. "Yep, but I'm claiming my destiny tonight."

"Well...fuck." Nova shakes his head. "Destiny it is."

Are they seriously in this with me?

Two

Wendy

My virginity is not a commodity to be traded between men. My pulse pounds in my ears as I storm into the sex club, ask that I be added to the program, and join the other three ladies.

Bianca, Aurora, and Cindy are more than welcoming, even giving me a Christmas dress that will allow me to look as festive as they do—much better than my white sweats with 'BRIDE' written in silver down one leg. Aurora dusts me with body glitter. I love her for that, and I love that they don't ask too many questions.

I don't even have answers for myself. Like how did my father know I was still a virgin? And did he really think that it was appropriate to pledge my virginity as part of a business deal? If I hadn't overheard their conversation an hour before the wedding, I would have played the part of a fool—blindly believing a gazillionaire would be interested in me.

Ick.

A shiver runs up my spine…and back down…a couple of times. So creepy to hear that I was part of a contract negotiation. Scratch that. *I* wasn't the important item—the tightness of my vagina was up for sale. That's not okay. And that's way understating things.

The auction proceeds chaotically, but I barely register any of it.

I have one mission tonight—prove that virginity isn't a big deal. Sex isn't a big deal. The only reason I haven't had sex is that the moment, or rather the guy, never seemed right. I didn't want to have a crappy get-it-over-with first time.

Based on last year's auction, this is the perfect place to get my cherry popped while not worrying that I'll end up with a crappy memory instead of orgasms.

I don't want to admit that this plan has niggled in my brain for days, and I definitely don't want to admit that the glimmer of it started weeks ago.

In retrospect it all makes sense—the little comments and awkward moments that started as soon as I accepted his marriage proposal three months ago. A switch flipped. Hints that he thought he owned me morphed from fun to troublesome.

When the bridesmaids lined up, and the music shifted to one of the only choices I got to make in my own wedding, fear of my future finally screamed loud enough for me to trust myself.

Ironically, the only thing scarier than the life my father had set out for me, is not having his support and his certainty. I've lived a precious life because of the legacy he's creating.

But I didn't understand I had to pay for it. I can't imagine how furious he is.

A ruckus disrupts the auction and a faint rumble of motorcycles filters backstage. Cindy and I sort out that Aurora's brothers are demanding she go with them. But my brothers enter, and I might have a bigger problem.

Are they going to drag me back to my wedding before I have a chance to complete my mission? They don't like my father but they respect him. They would follow his orders to save the day.

The world is a blur as I step onto the stage. I'm aware that all of the other women were bought by their stepbrothers. If they get to live in a fantasy world, is it too much to ask that I live there too?

All of the hope that's ever existed wells in my heart when the bidding starts. My brothers bid on me as a group. Knight is the one raising the paddle. The look of sheer determination on his face and the glare he gives anyone else who bids on me, leave me uncertain as to his motivation.

Nova's expression is softer as always. It's through the ease on his face that I sense they're not going to take me back to the wedding.

And Axel? He would have come backstage and told me we had to leave. He doesn't tolerate nonsense.

But if they're not here to take me back, why are they here?

The auctioneer seems to be calling for a million dollars and other paddles continue lifting into the air. Knight's lifting motion grows firmer each time. His scowl deeper.

Are they bidding to protect me, or... I almost hate to let Fantasy Wendy run wild...bidding to *win* me.

Is it foolish to ask my stepbrothers to claim my virginity?

"Two million," Knight growls. I've never heard him like that. Never seen the dark possessiveness as he looks to the stage. Never wanted him so badly, and that says a lot because Fantasy Wendy has a lot of fun with her brothers and a vibrator.

The auctioneer stops.

Knight continues, "I'm not about to let any of you assholes get your hands on my des—" His words cut off then he resumes. "my stepsister."

The grumbling amongst the attendees rattles around incomprehensibly in my head. It's the statement from the auctioneer that makes it through. "Two million! Going...going...sold!"

I make a mad dash off stage and switch back into my clothes so nothing happens to Aurora's dress. I already ruined one dress today. And if I have to face my father, I'd rather not have to explain where I've been.

"Come with me." Knight is storming toward me when I step back onto the stage.

With clarity, I say, "I'm not going back to the wedding."

"I'm not taking you back to the wedding."

"I came here for one reason. I have to have sex tonight. I have to take away Dad's power to use me like property."

"What the fuck?" Knight says as our brothers catch up to him.

"My virginity was part of a business deal."

They all look shocked, but Knight sets a hand on my shoulder. The contact is comforting and seductive. His jaw clenches. "I didn't know it was a business deal until after you left. And I didn't know—"

"No reason you would know about my sex life. And I didn't know about the business deal until right before the wedding."

"Your goal is to have sex tonight?" Knight's voice catches.

"Yes," I say more firmly than I feel.

He turns to the people who haven't left yet. "Get out of here unless you want to see me fuck my stepsister."

Fantasy Wendy isn't going to have to do all of the work tonight, but I'm not sure a public announcement is the right approach. Father will be humiliated if his children have sex. Serves him right.

Three

Wendy

Knight trails his fingers down my braid. "It was risky of you to do this."

The intimate gesture is prolonged as he toys with the white ribbon securing the bottom.

I want to say the right things to ensure Knight will help me. Can he see my reasoning? "Auctioning myself for sex didn't seem so bad in comparison to actually being sold. One night, four hours, however you want to look at it."

His hand shifts and he tugs my braid, tipping my face up. His deep blue eyes storm with thoughts. "You have no idea who could have bought you."

"Then I guess I got lucky."

Nova steps close. "I'm sorry Dad treated you like that. I would've helped sooner if I'd known. Promise me you won't ever pull a stunt like this again. Come to us if you have a problem."

"If you help me tonight, I won't have this problem again." I suspect Knight is most likely to be willing to have sex with me, but Fantasy Wendy leaves our options open.

Nova's jaw strains. Axel joins us but remains caught in his head. Their combined body heat and musky scents do a number on me.

I take advantage of the pause. "I've thought this out. Let's keep it impersonal, just to get the job done. I won't even take my shirt off."

"Oh, no, Baby Doll, that's not how this works."

I hold a finger up. "Are you missing the point? I'm not having men dictate my life. You heard my offer, take it or leave it."

Which is completely contrary to my body's reaction to the nickname.

Knight lets his hand trail from my braid to my shoulder, down my back, and I'm ridiculously swoony at the sensation of his strong hand guiding me from behind. "Get in this room."

"We should go home."

"We're doing it right here. Right now. You want to prove that your virginity is gone. You're going to need witnesses."

"But..."

"No buts. I plan on giving you exactly what you want; proof that you've had sex." He has a point. Not everyone was deterred by his statement that he was about to fuck his stepsister. Several people have gathered around.

Inside the dimly lit room, I give one last thought to closing the curtains in front of the glass wall to block the view for those still present. Fantasy Wendy turns my attention to a leather padded bench that's about waist height. I lean over the bench, unsure what the ideal height would be.

Whatever it is, the warmth of Knight's hand caressing my clothed ass makes this height perfect. My body betrays me with a shudder. His other hand reaches up, tugs on the ribbon in my hair again, and forces my head to the side.

Pull harder. Fantasy Wendy makes a note. *Hair pulling. Check. Love it.*

Nova steps beside me. "Are you sure you want it like this?"

"Yes." I gulp down my answer.

Knight spins me to face him. His thick fingers tuck into the waistband of my white sweatpants. The glittery 'BRIDE' label I'd been so eager to earn might as well have spelled out 'PROPERTY'. How will I ever trust a man again? How will I trust myself?

He kneels, slowly and reverently. The lowering of my sweatpants over my hips removes the once-exciting label, revealing my white satin panties.

Knight abandons my sweats just above my knees. Awkward.

He's staring. Even more awkward. Should I ask one of my other brothers to do the deed?

Knight's hands wrap around my hips, stopping words from being able to leave my mouth. His firm, intimate grip has

Fantasy Wendy screaming from the cage I've locked her in. *Let us out. Let us have a chance at reality.*

Yeah...no. I'm not stupid. This is a transaction. We'll have sex. I'll no longer be a virgin. And by the grace of escaping my wedding, I belong to no one but myself.

Fantasy Wendy objects. I give her a lollipop and tell her to sit quietly in her cage. Her obedience is vital for me to maintain my façade of indifference. Getting attached to a man, or men, is not tonight's plan. Not a plan I can ever have with my stepbrothers. They are strictly fantasy fodder.

Knight slides one thumb forward, stroking the front of my panties, and pauses on the two tiny rings held by a bow.

Guys are so out of touch with pretty things. He leans forward, pausing an inch in front of my sex. I take in a breath since I seem to have stopped breathing.

Why the staring? Why aren't we having sex? Why does the warmth of his breath send pulses of excitement through me? Can warm breaths actually melt my legs? I'm on the verge of not being able to support—

He closes the gap. He bites the bow and rings. My panties are caught in his mouth as he yanks his head back and to the side.

A ripping sound is followed by the slap of my panties back into me. I'm staring now as he spits the tiny jewelry onto the floor. The once-decorative white ribbon and miniature gold bands clink as they hit the dark marble then skid another few inches.

He growls before looking up at me. "That prick doesn't deserve to be anywhere near you."

"I know." I'm not sure the words exit my mouth.

"This isn't the way your first time should be."

Fantasy Wendy clanks her lollipop over the bars of her imprisonment like a felon. Why am I having to dig so deep to keep my façade in place? I take control.

Fantasy Wendy, your judgment can't be trusted. You believed a man thirty years older than you could be our true love. That he could actually be interested in an eighteen-year-old roller derby, graphic artist. Our heart is on lockdown until further notice.

Thanks to my imagination, I shove the lollipop back into her mouth and divert my eyes from Knight kneeling in front of me. Shifting my attention across my selection of stepbrothers, I say, "If you're not up for it, I'll find someone who is. But never fear, I'll make good on the four hours of holiday help you won in the auction."

I'm so busy applauding myself, I don't register what's happening until it's over. Knight grabbed my panties on both sides and ripped them from my body.

Fantasy Wendy drops her lollipop. I'm pretty sure she's drooling, but Knight has my attention.

"Fuck the auction, then fuck me." His voice is low and possessive. He stands and unzips his pants. I hand Fantasy Wendy her lollipop so she has something to suck on. It's not like I haven't seen a penis before. I just haven't seen one that makes me want to drop to my knees while simultaneously riding it. Sure, it's physically impossible, but my eyes flit to Axel and Nova. We could improvise.

What is wrong with me? And why is my brother letting me stare when I return my eyes to him? Nope. This isn't a four-hour porn session. I just need to lose my freaking virginity. Tab A. Slot B. Let's go.

I turn around, bending over the bench. His tip prodding at my sopping wet entrance might as well be a cattle prod. Electricity zings through my entire body. His pressure is enough to shove my body forward into the bench, but not enough to enter me.

My core knots with an insane intensity. Way better than my vibrator.

I shove my hips back, forcing his tip into me a tiny bit. My lips strain and stretch around him. The sharp sting is eclipsed by his groans and the pain of his fingers digging into my hips. The pain is nothing worse than I put up with in roller derby, and the good parts are way better.

I can't believe it. I'm having sex for the first time. I'm officially not a virgin. I want to have a party. I want to scream it in my father's face—to the world, that virginity is a stupid way to gauge a woman's worth, but all I can think about is how much I need the rest of Knight's cock inside of me.

I use the bench for leverage as Knight pumps slow and hard behind me. One of his hands returns to my hair, fisting a braid, pulling my head back. My entire body is alive. I wish I'd taken my clothes off. My nipples are beaded so hard, I can feel them dragging across the bench through my bra and shirt. I want to feel his entire body the way I feel his cock. I want to slide over him, our skin slick with perspiration.

I *need* this to end as quickly as possible. That's going to be easy. I'm plunging wickedly fast toward the abyss of release. The moment I lose control, a rhythmic pulsing of my sex tightens and relaxes around his shaft. His hand slides from my hair onto my shoulder, and he drives himself into me, thrusting hard and fast.

The throbbing of his cock matches the growls pouring from him, and is followed by the warmth of his release streaming down my legs, then the warmth of his body leaning over me. I could get used to this.

No! Fantasy Wendy, get back in your cage.

His still-hard cock makes it hard for me to think rationally. I need to end this. We're not here to cuddle. Movement catches my attention and helps a few brain cells fire up. I'd forgotten all about the people watching.

One man has his arms wrapped around a woman. His fingers are tucked between her legs, and based on her mouth hanging open... Oh my gosh! I'm watching her orgasm. It gets my insides ready to go again.

Shoot. This isn't going right. I need to get out of here before I jump all of my brothers.

"Thank you." I find the words tumbling from my lips as his cock twitches inside of me. "Mission accomplished."

Normally my awkwardness would distract the people around me, give me a chance to escape, but Knight wraps his arms around my waist, keeping his lips at my ear.

"Don't call this a mission and don't call it accomplished."

"Well, it is. I needed to have sex."

"And you can keep having it." Why does his low voice make me warm inside?

"No need. We've already overachieved. Made sure there were witnesses."

He slides his cock from me and Nova offers his pocket square. It's like using a tissue to clean a gallon of spilled milk, but I try.

"Wendy, I don't want this to end."

My name on Knight's lips makes the moment oddly personal.

"It has to, Knight. You're my brother."

"Your *step*brother."

Four

Wendy

None of us knew how to handle what happened last night. Under the 'mission accomplished' pretense, I went home. Thankfully, I'd moved out of my dad's house, but I paid for my little house with his money.

I would take comfort in having a job, but it's at my dad's company. The family that once offered me security has a stranglehold on my life.

Without a honeymoon to rush off to and no desire to use my ticket in case my supposed-to-be husband decides to use his, I go to morning roller derby practice. At the very least I need to field the questions my bridesmaids will have about the wedding.

I only turned my phone on to let the team know I was coming. In one fell swoop, I dismissed all of the messages that piled up overnight. I texted Mom and Dad, asking them to take a few days to consider my position, and told them I'd be in touch. Then I blocked them.

I arrive at the skate rink and my phone rings. I turn the volume down.

Barely inside the door, Nikki, the bridesmaid I'd given the terrible task of notifying my father, catches me. "Hey, are you all right, Wendy?"

"I'm sorry I bailed. I had to escape."

I let my gear bag thunk on the ground and sit on the long wooden bench. I toss my phone in my bag, ignoring it vibrating. She joins me in lacing our skates.

"What happened?" Nikki asks. She glances toward my buzzing bag and I wave it off.

It's good that she doesn't know since she works at my dad's company. It means the rumor mill hasn't explained that I let my stepbrother claim my virginity in front of people at the sex club. Supposedly they take privacy breaches very seriously, but we all know what money can do.

"I was being married off as part of a business deal. Every time he said *I love you,* he meant he loved money and power. I was just the tool to secure it."

"No shit." Nikki's fingers stop moving, leaving her laces dangling.

"Yeah. Part of the drawback to having an uber-powerful father— He thinks he can do things like that."

"That sucks," another teammate, Beatrix says from nearby.

"But you got out of it, right? You're not in an arranged marriage?" Nikki asks.

"For now." I stand and adjust my spandex shorts, avoiding explaining the whole virginity thing. "I just want to get my life back."

Nikki slaps me on the ass. "Yeah. Come on. Let's..."

My phone buzzes from inside my bag again.

"Maybe you should check that," Nikki says. "We'll start skating laps. No one expects you to be ready today."

I unzip my bag, curious who it could be. It's Knight: *We're not done with you*

I type back: *We?*

Like an idiot, after I send the message, I see that Axel and Nova are in the group chat. Not that there was much question.

Knight: *I'm not done with you*

Axel: *If you need to be extra sure you're not a virgin, I can help*

Me: *I'm pretty sure it's one-and-done*

I'm cracking up at this text exchange. No use reading anything into Nova not responding.

Knight: *We have an offer for you*

Me: ???

I'm fairly certain Fantasy Wendy got control of my fingers. There's no rational reason I would have a text exchange with my brothers about sex.

The phone rings and it's a number I don't know. I'm not in the mood to talk to a stranger but my finger accidentally taps the answer button instead of Reject Call. Gah! I cautiously lift it to my ear.

"Hello?"

"What the hell were you thinking, Wendy?" It's Dad. Not sure who's phone he's calling from. My heart sinks as I watch my friends skate around the track smiling, laughing, sling-shotting each other in practice moves.

"I said I'd be in touch in a few days. I'll be at work Monday." My head drops backward. Ugh!

"No need. If you can't respect the importance of this wedding, you're fired."

I snap upright. It's not that I don't respect authority. It's that I don't respect it blindly. But I know how Dad is. There's no point arguing. I'm no more than an employee who messed up a giant contract.

I offer a simple, "Okay," then drop my phone in my bag and push off to join my girlfriends in the rink. They're my found family. They accept me for who I am. I don't get treated special here. I'm not the girl with all the money and the legacy. I'm just a girl who's willing to skate and shove people around and have a really good time.

The thoughts in my mind settle as I skate warmup laps. My dad didn't mention sex, just the wedding. Surely he would've mentioned my public stepbrother fucking if he knew.

Fantasy Wendy tries to get me to leave the rink and text my brothers to see what their offer is. I almost agree.

But, it would be a family disaster. One screwup of a child is almost expected, but two...three...four. That's too much. I have to end this nonsense. I'll deal with that later, though, when I can take time to leave a clear message—this is my life and no one is going to control me.

The tough façade I put on last night needs to become my daily wear until this passes.

In truth, I want love and support. I want people that I can lean on. That's what the roller derby team is. Roller derby's also a great place to get my frustrations out and let my inner badass shine.

Five

Nova

"I don't disagree with you, Knight." I shove dishes in the dishwasher instead of joining my brothers in texting Wendy.

Knight slams a pile of papers onto the kitchen counter as he sort of straightens them. "Then what the fuck is it, Nova? You're either in or out. Don't confuse her. And don't fucking pout when Axel and I rope her in without you."

"I'm in. I want her."

"Then send a text. Let her know." Axel grabs an energy drink from the fridge then slams the door shut. "We have to be clear."

I can't get out of my head. None of us has had a successful relationship, thus why we're all single. But I've given my heart away twice—in the form of diamond engagement rings. Once, I made it to the altar. My fiancée didn't.

Knight adds, "Wendy's unsettled. She's young. Our father manipulated her. We can't have her thinking we'll do the same. We have to go in strong and show that we can take care of her."

"Yeah, I get it."

Axel pops the top on his can. "I can see you might be worried after...your past. Don't let it fuck this up."

I can't keep up with them. "She was a runaway bride yesterday. What makes you think she's ready to shack up with three guys she's never dated? Oh yeah, she hasn't dated them because they're her brothers. Do you hear how insane this is?" I shut the water off and sort a handful of silverware into the basket. "Besides, you had sex with her in front of us and other people. That's not the kind of relationship I want."

"How would you know? You haven't been with a woman in how long?" Knight's harsh about my situation. He's also wrong. I've never been *with* a woman, which makes this all the more awkward. If we were teens, sticking my dick in my stepsister would be one thing, but now?

My cock volunteers to give it a shot. I turn back to the sink so my brothers can't see. Wendy's everything I love in a woman. Feisty and free. But she's our stepsister. How does that not bug them?

"We're not talking about having sex in public all the time," Axel says. He's so private, it would shock me if he ever did, but they're acting crazy about Wendy. "This would be a thing between the four of us."

"Have you two shared before?" I ask them.

"No, but there's something special about Wendy. We'll give her a choice, but we'd rather share her than lose her to someone else. Axel would be a pillar of stability and practicality for her. I would be the one to make sure she's pampered. And you could round it out, always keep things peaceful for her? We each have something to offer beyond our cocks."

I'm seeing red as the conversation opens too many wounds. Turning the tables, I ask, "Keeping things peaceful? Did I do a good job of that when my fiancée got a boyfriend? Did I handle it smoothly when my bride *didn't* walk down the aisle? Is this the trifecta to round it out? Guarantee I'll face another..."

I turn the water on and run the garbage disposal to drown everything out. How can they think this will be anything more than having a fuck fest with our sister? Will any of us survive the adventure? Will we take our entire family down? Have we already?

Our phones buzz and there's a message from our stepdad. The man's a fucking mind reader.

Dad: *Cut off all communication with Wendy*

What the fuck? I read it then lift my gaze to see what my brothers think. Knight is rubbing his chest and Axel just stares aimlessly at his phone.

"How do you plan on dealing with him?" I ask.

Knight tosses his phone on the counter. "We can deal with *him* or we can deal with *her*. I know which side I'm taking."

"He'll find out you fucked her. How eager are you to make it worse?"

Axel explains, "We'll talk to her, see if she feels the same, but I can't see a future without her. I've never hated anything as much as attending her wedding. I couldn't understand why one of Dad's business partners would show so much interest in her then pounce on her with a marriage proposal at her eighteenth birthday party. I can't believe I didn't see it."

"I'm in the same boat as Axel, Nova. I can't explain how, but I know I'm supposed to be with her. What do we have to lose?"

"We're putting our future in the hands of an eighteen-year-old roller derby girl. Do you think we don't have something to lose?" My voice raises. I never knew my brothers felt this way about Wendy. They're saying all of the things I've denied. I swore I'd never fall in love again, but Wendy...she threatens my control daily.

Knight slams his fist on the counter hard enough that his phone bounces. "Quit saying you're in then making excuses."

They've got me cornered. My heart is too fragile to handle another breakup. But watching them be with her and not participating, would destroy my relationship with them.

"I need to talk to her." I don't have a fucking clue what I'm going to say, I just need to get away from this conversation.

Six

Wendy

After a physically exhausting derby practice, I fear being inside my house alone. I want a shoulder to cry on. I want to feel loved. I want to see my stepbrothers. Should I check with them to see what their offer is?

Gasoline meet fire.

I tried watching some self-help gurus last night and they suggested that sitting alone with yourself can be the hardest thing to do. It can also be the most cathartic if you use the time to get to know yourself rather than wallow in your pain. I can try. I can also update my resume and search for a job.

Turning onto my street, something isn't right. A car is in my driveway. It belongs to Knight.

The endorphin rush from practice fades as fear niggles through my mind. Were their texts a trick? Did Dad tell them to bring me in? That's exactly something he would do. Or are they here to break my resolve?

My futile effort at losing my virginity probably doesn't even matter to Dad's business partner. I refuse to acknowledge the man by his name, all he'll ever be is my dad's business partner. I've had enough time to realize the loyalty created by marrying our two families is the real selling point. My virginity was merely a bonus feature, or maybe an upsell. Would you like fries with that?

So basically, I fucked my brother at a sex club to keep someone from getting fries with their burger. Very mature.

I might as well get this over with. My brothers get out of their car when I turn into the driveway. I pull past them and park in the garage. It gives me a brief moment to fortify myself.

Heading to my door, I say, "We're done." I wave them off as they follow me. "I'm not interested in whatever you have to say."

"We think you might be," Knight says.

"Are you here because Dad told you to be?"

"On the contrary, he told us not to communicate with you."

"Then you should probably listen to him." Isn't that interesting? My dad and I agree on something.

Nova says, "We just want to talk. And since you backed out of your wedding and then auctioned yourself, we're guessing you need someone to talk to."

I direct my lie to Knight while fumbling the keys at the front door. "Are you going to get all needy? It was just sex."

Knight steps behind me, his fingers wrapping around my pigtail. He gives it a little tug, A shiver betrays how much I like it.

"Was it?" he whispers beside my head.

I drop my keys. Dammit. I turn sideways, bumping him, and thankfully he gives me space to pick them up. I focus on sliding the key in the lock, which ends up teasing my sex as I remember how good it felt when he moved inside of me.

"It was sex, mission accomplished remember?" I need to convince all of us.

"That's what you said, but your body told me something else. Let us in so we can talk."

There are so many penalty whistles and red flags going off in my mind, but my free spirit convinces me that inviting my brothers inside is nothing compared to running from my wedding.

If they were carting me back to dad, they would have shoved me in the car already.

What's the worst that can happen? I take Axel up on confirming that my virginity is gone?

They decline drinks and find places to sit in my living room, which is decidedly small with the three of them.

Knight goes first. "Would you consider a relationship with us?"

Whoa. Us? I play it cool while trying to figure them out. "I wouldn't know how to pick."

"We're not asking you to pick."

Nova wrings his hands and is the only one of them not staring at me.

Axel says, "We're sure you're fully aware of other sibling groups and unusual relationships in the area."

Words fail me because if I admit this, I'm admitting so much more, so many hidden desires. But getting out from under my father's thumb, only to submit to my three brothers? Is that what Real-World Wendy wants? Fantasy Wendy is banned from voting.

"I am aware of them. I just don't think it can work for us." I lower my eyes. "I already got fired for running away from my wedding. If we..." I motion between all of us. "If any of us become a thing, Dad will hold it against whoever's involved. I can't take you down on my sinking ship."

Knight says, "If you're on a sinking ship, I want to be by your side to save you from drowning."

I glance at Nova and Axel. They both nod.

Axel says, "We can pull this off. We can keep it between us at first, test drive the relationship before any reveal. We want to be on it with you."

The last thing I want is a relationship but Fantasy Wendy seems to have found a way to ball gag me when I open my mouth. I reach a compromise with her so I can do more than stand there gaping.

She allows me to ask, "How can you know you want a relationship with me?"

Knight says, "It's hard to explain."

"Yeah, like trying to explain flight to a snail."

Axel laughs. "You're hardly a snail, but I've always thought there was something special about you. I kept it quiet, a taboo thought, wanting my stepsister. But watching Knight fuck you, my future has never been so clear. I need you."

Need? Fantasy Wendy loves Axel's word choice. I attempt to dial it back. "You want to have sex with me."

"I didn't mean it like that. I feel a sense of freedom when I'm with you. I don't get as caught in my head when I have a conversation with you. It's easy to be with you. I've never felt that with anyone. I'm a better person with you."

Axel makes me feel safe. He thinks everything out. Is considerate of his words. And I make him better? No. "You're a good person period."

"I have to disagree. I want a life with you so I can be the man I was meant to be."

That's too much. "You want non-sexual things?"

"Yes."

"Name one."

Without missing a beat, he says, "I want you to come on the toy run with us. We go to a bunch of locations that have been collecting toys, stopping briefly at each one so kids can come out and look at our bikes. Then we ride off with our big red Santa bags. Back at the clubhouse, we sort, wrap, and organize the toys for delivery."

"But Dad said not to talk to me. If he finds out, he'll be furious."

"He can't be furious that you helped with a children's charity event. The media coverage is huge. Always a win for our family."

"A win for the children," I correct.

"Right, but all Dad sees is how good it is for the family image. He'll get the fuck over it."

No longer trusting my judgment, I can't tell if this is an example of poking the bear, or an effort to remind Dad we're still a family. "Okay, let's do it."

Seven

Knight

We pick Wendy up at her place. I called dibs to drive her from her house to our starting point, but I'm not sure I remember how to ride a motorcycle. The hints of white leggings in the gap between her black, thigh-high boots and her dress make it hard for me to think.

If she's cold on the ride, I'll have to rub on all of her cold parts. What the fuck? I sound like a perv.

Seating myself between her legs, my inability to think escalates. The pressure of her legs splayed around me, knowing that her pussy is open, has me ready to spin her into my lap so I can sink inside of her.

My innocent little stepsister has ruined me, even with the fast and impersonal sex she insisted on. It's killing me not to have sex with her again so I can take my time making love to her. More important than what I want though is what she wants...space.

She's had enough of men negotiating her pussy lately. My stomach turns every time I think of our father writing her into a contract.

If time will help her accept us, I'll give it to her. Axel was a genius to invite her to the toy run.

I hate that she's going to be on the back of Axel's bike when we drive to the second location, and Nova's bike on the way to the third, but she's the best addition we've ever made to our toy run.

The kids are enamored with her. She helps them on and off the bikes. She corrals the little ones with ease, getting them to line up for pictures with the row of Harleys. She has a good eye for staging.

Our father is a dumbass for firing her. She's the best graphic designer the corporation has, even without formal training. She's going to school so she can up her game even more, but she already eclipses the other employees.

Visual organization isn't the skill I want to help her develop. That's just the thought I allow myself to have.

The thought I'm tamping down because it would get me arrested for public indecency is my desire to fuck her right here. Watching her light up as she talks to the kids, I'm ready to pump her full of babies. I hope I already have.

The Aubergine Affair normally has a birth control policy, but since the auction wasn't actually for sex, the policy was waved. I didn't bring it up because I wanted to get her pregnant. That has to be a pipe dream. Surely she wouldn't have been willing to let any winner get her pregnant.

Her cheeks get rosier as the night goes on and I fall a little more in love with her at each stop. She's as cheerful with the last kid as the first. She was made to be a mother.

When we get back to the clubhouse, Axel grabs a mug and packet of hot chocolate and preps it for her. When I pour shots of whiskey for the rest of us, she says, "Hold on a second. I like cocoa, but why don't I get that?"

"Because you're underage." And you might be pregnant, but thankfully I shut my mouth before saying the last part.

"After what we did at the sex club, you're going to call me out on that?"

"I have my reasons," Axel says.

She relents with a pout, then sips her cocoa, her tongue darting out to lick the chocolate from her lips. My cock's hard again. I really need to get a grip on this. Would this be the drawback to being with her? I'll walk around with an eternal boner? That's acceptable.

Other MC members continue bringing bags in from the back of the truck that we took around with us. While it's a good visual to have us riding with huge Santa bags on our bikes, we pick up too many toys to handle all of them.

The four of us sit in a side room. Somebody left cards and dice on the table but that's not how I want to pass the time with her. Wendy has both hands cupped around the mug, and I wrap my fingers around hers.

"Hey, Nova, go turn up the heater."

She says, "It's okay. I'll be warm in a second."

Nova heads to the thermostat. "I'd rather you be comfortable now."

I want to hear her talk about the kids. "Did you have fun tonight?"

"Yeah. I can't believe how many toys you picked up. I've heard about your toy run before, but I didn't realize how big it is."

Axel mumbles, "That's what she said."

I sure as hell hope Wendy didn't hear him but she snickers. At least the overused joke didn't offend her.

"Now it's time to sort the gifts." I hop up and grab a notebook from the cabinet. Flipping it open in front of her, I explain, "Here are all the kids, their ages, and types of things they're into. We usually do a pretty damn good job pairing the stuff we collect with individual interest, if I say so myself."

Nova adds, "It's easy to pick out the kids who like fantasy and make sure to give them the toys that fit that. The kids who are thinkers get the more educational stuff. The kids who need creative outlets get the artistic items. It's fun, and if we get it wrong, a kid might try something new and find out they like it."

"Are you glad you're trying something new, Wendy?" I ask her as I tighten my hold on her hand.

"I'm glad I went on the toy run. But..." She pulls her hands into her lap.

Dammit, with a simple question, I pushed too far. "Thank you for going with us. I didn't mean to pressure you."

"I don't want to lead you on. I'm not looking for a commitment. I still haven't fully processed that I've been groomed my whole life to belong to a man."

"We're not asking for a commitment."

Axel clears his throat.

"I take that back. We would love to commit." And if I put a baby in her already, I've secured my commitment. Fuck. Does that make me the worst brother ever? I want to make a family with her so badly, I avoided the birth control conversation. But so did she.

Wendy toys with the dice and I notice they have sex words instead of dots. She furrows her brow and reads them. A smile is short-lived when she says, "I know a lot of women are playing wife to more than one man and it's working for them. I just don't know if it's my role."

"You know how you find out if you're right for a role?" I ask.

She narrows her gaze at me.

"You audition."

Her smile returns half-heartedly. "I don't think it works that way for relationships."

Nova looks nervous but Axel catches on. "Why not? Have fun with it. Roll those dice. Audition us."

"Don't we need to sort gifts?" She taps on the open page in the notebook.

"We have all day tomorrow to sort these gifts, plus the rest of the MC helps. We can have a little fun tonight."

She rolls the dice, then her eyes get big.

One die reads, "eat pussy." The other reads, "on the table."

"I'll audition for that role." Axel shoves his chair out from the table, takes her hand, and guides her to standing. They stare into each other's eyes.

He wraps his hands around her waist and sits her on the table, her skirt flaring out around her. He kneels, unzipping one thigh-high boot, removing it, and massaging her foot before doing the same with the other boot.

"Hop down for a second, Princess." Appropriate nickname for his kneeling position.

She stands, and he reaches his hands under her skirt. In seconds her tights are thrown across the floor. I consider grabbing them and sniffing that sweet scent of her pussy, the one that lingered on my cock that I could smell each time I jacked off the other night, but I'm too captivated to move.

He pulls her head forward to kiss her. Their lip lock is epic. They work together in perfect synchronicity. Damn, I'm jealous I didn't have that. The way they're staring into each other's eyes while their tongues mingle strikes me as more intimate than getting to put my dick inside of her from behind.

Then he pulls away and says, "You ready to do what the dice say, Princess?"

"Is there anything I need to do to get ready? I've never had a guy do that?"

Oh, sweet Jesus. We're giving her all of her firsts. That's the only positive thing I've been able to find about the 'just business' marriage. He didn't get anywhere with her.

"Just spread these sweet legs." Axel grabs just below her knees and lifts her feet onto the table as she reclines. "All you have to do is relax and let me make you come."

The sound of his mouth on her pussy is the hottest thing I've heard, second to my cock sliding in and out of her. I'd been shocked by how wet she was. I swear to God her sex juice is honey because my mind is absolutely stuck on her sweetness.

I kick my chair out of the way and stand beside the table, stroking my fingers through her hair. I want her to see me when she comes. I want her to think about yesterday.

"You like that, Baby Doll?" I get her to look at me.

"Yes."

"I bet you'd like it if my cock was inside of you while he licked your clit."

She moans. She definitely didn't object. Nova leans forward on the other side of the table. He's taken a keen interest, splitting

375

his attention between watching Axel eat pussy and the ecstasy on Wendy's face.

Axel moves a hand to her belly. I'm tempted to get my dick out and spray her belly with cum. He could rub it in for me. She's going to look so good when her belly's rounded with my baby.

Then her eyes roll back, her moans escalate, and her hand slaps out, grabbing my forearm. Her fingernails dig in. I hope she leaves her mark on me. She's doing the same to Nova on the other side. Then she splinters apart.

Her body falls limp, her chest heaving as Axel eases his drenched face away from her sex. He rubs a hand over his mustache and beard, inhaling deeply.

"Let me do that to you every day, Princess."

"Uh-huh," she says.

I'm going to take that as a commitment.

Nova's shoulders are bunched up ever so slightly. He keeps shifting from one foot to the other. I get that he has commitment issues, but how can he resist Wendy?

He bites his lower lip and is a little too fidgety with the way he holds her hand. What's going on with him?

Eight

Nova

"No commitment, right?" I tread lightly before making my big admission. I'm worried that if I wait, I'll miss my chance. The evil glare I get from Knight tells me he doesn't approve.

"Yeah," Wendy says, sitting up and sipping her cocoa.

"I need to tell you something." There's not a breath deep enough to make me feel ready for this.

"Okay," she says, but they're all staring at me.

I blurt out my secret. "I've never had sex."

She spews cocoa onto my shirt and the floor. "Oh my God, I'm sorry." She starts to jump up, but I hold her in place.

The shock on Knight's and Axel's faces is what I expected. "Keep your comments to yourselves, guys."

I turn to her. "Let one of them clean the floor. Here's the deal. I'm not ready for a relationship. You're not ready for a relationship, but I want to give this a try."

She shakes her head. "Your nickname is Nova but I remember it used to be Casanova. I assumed…"

"Just how guys razz each other. Casanova because I gave my heart away too easily. They reduced it to Nova as a joke. A loose translation to 'no go' in Spanish, since I quit dating." I rub my thumb over her lips. "But I want to explore this with you."

She grabs my wrist, kisses my thumb, and it's the best confirmation she can give me. "Do you want me to roll the dice?"

"No dice needed. I know what I want." I reach around her, unzipping her dress.

"No commitment." She unfastens my belt.

"Why set ourselves up for failure? Relationships never work." I lift the dress over her head.

The way she lifts her arms, and the little wiggle she does is almost enough to send me over the edge. Her hands sliding over my strained underwear are no help.

"And a relationship like this... Our family would never approve." She tackles my shirt, and while I'm happy to be one step closer to naked with her, I miss her touch on my cock.

I unfasten her bra. "Which is why we have to keep this a secret. Unless we're sure..." Damn her tits are perfect. I hold them in my hands, dragging my thumbs over her tight rosy nubs.

She works the waistband of my underwear over my erection and pushes them down. "Which is why you have to audition. We might try it out and decide it's not for us."

I don't think that's going to be the problem, but I can't bring myself to say it. I just don't understand how I could give my heart away to women who didn't want it. I guide her to the counter.

"Perfect. I can just lean over this. It keeps it not personal, that's what I read on the blogs."

Blogs? I spin her around. "You're not getting away with that shit." I plop her onto the counter, her ass smacking against the Formica, and scoot her to the very edge.

"The blogs also suggested dirty talk. Can we try that?"

"That one's fine. But you have to face me so I can watch you come." With my cock pressed between us, I lean in and kiss her lips. It was so fucking hot watching Axel kiss her, just like watching Knight fuck her, and now I get to do both at the same time.

I line my cock up, pressing into her sweet pussy lips. They barely make room for me. Her legs are spread wide, her hands run up and down my arms. This is going to be harder than I thought.

Every time I woke up last night, and then several times today, I yanked one out, trying to prime myself. But her scent is a sugared version of crack, and her big eyes looking up at me, and those lips that are red and swollen from our kiss. I can barely hang on.

"I'm ready for your big fat cock to fill me," she says.

For fuck's sake, she went for gold with the dirty talk. I close my eyes to eliminate the visual, and I quit breathing to cut off her scent. I even try to pull back and wrap my fist around my cock to gain control, but I can't. My balls blow load after load onto her.

I force my eyes open so I can watch. One white splat after another coats the dark curls of her pussy, her ivory skin, the countertop. Shit, I shot some on the backsplash and some up on the cabinets. She laughs and her tits bounce, giving me a moving target. I hit those too, streaking her rosy nipples with white stripes.

Fuck. The laughter starts behind me. They're never going to let me live this down.

Nine

Wendy

"Thanks for picking up this extra shift, Wendy. Now that the line's down, I may take off," Liz says then escorts a brother and sister away from Santa. She was one of my bridesmaids.

With a sudden lack of employment, I'll pick up all the extra shifts I can get. I tweaked my resume and spent a few more hours applying for jobs this morning. Or maybe it was a few minutes. Even now, as I think of last night, my hand migrates to my belly. I stop it before it dips lower.

My 'no commitment' approach is faltering at the hands of my stepbrothers.

I motion to the next family in line. "Your turn."

The mom has a baby in her arms and a little girl by her side. They're adorable. She holds her finger up. "Hang on a second. I was holding a place for someone." She turns to the side. "It's your turn, Sir."

Forcing my hand from my belly, I question the insanity of my rebellion. Running away from my wedding was self-preservation. Having unprotected sex with my stepbrothers is fate-sealing. My father would say I'm still a foolish, invincible teenager in need of guidance from wise men like him...and his business partner.

Can I get a vomit emoji? Oops, bad choice. I chuckle to myself. Vomiting after unprotected sex would indicate something I can't believe I risked. I was so caught up in the moment and the safety of my brothers, that my mind went on Christmas vacation early.

Santa says, "I can't believe you're back at work so soon after the fiasco. Don't get me wrong, you did the right thing, calling off the wedding." Santa's fairly understanding. He's one of my brothers' friends, Mammoth, in the local MC. Apparently, he and my brothers had talked about the marriage not seeming like a good thing.

Was it obvious to everyone except me?

Santa freezes, then leans to look past me, and raises a white-gloved hand. "Hey, didn't expect to see you here."

I turn, curious who showed up. The weakness in my knees, the fluttering in my chest, and the exhilaration that's zinging through my insides faster than Santa can circle the globe on Christmas Eve tell me exactly how I feel about my stepbrothers.

Knight, Axel, and Nova walk toward us on the red carpet laid over the fake snow. The lady with the kid and baby is smiling. Is this who she was holding a place for? Shit.

"Hey guys, do you need something?" I stammer.

Knight winks at me. Yes, I need that too. No, I can't think about that here.

"I'm at work. So seriously, did something come up?" I almost sound normal.

Axel snickers.

I try to step to the side to signal to the woman, but Nova grabs my arm. "Hold on. It's our turn."

"Your turn for what?"

"To make a wish." He points at Santa.

"This is for kids."

Nova leans to the side. "Santa, do you discriminate by age? You know you can't get away with that anymore."

Santa stays in character and does the deep belly laugh. He pats his leg. "Step right up. Tell me your deepest, darkest wish."

Oh, shit.

Nova says, "If you don't want us to sit on his lap and reveal our wishes, you can promise us another visit." He leans closer and lowers his voice. "I'll do better this time."

Better? He may not have fucked me the way he wanted to, but after he nutted all over me, he got me off with his hand. Being covered in the musky scent of his release intensified my orgasm to the point he had to carry me off the counter and hold me until I drifted back.

That's when I panicked and insisted they take me home. His strong arms holding me against his thick chest. His lips trailing little kisses in my hair. And the little murmuring when I swear he said, "I love you."

It all felt too good. And here they are making me want them more than ever. I'd planned on proving that sex was no big deal. I've never been more wrong. But I'm too afraid to say how much I want them.

"So be it." Nova smirks then lets go of my arm. He sits on Santa's lap while Knight and Axel stand on either side. The cameraman snaps a photo. It is fucking adorable. I'll give them that.

Santa takes it all in stride and gives the same line he's said a hundred times tonight. "What's your wish?"

My heart is caught in my throat.

I turn to Liz, "You can go. I've got—"

Knight's voice cuts me off. "We wish for a woman who'd be willing to share the three of us."

Axel says, "Who can handle our sometimes inappropriate humor."

Nova adds, "Who makes us as happy as we plan on making her."

I make Nova happy? And he plans on making me happy? He was my main partner in the 'no commitment' arena.

Santa says, "This will be a fun delivery. She can sit on my lap while Rudolph pulls my sleigh."

Knight objects, "Oh no, Santa. If she's sitting on a lap, it's going to be one of ours."

"All right. So what do you want her to look like?"

The guys talk over each other asking for light skin, long brown, straight hair, a wide smile that shows off her pretty teeth, but not in a weird way, a perky little nose, long legs…

Santa winks at me as I worry my lower lip. "Would you be happy if she was named Wendy?"

The guys laugh, but a public admission that they want me is scary.

Liz hasn't left yet. I'm sure nothing could compare to this freak show. She steps closer to me. "I know you're hesitant to commit right now but recognize an opportunity when it presents itself. Why not try this thing with your brothers? Hell, if you won't, I'm close enough to that description. I could let them call me Wendy."

She's joking, but the jealousy that flares through me makes it clear how I feel. Again. Am I going to keep denying all of the signs that things are good with my brothers?

"That's what I thought," she continues. "Instead of me leaving, you need to."

"I told you I'd take this shift."

"It's okay. I was just going to watch Hallmark Christmas movies and search online for new sparkly derby shorts. I can do it a different day."

Ten

Knight

Wendy agrees to meet us at the house. I'm tossing dirty laundry into the washing machine while Axel cleans the bathroom and Nova tackles the kitchen. We want to make a good impression when she gets here.

Santa, aka Mammoth, let us know that Wendy was taking a shift unexpectedly today and we rushed to meet her, not thinking ahead to what would happen if she accepted our offer to come back to our house.

She's so cautious right now, insisted on driving herself. She wants a way out. I can't falter for being hesitant about getting trapped. She's been trapped for way too long.

The doorbell ringing is a straight shot to my heart. How can we make so much mess?

"I wasn't sure if she was going to show," Axel says, "I thought she might've agreed just to get rid of us."

We help her with her coat and sit casually around the living room. It's anything but casual. We had to promise each other not to fight to sit next to her. Give her space. She chooses a spot on the couch.

She must have gone home and changed because she's not wearing the Santa's helper costume from the mall. The red and white striped stockings had me wanting to lick her like a piece of candy. That hasn't changed.

She switched to pink sweats and a T-shirt. She looks comfortable. That's how she should be. In fact, it makes the moment homey. Perfect.

"Did you bring a bag?" I ask, "You know, in case you decide to stay for the night."

"Mi cama es su cama." Nova grins.

"It's *mi casa es su casa*, amigo," Axel corrects.

"I meant what I said. Cama's bed in Spanish. You've got a place to sleep, or whatever. I'd like another chance to prove myself."

She lowers her face and tucks her hair behind her ear. "I'm sure you will. We can learn together."

This opens the conversation for what I've been wondering, and also a chance to razz Nova. "I'm happy to play the role of teacher. First of all, Nova, you're supposed to come *after* you put your dick in her."

"Fuck off, Knight. How about we start with a lesson about not judging each other? Tell us what you want to learn, Wendy," Nova gives me an understanding smile.

"Dad didn't let me date, so I've only stolen a few kisses. Then the heathen, because I refuse to say *his* name, first expressed an interest in me on my seventeenth birthday. At first, it was a badge of honor to have an older guy want me. I thought I was special. So naive. Now I know it's all a farce. I'm not special. I was a contract. So, basically, I need to learn everything."

"Whoa." I jump up, walk over to her, and drop to my knees. I take her hands from where she shoved them between her thighs. I hold them gently. "You are special. He's just a fucking idiot. And our Dad, he's power hungry. He always has been. It's why the three of us started our own accounting firm. We didn't want our legacy, if we even have one, to be tied to him. We wanted it to be something *we* made."

Axel cuts in. "Sorry we didn't think about you, sis, that he would leverage you like this."

I tread lightly, "Believe it or not, something seemed off and I was going to object to your wedding in that 'speak now or forever hold your peace' moment. But you beat me to it. You didn't need a hero." I take a breath. "I hope you want one, though."

"A hero... You were going to object?"

Axel says, "You wouldn't have done that. You're bullshitting."

Nova rubs his hands over his face. This is bound to dredge up discomfort.

"Check the inside pocket of my tux jacket."

"What's in it?" Wendy asks.

I lead her to my closet and point to the tux.

She side-eyes me then reaches inside. Retrieving the two pieces of paper, she holds them side by side and reads the fortune: *Claim your destiny with your heart, and the important things will fall into place.*

Axel takes the papers from her hand. "You had that at the wedding. Dad ripped it trying to get it from you."

"Yeah."

"You were going to object? And Dad knew?" Wendy says softly.

"Dad saw the fortune but had no idea what I planned on doing. I was going to object to protect you."

Nova says, "But she went with the runaway bride option, no hero needed." His voice cracks as he steps away from the closet. "I didn't realize Dad would stoop that low."

Damn him for killing the mood. Wendy tucks the fortune back into the pocket.

I say, "We could help you. We'll take care of you if you'll let us. We're a package deal. And if one of us turns into a jerk and tries to do some power play shit with you, the other two promise to kick his ass. Right, guys?"

Axel nods more enthusiastically than Nova. I add, "We'll set up a trust fund for you if that would make you feel better. Whether or not you are ready to commit to us. Just a gift to our sister. No strings attached."

"Please don't go setting up any trust funds. I'm applying for jobs and want to prove that I can take care of myself. Just like you did. I've been reading interview skills on the internet and doing practice questions out loud in front of the mirror."

"Hold on, I see an opportunity," I say. "We've conducted a lot of interviews. We could help you practice. In fact," I stand up and head to the kitchen to grab my keys. "We could go to the office and role play."

"I love role play." She practically leaps from the couch. In seconds we're all piling onto our bikes. I make sure she's on the back of mine.

At the office, she sits in the lobby instead of heading down the hallway with us. "Come on. Let's do the interview."

"The secretary has to call me back." She picks up a magazine, crosses her legs, and ignores us.

"Axel, you take the desk. Nova, you'll be with me and we'll do a panel-style interview. Axel, once you finish your role as secretary, join us."

We take our spots in the office that has minimalist decor, a neutral place for conducting interviews, away from our personal offices. Rather than sitting at the desk, I grab pens and paper then lead Nova to the oak table. It's sturdy enough to support us climbing on top of it.

"Set her chair out there." I motion a few feet from the desk. It will give me room to kneel in front of her.

Axel knocks on the door, then pops his head in. "Mr. Russell and Mr. Russell, are you ready for the interview?"

"Yeah, bring her in." Rather than looking up from the paper in front of me, I lift my hand and wave a couple of fingers. "Come on in..." I pretend to be looking for her name. "Ms. Cooper."

"Thank you, sir."

"Have a seat," Nova says.

Axel continues as secretary, taking pretend notes. We go through a few formalities and her poise impresses me. But we're not really here to practice. Time to segue to the fun part of the interview.

"Ms. Cooper, how would you rate your multitasking skills?"

"I like to think that I'm good at multitasking. I can handle multiple things in motion at one time, but I've read numerous studies that say it's more efficient to focus on a single task. But I'm versatile. I'll do whatever the job dictates." The lightness in her voice indicates she knows I'm up to something.

"Interesting. How about this?" I walk around the desk and drop to my knees in front of her. "May I?" My hands hover above her thighs.

"Of course, sir. It's your office. Whatever you want. I want to ace this interview."

"Okay. Let's test your multitasking skills. Nova, my partner, is going to continue asking you questions while I feast on your pussy. Let's see if you can truly do two things at once."

She allows me to slip her sweats and panties off. I'd rather ditch the role play, but it seems to help her relax. My erection is about to bust my jeans open.

I spread her legs wider, but when the edges of the chair prevent me from splaying her open, I reach around and pull her ass forward. It's like pulling the buffet table to my mouth. I want to dive in with full gluttony.

With mock professionalism, I kiss my way up her thighs and over her pussy before sliding my tongue between her sweet lips. Her swollen nub grows harder as her breaths become more erratic. Her answers to Nova's questions take increasing time and are less coherent.

There's nothing I love more than making her lose control, except for doing it with my dick.

When she cries out, I slow my pace, easing her through the climax. Her head is tipped back, her hands tangled in my hair, and her mouth open. I sit back on my heels. I'm not ready to return to my seat, so I hang out in heaven between her legs.

Continuing the interview, I give her a minute then assess the situation. "Screw the studies. You did a great job putting your primary focus on having an orgasm. Your secondary focus shifted to tangling your fingers in my hair. I'm giving that a thumbs up. Let's get Nova's report."

Her smile takes my focus away from my cock. My heart is full. I want to make this woman happy for the rest of my life.

"The more she focused on orgasming, the more trouble she had answering questions. But that's only one test. I'd like to try another situation if you don't mind. And if Axel can stop taking notes, I think we should all participate."

Axel slaps the pen and notebook on the table. "Tell me what we need to do."

"Okay, Ms. Cooper, I'd like you to strip naked, then lie down on this table. Would you be comfortable with that?"

"I think I'll be comfortable with anything you ask me to do."

"That's a very teamwork-friendly answer. We like that."

"What kind of multitasking do you want to test this time?"

"I'm going to fuck you and you're going to either have your hand or your mouth on their cocks. Do you think you can focus on all three tasks at once?"

Way to go, Nova.

The façade of role play cracks briefly with her laughter. "I think I'm perfectly suited for this."

The scent of her sex already fills the small room. My cock throbs and springs free when I strip my clothes. I've never been naked like this with my brothers, the key factor being the naked woman climbing back onto the table.

I tip her face to the side and tap my cock on her mouth. She scoots toward the edge to reach it easier. Poor Axel will have to go for her hand. Although watching her bright pink manicured nails wrap around his shaft, he's not losing much.

There's still no conversation about birth control. Everyone has to be thinking about it. Nova positions himself in Wendy's curls. He gets his footing stabilized. Pre-cum drips out. He could be getting her pregnant right now.

Wendy's tongue roams the tip of my cock but all I can think is that Nova needs to hurry.

He drags a thumb over his pre-cum, rubbing it into her glistening curls.

"Fuck."

His eyes meet mine and I realize I said that out loud.

His evil grin gives way to him saying, "I'm putting this inside of her to make sure she's ready."

Lowering my eyes, my cock twitches. Nova catches another drip of pre-cum from his tip then slides it into her cunt. He's teasing me, the little shit.

She shudders under his touch for what seems like an eternity before he fists his shaft and pushes his strained head into her wet lips.

"Remember how much cum I had for you last time?"

She pulls away from my cock and offers a breathy, "It was everywhere."

"It's all going inside this time. I'm going to fill you up." Nova's eyes roll back as he slides inside of Wendy for the first time. I figure we don't have long. He grips her thighs, then repositions, lifting her legs so that her feet are at his shoulders.

He wraps his arms around her legs, holding her into him as he thrusts. Grunts and groans rumble from him.

Wendy licks my tip until Nova sets his rhythm. She opens her mouth, taking me in while stroking me with her tongue. Her beautiful red plump lips seal on my shaft, locking in my pleasure. She's sucking me into oblivion. She certainly doesn't need any lessons on cock sucking.

I fist her hair, guiding her head carefully so that she doesn't have to move much while getting railed. As I work my hips, I'm getting close, but hold my release back. I shift my attention between watching Nova fuck a woman for the first time, Wendy's hand driving Axel crazy, and her mouth stretched around me.

We make a great team. I could exist here forever. We could rotate around this desk, each taking turns pleasing her.

On this rotation, her moans vibrate my shaft, building my orgasm to heights I haven't been to before. Then Nova growls out his release. Good thing nobody's in the building. They could have heard it on every single floor.

He promised to fill her, and he did. I watch between her legs as his seed spills out. The sound of bodies, slapping with wetness, sends me dangerously close to the edge. I thrust forward and fill her mouth with my release.

She gags and gasps for air so I fist my cock, keeping the tip in her pretty lips. Like a trouper, she regroups, seals her lips on my shaft, and sucks for dear life. When I can breathe again, I say, "Such a good girl."

She smiles up at me with my cock still in her mouth. At least I think it's a smile, but a white flash interrupts our tender moment. Axel's pumping cum across her tits, even hit me. Fuck. That's messed up.

But while she keeps pumping Axel's shaft, she keeps her lips on me.

Fuck, what's happening. My balls grow heavy, tighten, and blow another load down her throat. Damn. I've never had a double release before.

There's no way I can let her go.

Eleven

Wendy

Braiding ribbons into my hair, I get ready for the special Christmas fundraiser roller derby bout.

My legs are weak after an evening with my brothers, but if that had been a real interview, it would be safe to say I'd get hired. The question is if I want to be hired...as their girlfriend. Is that what I'd be? Or just fuck toy?

I keep trying to tell myself that's all I want—Brothers with benefits. Fantasy Wendy keeps interrupting to insist that I commit.

My video messaging app rings. It's Dad. I quickly get to the end of my braid and tie a bow around the end. I forgot that we'd connected on here before.

Deciding to stand up for myself has been a big move for me, and if I'm going to do that, I might as well talk to Dad now. If we can repair our relationship, great. If he can't see that what he did is wrong, I'll get my frustrations out during the bout.

"Hi, Dad," I say.

"Wendy." He nods.

I take a deep breath. Don't let it get to me that he's impersonal. He's never been personable. "I only have a few minutes. I have a roller derby bout, but I want to talk to you."

"Since you mentioned roller derby, are you still doing that?"

Duh. "Yes, it's very important to me, Dad. We do charity work, plus it's great exercise."

"It's not appropriate for a woman to go out and act like that."

"My teammates disagree." It's a bold move for me to say that, but I feel supported now that my brothers are on my side. "It's one of the many roles I play in this world. If you want to judge me, then we can end the call right now." I reach for the End Call button.

"Wait, don't hang up. Your mother and I have talked and she asked me to make amends with you."

"Okay." I'm cautious since the call got off to a bad start.

"This is me officially saying that I can see how you would be unhappy about the marriage. You aren't old enough to understand how difficult the business world is and the importance of family legacies. That you wouldn't want to be *used*. That's your mother's word. I could have been clearer with you at the outset about why my friend was interested in you."

I take a second. Does he believe this is an apology? "Used...yes. And worse, traded, treated like property..."

"It doesn't sound great when you put it like that, but when you're older you'll understand love is overrated. But with skilled negotiating on my part, the partnership talks are continuing. He'd still prefer that you be involved, but if you refuse, he will still consider partnering with our company. He sees the value in what I've built even if you don't."

"Dad, this isn't an apology. You tried to sell my virginity?"

"What on earth are you talking about, Wendy? How would I know if you're a virgin?"

Shit. This is embarrassing. "Oops, that one's on me. I drew a conclusion."

"Did he try..." My father's voice wavers with a shred of decency.

"No. Never." Oh boy, that makes the auction thing a ridiculous choice. Good thing we don't have to discuss that.

"Good. I've built myself up from nothing and I don't want you to have to do the same."

The sad truth is that as angry as I am with my dad, I still love him. I know that he means well. He'll have to earn his spot in my life though.

"Maybe I don't mind doing the same. I need to learn who I am, and it's not a contract bride. I'm a human. I'm your daughter. I need time to get to know myself with or without you."

"I can agree to those terms."

Those terms? I stick that irritation in the front of my brain where I can pluck it out to use during the bout. But guilt pangs inside of me for not telling him the full story. I try to speak on his terms.

"We have to make risk assessments, right, Dad? I've listened. I've learned things. Just give me a chance to sort myself out."

He smiles when I say risk assessment.

"That's what your mother said. I have to give you time. I'll do it, but I can't guarantee which position I'll have open for you whenever you decide to come back."

"Dad, I need you to be my father, not my employer. I need someone I can turn to when I have questions about life, when I need support, when I feel like everyone turns against me."

"That's hard for me. I'm not the emotional type."

"Can you just be there to listen? You listened to mom and you're on the phone with me, that's a start."

He smiles. "I suppose I can commit to listening. I do love you, Wendy."

"I know you do, in your own way, but not working together will be the best way to nurture that."

Nikki rolls into the locker room. "Five-minute call."

"Sorry, Dad. I've got to go. We can talk later."

"I'll have my people call you and set up a time."

"No, Dad, we're not going to have our people talk. We're going to do it." For the first time, my dad might truly respect that I'm not his property.

How damaging will my secret relationship be if he finds out?

Twelve

Axel

We showed up for Wendy's roller derby bout, but in the interest of making it less obvious, we invited the whole MC. It was pretty easy to convince the rest of the gang to come watch girls in spandex get rough and sweaty with each other.

"Our sister's off-limits," I remind my brothers. Not my birth brothers, my found family of brothers in the MC. "She's number twenty-three, Roll Play."

It's hard enough for me to share her with my brothers. I want her to myself.

Catcalls and general rowdiness erupt as the derby girls take the track. They joke about my claim, but I know they heard me.

I get lost in thought. Her derby name...Roll Play. She likes pretending. Is that because she's been escaping the reality of her world, even if just subconsciously knowing she wasn't loved for herself? It hurts. How the hell does she deal with it?

Is there similarity to how I get caught in my head, missing things that are right in front of me?

I want to ride home and tell Dad to apologize for everything he ever said that made her think she wasn't enough, and to give her job back. But mostly, I want to take Wendy in my arms and hold her, protect her from the world.

Could I do that with Knight and Nova by my side? We could make sure she's safe to be herself. Nobody fucking judging her or telling her what to do, and with the extended family of the rest of the MC, she'd never be at risk.

Watching her skate and crash into other women, the intensity on her face is insane. It's a little reminiscent of when she was younger and would try to get a toy that we were keeping from her. She still has an innocence about her, but she's jaded.

Rightly so. I fucking hate everyone who's done that to her. I can't think about it.

My eyes are glued to my sweet princess, Roll Play, as a member of the other team makes an illegal move and shoves her out of bounds. My girl is smart. She knows how to fall. I hate that she's had to learn that.

Shit. I'm all messed up. She chooses to learn that so she can skate safely. She doesn't need me there to catch her, to protect my little sister.

I wish I could get a better read on her. It terrifies me that our relationship doesn't feel superficial to me, yet I'm not sure how she sees it. After the wedding fiasco, we might never be able to break down her walls and convince her that love can be different.

Sitting in the bleachers with Nova and Knight, knowing that they feel the same for her as I do, and the rest of our club surrounding us, I realize that what works about this is that we are willing to share her.

That's what works in our club. We share responsibility for each other. In that light, it's fine to want Knight and Nova to be part of the relationship. We'll share responsibility for Wendy.

We have a big mission ahead of us—convince her that she's special. I hated her saying she wasn't special the other night. The truth is that my brothers and I might not be worthy of her.

But she may never be ready to go public with us. She might have her fun then pick guys her own age. A headache sets in. I wouldn't be able to handle her dating another guy. I scan the bleachers, my eyes landing on a guy her age, and I automatically want to strangle him.

The crowd goes wild as the final whistle blows. I stand and cheer. Our girl's team won. Time to celebrate by doing some more role play with Roll Play.

Thirteen

Wendy

The ends of my braids blow backward below my helmet as we fly down the road. I'd gotten a ride with Beatrix to the derby arena, so no problem figuring out what to do with my car when my brothers offered to take me home.

The ride to my brothers' house gives me time to sort my thoughts. Hearing them and many other members of their MC cheering us on, I realized how much they support me. How much each member of the MC supports all of the other members. They're more of a family than we had at home.

Our parents don't approve of the guys being in an MC any more than they approve of me doing roller derby. None of us kids grew up the way our parents wanted us to. That's not my fault, or my brothers'. We are who we are.

It's a turning point for me to realize I'm not wrong. I can choose my path. And right now, the path I'd like to explore is with my brothers. But that's all it is—an exploration.

We turn into the Cherry Ridge foothills, winding our way to their isolated home. Good thing they pay someone to keep their road plowed, the snow is starting to stick. The bumps and bruises that plague me after every bout seem less with my new sense of freedom.

Pulling up to their house, Axel lowers the kickstand, then hops off. I start to dismount but he sets his hand on my shoulder. "Hang on."

He helps remove my helmet. "I've had a goddamn boner watching you sweat and grind with all those women. I need you, Wendy."

"I need you too." Being consumed by a physical need for someone is new for me. And we get along so well otherwise. In our little bubble. We're a long way from exposing ourselves. Clouds move in front of the full moon, protecting our space with darkness.

"I want to fuck you out here where it's wild and raw under the night sky. Nothing between us and the world. You good with that, Roll Play?"

The play on words of my derby name rings so true with my guys. "Which role should I take now?"

"Be mine."

That feels too intimate. I don't want them to think I'm committing to more than I'm ready for. "Axel—"

He puts a finger on my lips. "Shhh, just let me have you."

My heart says yes, but my head is still a mess. Is silence my way of chickening out, not being clear that I'm one hundred percent ready to commit physically but struggling with the rest? Or is my surrender enough?

He grabs the ribbon holding one of my braids, pulling a single end slowly as he watches it untie. Then he fishes the other braid from behind my shoulder, pulls it forward, and removes that ribbon. He hands one to each of our brothers.

"Get her naked and on my lap, then tie her hands behind her back."

There's a pause while they visually check in with me. I nod, my breath coming with audible heaviness. They strip my lower half bare. I should be cold in the winter night air, but they're close and my body's on fire.

Axel tosses his clothes aside and sits on his bike, his erection standing tall in front of his ripped abs. Our brothers lift me onto his lap and carefully position my feet so they don't touch anything hot. I question if I'm hotter than anything on this bike.

Nova and Knight work together to bind my hands. The position thrusts my breasts shamelessly at Axel. My sex is open for him. His cock stands ready for me. Correction to my earlier thought. Now, I've never felt so free.

The dark sky with twinkling stars. The light breeze that can't quite cool me off. And the freedom surrendering to my brothers. This is how I want to live.

Axel's hands wrap around my waist and he adjusts his hips to notch his cock at my entrance. I slide down. My body stretches around him. I stare at him, wondering how I can feel this good.

The other two brothers stay close, making sure I'm safe since I can't balance myself, but also making sure they're involved.

"You look so fucking good riding him," Knight says.

"If you were doing this to anyone but my brother, I'd have to beat the shit out of someone," Nova says. "You fucking make my cock eternally hard."

Axel kisses my neck, and massages my breasts. Knight and Nova are intimate with me from either side, but I can't touch any of them. All I can do is accept what they offer, and give in to every thrust of Axel's shaft as he makes me whole.

And possibly more than whole if our unprotected sex has consequences. Am I finally ready to admit that Fantasy Wendy was right?

It's a dangerous thought, made even worse by how quickly I come and how quickly I pull his release from him. I'm limp in his embrace. I'm completely at their mercy. I've surrendered and I'm happy.

Physically we're perfect together. But a relationship has to be more than a physical connection. We need to be friends too. And we are. We have to respect our differences. And we do. But I thought that with he-who-won't-be-named. It was too perfect, just like this. Well, not *just* like this.

Axel whispers. "I love you, Wendy."

Knight joins him, "Damn, I love you, Wendy."

Nova looks away. His chest expands and releases. He faces me, and his words are intentional. "I love you, Wendy."

It all happens so fast, I can't stop them before they all say it. Anxiety wells inside of me. How can they know they love me? What even is love? And why did Nova have to say it? Is his declaration proof that we're moving too fast like he's always done?

The intimacy comes crashing down. The bright light of the full moon shines like a glaring spotlight in my eyes, exposing me, blinding me. I'm uncomfortable. I turn my face away, unable to defend myself.

Only one other man than my father has said he loved me. He didn't love *me*, no matter how good it felt to hear his words.

"Untie me."

"Hey, hey. Slow down." Axel grips me with both hands.

I twist my shoulders. "Untie me now."

"We will. Calm down."

Knight takes control. His hand around my wrist is met with sudden freedom as the ribbon falls free. "What's wrong?"

"This isn't love. This is lust and sex and... Just let me go."

Nova looks sick as he turns, walking away from us.

Axel says, "I thought we were—"

"You can't say love. That's not what this is."

The hurt in their expressions tells me I might be wrong.

Axel wraps an arm around my shoulder as Knight helps me get my clothes on. No one's worried about the cum dripping down my leg. No one needs to be. The worst problem is what's left inside of me and what they put inside of me previously.

I am just a foolish girl. My dad was right. I'm too screwed up to trust that people can love me.

Fourteen

Nova

I knew better than to say those three little fucking words. Why couldn't I keep my damn mouth shut?

Anger flows through my veins. Why did I storm away from them? My bike was right there. My hands itch to grab the handlebars, rev the throttle, and put miles between us.

Wendy's going to break my heart.

Reaching in my pocket, freedom is offered by the small metal key. I pull it out, ready to ride. Ready to be anywhere but here. Ready to...

I turn toward my bike and see Wendy. I see her pain. Something happens inside my chest. She's as hurt as I am. We're all pawns in someone else's game.

I step toward my bike. Toward freedom. Just get on. That's all I have to do to escape this shitshow. She made it clear she doesn't want to go public with our relationship. We're just fun to her. Even her goddamn roller derby name proves it. She just plays roles, pretends, and has her fun and leaves.

My chest tightens. I press my hand into my shirt, but the pain doesn't let up. Fuck! Am I having a heart attack?

Two more steps to my bike, and my chest hurts worse with each one. I won't be a coward. I'm man enough to say goodbye. I angle my head.

Her eyes meet mine. She's so young. So talented. I don't deserve someone like her. The three of us ganged up on her, not giving her time to breathe after one of the hardest decisions of her life—standing up to Father.

Wendy makes me a better person. I take a lesson from her and face my fear.

"Fuck!" So many emotions storm inside of me, I unintentionally scream to vent. All eyes land on me.

The key falls from my fingers, nestling itself deep in my pocket.

Knight and Axel will be pissed. They don't matter. The foolish belief that we could all take care of Wendy is our fault. Not hers. When it's over it's over, I've certainly become an expert on that. She doesn't want us and we need to accept it like grown men.

Wendy slips a sock on and ties her shoe.

I nod toward the house. "Give me a minute with Wendy."

When we're alone, I say, "You've been clear with us from the start, we just didn't want to see the writing on the wall." Motioning to my bike, I continue, "Hop on, I'll take you home."

411

Fifteen

Wendy

A pain in my hip wakes me from the minute of sleep I managed for the night. I roll onto my back and rub the sore spot. I remember all too clearly bouncing that hip off the derby track last night. I rotate my leg to get some blood flowing and ease the pain a little.

If only I could mend my heart so easily. It hurts worse than any other body part. I lift my pajama top, sure there will be a bruise on my chest. There's not.

A sleepless night has turned into a day I don't want to face, and a decision I don't know how to make.

There was so much hurt in Nova's eyes when he gave me the option to go home. I flop an arm over my eyes.

Why did I have to freak out the second he said he loves me? Can I blame it on the rebound?

I can't be the woman three men, who happen to be my brothers, need. I'm just an eighteen-year-old, trying not to get married as part of a business deal.

They were there to catch me when I fell, and look how I repay them.

My heart pumps a different emotion with each beat. One beat I'm angry with them for being older and knowing better. They shouldn't have put me in this position.

Then it beats sympathy for them. They offered and I accepted. I can't blame them.

Then it beats sadness that there's so much strife in my family right now. Another beat, resentment for the way my father treated me. Another beat, disbelief that my mother would allow my father to do that. She may be my stepmom, but she's the only mom I remember.

The next beat is mushy and wiggly. It doesn't make sense. It's an emotion I haven't dealt with before. It begs me to trust it, but how do I trust the unknown?

I won't be fooled. This is Fantasy Wendy. She's wild and carefree. She's also imaginary. She doesn't have to live with consequences.

I have to end this. I have to find my worth, no matter how good it feels to be with my brothers. No matter that my favorite role is to be theirs. I need to play the role of Wendy first and figure out who she is.

The video app on my phone buzzes. It's Dad. I'm not up for a video chat. I showered thoroughly last night, trying to convince myself that I had to wash myself clean. Free from my brothers, free from everything except me. No smeared makeup, no sweat, just me.

Dad won't be happy knowing that I've slept in until... I look at the clock on my phone. It's after nine.

I sit up and clear my throat before accepting the call with audio only.

"Hey Dad, can't put you on video right now." I stick with the truth.

"That's not exactly what I wanted to hear. Are you with your brothers? Are you having sex with them? Don't answer that. I heard about what happened at the sex club."

I'm too stunned to say anything. He doesn't need me to.

"The humiliation that you're bringing to this family is unequaled. Do you think you're one of those people who's going to find fame and celebrity by leaking a sex tape? Do you think that because we have money, you can do anything you want? I absolutely will not have that in my family. You can watch your email for an official notification from the lawyer that my will has been rewritten and you are no longer in it. And your mother is in full agreement."

The call goes dead, on par with my soul.

A few seconds pass before my mother's strained voice adds, "I'm in full agreement with your father. This is unacceptable behavior."

Did I get what I asked for? I get to figure out who I am with no access to my family's fortune. I resist opening my bank app to see if he closed my account. I don't think he'd want me to live on the streets, but I'm not ready to be sure.

My parents continue to drive their point home and I half-heartedly listen.

I'm not ready to face the world so utterly on my own. A million ideas run through my mind of how I can minimize my lifestyle.

I flip to my email to see if any of the companies have responded to my job applications. Not yet. I'll send more applications today. It's time to take care of myself.

Sixteen

Wendy

I text Nikki to catch her up on things and she offers to come over, but I need to get my big girl activities done before I chicken out.

I text back: *Thanks. I may take you up on it later*

Nikki: *Are you sure? I'm grabbing my keys*

Me: *No, I need to handle this*

She sends a GIF of a car fishtailing as it speeds around a corner.

Me: *I promise I'll be in touch later today*

I pull up the sibling chat. *Can we meet?*

I swear the message hasn't even had time to send when all three guys respond.

Nova asks: *Where*

Knight: *When*

Axel: *yes*

We agree to meet at their office because I need to be somewhere that I can try not to fall apart. I need to be somewhere to remind myself of professionalism and responsibility. And they're already there, so that makes it easy.

The secretary tells me they're wrapping up a meeting and directs me to an empty conference room. The interior blinds are closed so no one can see in. I take a seat.

That wiggly, squishy, evasive feeling hasn't left my chest. Sitting alone, I try to figure it out. It reminds me of snuggling on my grandfather's lap while he told stories of his childhood. Of hanging out with my best friends in high school. Of getting the boss's approval of my graphic designs. Of getting accepted onto the roller derby team.

All good feelings. All supportive. All about belonging. The emotions grow stronger and stronger as each realization hits me. Oh crap. I think this might be love. Everything starts clicking into place.

Fine time for the revelation. Or is Fantasy Wendy getting more savvy, and tricking me since I'm a bit desperate?

For now, stick to my mission... I owe my brothers a gigantic apology. At the very least, I need their friendship.

Cindy pops her head in. I'm so self-absorbed, I forgot she'd be here since she works for my brothers. She was in the auction too, also won by her stepbrothers. I guess she hasn't quit her job to live a fantasy life with them.

"What's going on? Is everything okay with your brothers?"

"I can't blame them." It's hard to finish my thought.

"What happened?" She looks worried.

"Is it terrible to have sex with our stepbrothers?"

She rolls her eyes. "I took two wrong turns driving here. I might not be the best person to ask for advice." She sits next to me and takes my hand. "Are you concerned about the act of sex, or is your heart the question?"

"Have you told your parents yet?" Living in a bubble versus living openly makes a big difference.

"No."

"My dad was upset that I walked out of my wedding, which he'd carefully crafted as a business deal. And when he found out I hooked up with my stepbrothers..." I flop my hands as if presenting myself. "Who wants tarnished goods? He was so mad he wrote me out of the will and said I better hang up my roller skates and get a real job."

"There are so many things wrong with that. You're far from tarnished. You only do roller derby for fun. And who—"

Knight, Axel, and Nova file into the room looking insanely stern. Cindy and I wish each other well and she leaves.

"We're glad you're ready to see us." Nova rushes to my side.

"I'm so sorry for the way I treated all of you."

"You didn't do anything wrong," Axel says.

"I did, but I've come to my senses, and I have to be completely honest with you so you don't find out otherwise. Dad wrote me out of his will. And I realize I said I wanted to figure life out on my own, but family was my safety net."

Saying it out loud, I understand why my brothers separated themselves from my dad's empire. They didn't want to be controlled like this.

"That's what family is supposed to be. In our case, it's money. In other families, it's warmth, compassion, and support."

"And now I have none of that."

"You do, you have all of it with us." Knight waves me off when I open my mouth to speak. "We've been talking this morning. There's something we need to know. If we weren't your brothers, would you have been open to a relationship?"

I'm stymied by his question. Did I have trouble with the timing, the sibling thing, the number of guys, the speed I fell for them? "It's so hard to say."

"You were auctioning yourself. Anyone could have bought you. If you'd hit it off with strangers, would you have committed to them?"

"I can't answer that question."

"Why?"

"Because I just figured it out. I know who I am. I am a woman who's admired the way you stood up to my dad. Without him, you built your business from the ground up. You were a role model for me to escape my wedding. And even when I was clinging to him for understanding, you clung to me. You found your own supportive family in your motorcycle club. I want to be a part of that. I want to not just have one man, but three men who love me."

It's their turn to be shocked.

"I don't just want to role play sex games. I know which role I want. I want to be your..." I stop Fantasy Wendy just in time. She jumped in and was about to say 'wife'.

Knight kneels and takes my hands. I love it when he does that.

"You don't have to say anything you're not ready for. You've been through a lot. And I know I can speak for these fuckers when I say, you've just made us the happiest men in the world."

We end up in a hug that I'm finally happy I can fully enjoy. Fantasy Wendy joins us. Maybe Real-World Wendy and Fantasy Wendy aren't all that different.

"One more thing. I'm ready to commit to the three of you, but I have one important requirement." I pause.

Knight says, "Hit us with it. I'm sure it will be fine."

"We have to tell our parents." I'm not sure how I expect my brothers to react, but Knight's smirk isn't it.

Seventeen

Nova

Axel and I join Knight kneeling on the floor and I spin Wendy's chair so she faces me.

"Consider it done."

Wendy bites her lower lip and catches Knight and Axel nodding at me. Before she can ask what's up I go for it.

"We want you to understand how committed we are to you, even if it means giving you more space than we want." I reach into my pocket and pull out a black box, opening it to display the diamond ring. "When the time is right, this ring is yours."

Her hands fly to her mouth and her first few attempts at words come out garbled. Knight rubs her back, helping her calm down.

"When did you buy this?"

"Knight had it before your wedding. And when this group thing happened, we took it to the jeweler to modify it to represent all of us."

It's beyond gorgeous. I suck in a breath to calm my threatening tears. "That's so sweet. But why would you do that?"

Axel says, "We knew we wanted to marry you."

Knight adds, "And wanted to knock you up. If you didn't notice, we didn't ask about birth control."

"So I'm not crazy for being careless," she asks.

"It's fine, as long as you're only with us," I say.

Knight explains, "I bought it before I ever had sex with you, even though you couldn't know that. I hoped that if you ever got worried about why we were with you, we could use it to show how far we'd fallen for you. We weren't just with you because you're the best sex any of us have ever had."

Axel quips. "Especially Nova."

I glare at him. No time for sibling bickering though.

Knight says, "Remember the fortune?"

She nods. "You might be as caught in fantasies if you think a fortune could tell you we were supposed to get married."

"Trust me. I've never paid attention to wisdom from a cookie. But, I got the fortune at your eighteenth birthday party. I had just broken the cookie open and was reading it when I overheard you accepting a marriage proposal."

"No way."

"Full honesty. That's what happened. I wasn't sure what to do, so I slipped it into my wallet. I'd denied my feelings for you, and the whole idea of marrying my sister seemed ridiculous until everything started falling into place."

I steal the show back from Knight. "We love you for who you are. We watched you defy Dad and join roller derby. We watched you choose your own career path in graphic arts instead of number crunching or market analysis or any of the other jobs Dad approves of. We watched you take control of your future when you realized he was using you to advance his business—"

"You mean *legacy*?" Wendy laughs.

"That too. Those are just the big things. You're strong. You've always known who you are. And if someday you choose to add *our wife* to that list, it'll be our honor."

"Seeing myself through your eyes, I don't feel nearly as screwed up." She extends her hand and we stare at it before I realize what she's doing. I fumble the box. Axel catches it. Knight grabs the ring and slides it on her finger.

"I'm more than ready to be your wife. And since I'm probably pregnant, the sooner we do this, the less explaining we'll have. So you're good with telling our parents?"

"We are," Knight says emphatically. "In fact, we had a long talk with Dad and Mom this morning. He called us, furious at what we'd done in the sex club and we told him to come say it to our face. So he did. We've been talking to them all morning."

Axel says. "He's not happy about it. Mom isn't quite as upset, but we convinced them to write you back into the will."

"What? They're here? And you convinced them?"

I take the seat beside Wendy. "Want me to call them in?"

Fortified by the presence of my brothers, and now fiancées, we sit around the table as they have the secretary get our parents. We're lined up on one side and they sit on the opposite side.

Knight insists on being the one to do this. "Mom. Dad. We appreciate you hearing us out this morning and rewriting Wendy into your will. Now we have one other bomb to drop."

"Really? Dictating how I conduct my affairs isn't enough? What more could you want?"

I consider saying that we want their blessing for our marriage, but we'll be fine without it.

"We're engaged."

Dad coughs and sputters and pushes away from the table. He stands and paces.

Mom forces a smile and says, "Engaged?"

I lift Wendy's hand to reveal the ring.

Mom's smile grows more genuine. "For real engaged?"

Knight says, "It's for real, the way Wendy deserves it. For love."

Eighteen

Axel

Mom and Dad are at our house for Christmas Day. It's the first time they've come over since our big reveal last week, which was promptly followed by Wendy moving in.

Dad does his best to remain cordial. He's truly trying to accept our relationship. Mom's openly good with our choice now that she understands we're committed to one another. She didn't know about the business deal marriage and had it out with Dad. She keeps him on a tight leash now.

But Wendy had a stroke of insight that we have to get our parents up to speed on everything. It won't be long before people talk about how quickly we're getting married, and shortly after that, they'll do the math on when the baby's due.

Wendy reasoned that we tell our parents about the baby now, so they feel included. That allows them to address it with friends and family however they wish.

Christmas dinner wraps up. The gift exchange is over. Dad's gift was the nicest of all. He stepped out of the business deal with the man who wanted to marry Wendy. It was a huge contract, so we appreciate the consequences of not going through with it. One of the nicest gestures he's ever made.

And now Dad's getting grumbly about heading home to watch the football game. "Thanks for having us. We better get going."

"Before you do," I say, casting a glance at my brothers and sister. They all nod, so I continue. "We sincerely appreciate your support for our upcoming marriage. We know it's not easy. And we want to be as open with you as possible."

"I'm trying, son. But teaching an old dog new tricks has never been easy."

"He'll come around," Mom says.

"Speak for yourself, woman." He smiles at mom. "I just don't understand why the rush on the wedding. It's not like you have a contract deadline to meet." At least he's able to take himself down a notch.

But we do have a deadline. "That's what we want to talk to you about. Are you ready for this?"

Mom's face lights up. I'm pretty sure she caught on. Her eyes move to Wendy's belly. There's a chance it was a coincidence because Wendy's holding a present, but Mom's smart.

Dad says, "Am I ready? How am I supposed to know?"

Mom swats him. "Hurry, say yes."

"Why?"

"You really can't think of a reason they'd get married quickly?"

"To spite me?" Dad's actually confused.

Wendy extends the gift. "Maybe this will help."

Mom snatches the present, rips the paper off, throwing it at Dad, and stares at the picture Wendy designed, trying to use terms he loves. It says:

Project: Grandparents

Status: in negotiation

Deadline: September

"We're going to be grandparents. Isn't that exciting?" Mom squeals then puts her arm around Dad, who stares at the picture silently.

The rest of us stare at him.

"They're sharing their lives with us. Be grateful." Worry tinges Mom's comment.

Dad takes a breath and when he lifts his head, I swear his eyes are a little shiny. He recovers quickly. "Maybe I shouldn't have written you all back into the will. You're doing your best to give this old man a heart attack."

I think that was a joke. My eyes scan everyone else. No one's sure.

"Congratulations," he says, and we breathe a collective sigh of relief. He shakes my hand then Knight's and Nova's before turning to Wendy.

He wraps her in a hug. "If they don't take good care of you, let me know. I'm going to try to be a better father."

"Thanks, Dad. That won't be a problem. They treat me better than anyone else ever has."

Epilogue

Axel

Dad escorts Mom down the aisle. It was Wendy's choice to have it this way, just like her first wedding. Fear ripples through me at how close we were to losing her that day.

The wedding planner nudges my shoulder. "That's your cue."

I take a deep breath before moving my foot forward. It's not that I'm nervous or have cold feet like other grooms. It's the disbelief that I've learned how to be more myself through Wendy, my little sister, my love, and soon-to-be my wife.

Knight and Nova fall into step behind me, just as Wendy wanted it. The three of us make our way to the front. We drew our order out of a hat because we couldn't find any rational way to choose, and the aisle wasn't large enough for us to fit side by side. So, not only am I first, but as I take my place at the front of the church, my brothers flank me. I get to stand directly in front of Wendy.

Thankfully she doesn't have horrible morning sickness like her friend Cindy. That wedding day got messy.

The bridesmaids enter, pulling me back to the moment, and I'm surprised by my jealousy. They've seen Wendy today. They know how divine she looks in her wedding dress, which we were expressly forbidden from seeing.

I glance down the line of women: blue hair, a pinup girl, an arm in a sling. She has quite the assortment of friends.

The music shifts to *Somebody Loves You* by Betty Who.

I turn my attention to the back of the church where the bottom of a full white dress appears in the entryway. How big is her skirt?

Why did she stop? Worry races through my mind that she could be backing out, getting cold feet. It wouldn't matter that she's pregnant, she doesn't *have* to marry us. It's her choice.

I glance at Nova, who looks as if he's about to vomit. Maybe today won't be much cleaner than Cindy's wedding.

But as I'm watching my brother, his expression relaxes, and pure joy covers his face.

Returning my attention to the back, I understand. Wendy rounded the corner. She's more beautiful than ever.

She's the last of the women who were in this year's Christmas Cherry Auction to get married. There was less urgency with her since she's only pregnant with a single baby. Honestly, it was an ego blow. My brothers and I felt like we hadn't done our job correctly. But since she's not as pregnant as her friends, it was fair to let the other women go first.

As pregnant...No. Our girl is one hundred percent pregnant. If it's possible for me to smile any wider, I do, although I'm starting to wonder if I'm going to look like a fool in the wedding pictures.

The photographer has his camera pointed at Wendy, so I clench my jaw and work my lips to relax my mouth. It immediately pulls into a smile again. I can't contain how happy I am.

In her big poofy, lace-covered dress, Wendy looks like the princess she is. But she doesn't get one prince charming, she gets three.

A chuckle rolls through me as I notice ribbons braided through her trademark pigtails, tidy little bows tied at the bottom, white this time, appropriate for today, although some people might disagree as to whether she gets to wear white. It's her day. She can do whatever she wants, just like every day.

She makes her way to the front of the church and takes her place opposite the three of us. We move through the vows until it's time for me to say mine.

"Wendy, you already know this, but I'm committing to it in front of everyone. I will be there for you for the entirety of your life, and beyond if I can figure out how. I no longer need to be the only man for you. And I never thought I'd say that in my wedding vows. It's just proof that you're special. You make me a better person, and I'm proud to stand up here and promise to take on the role of best husband ever."

Grumblings come from my brothers, but I ramble on nervously, since this is uncharted territory for me, being in front of people, exposing myself. Apparently, I have some desire to keep her all to myself as I feel like spending the rest of my life declaring how much I love her.

Controlling my mouth, I let the ceremony continue. Knight says something about claiming his destiny. I think he's quoting the fortune. Nova talks about the 'pain of the past' making the present even brighter. I'm too lost in Wendy's eyes to process anything until the officiant says, "You may kiss the bride."

It's a natural command my body responds to. I lean forward, my brothers moving in at the same time. I know we planned this out in the rehearsal dinner, but plans don't matter anymore. We go for it. We're all in there, loving her with wild abandon in front of everyone because this is her wedding and she should get what she wants—men who truly, openly love her for herself.

And we live happily ever after!

One last time...If you'd like more role play, grab the BONUS SCENE by signing up for my newsletter.

https://SylvieHaas.com

More by Sylvie Haas

SYLVIE HAAS

Christmas Cherry Auction
Sparkles and Spankings
Presents and Praise
Tinsel and Teasing
Holidays and Handcuffs
Wishful and Wanton
Baking and Blindfolds
Carols and Consent
Sugarplums and Submission
Ribbons and Role Play

Eggplant Canyon Phase 2: The Bratva Moves In
Virgin and the Bratva
Fake Engagement and the Bratva
Secret Baby and the Bratva
and more...